W9-ABW-255

The
SPOTTED
CATS

Also by William G. Tapply

The
SPOTTED
CATS

A Brady Coyne Mystery

WILLIAM G. TAPPLY

Delacorte Press

Published by
Delacorte Press
Bantam Doubleday Dell Publishing Group, Inc.
666 Fifth Avenue
New York, New York 10103

Copyright © 1991 by William G. Tapply

All rights reserved. No part of this book may be reproduced or transmitted in any form or by any means, electronic or mechanical, including photo-copying, recording, or by any information storage and retrieval system, without the written permission of the Publisher, except where permitted by law.

The trademark Delacorte Press® is registered in the U.S. Patent and Trademark Office.

Library of Congress Cataloging-in-Publication Data

Tapply, William G.
    The Spotted Cats / William G. Tapply.
        p.   cm.
    ISBN 0-385-30233-9 : $17.95
    I. Title.
    PS3570.A568S66   1991
    813'.54—dc20   90-23258
                                                          CIP

Design by Jeremiah B. Lighter

Manufactured in the United States of America
Published simultaneously in Canada

April 1991

10 9 8 7 6 5 4 3 2 1
BVG

For our friends Rick Boyer and Doc Adams

ACKNOWLEDGMENTS

For his expert advice on the medical scenes in this story I wish to thank Dr. Mark Robbins; and for their critical scrutiny of the manuscript in all of its many incarnations I am grateful to Rick Boyer, Jed Mattes, and Jackie Farber.

The
SPOTTED
CATS

PROLOGUE

• • • • • • •

IN ZAMBIA THE LEOPARD is called *Nyalubwe.* In East
Africa the natives call him *Chui,* and farther south he's
called *Ingwe.* But everywhere—in Africa, in Asia, in parts
of Europe and the Middle East—the leopard is the same animal: a perfect killing machine, the most efficient mammal
predator—aside from man—on earth. He kills people when
they're available, indiscriminately from other prey. Professional hunters do not believe that leopards fear man. Professional hunters do not believe that leopards fear anything. They
are tricky and cautious, patient and bold, lightning fast and
perfectly camouflaged. They kill what they can and they survive because it is their nature.

On the fifth day, one of the professional hunter's native
trackers found leopard signs. So they scouted the area for the
tree on which to string up the bait.
Finding the proper tree is important. It's got to have just
the right angle so *Nyalubwe* can climb it, and then it's got to
level off more or less parallel to the ground, so he can crouch
on it and rip off hunks of the bait. It's got to have lots of grass
and brush around it so he can slink up to it without being seen.
After they selected a good tree, they all piled into the
Land-Rover and drove to the river. They sat hidden among

the *miombo* tree scrub on a hillside for forty-five minutes. The professional hunter scanned the valley with his German binoculars while the client balanced his rifle across his knees. The native trackers and gunbearers crouched in the scrub, waiting with their stolid, infinite patience. Finally the hunter spotted a warthog trotting stiff-legged across the suncaked mudbank two hundred yards away. The client braced his rifle on his knees, lined up the animal in the crosshairs of his Weaver scope, and killed him clean. The wet chunk of the bullet thudding into the warthog's side echoed back to the men a perceptible moment after the report of the rifle had died.

The professional hunter clapped his client on the shoulder. "Good shot. Your first African kill."

"Bloody warthog," said the client. But he grinned with pleasure. It had been a good shot at a moving target. It wasn't his fault that he was only shooting bait.

The natives swarmed over the dead animal. They hacked away at the carcass, cutting off the nose and carving out the tusks, which their tribe prized. Then they heaved the body into the back of the Rover and drove it to the bait tree.

One of the trackers skidded up the trunk as nimble as *Nyalubwe* himself. The hunter stood off to the side where the hide—it's called a hide, never a blind—would be erected. He motioned to the native to cut away some of the branches, so that when sighted through the scoped rifle the leopard would be silhouetted against the fading light of the sky as he went for the bait. The tracker sliced off the branches with his machete and dropped them to the ground where one of the others carefully picked them up and loaded them into the Rover. Freshly cut branches would set off alarms in *Nyalubwe*'s survival-tuned brain.

The gunbearers and trackers pulleyed the eighty-pound hunk of already foul-smelling warthog up to the horizontal branch of the bait tree with braided buffalo rawhide rope, where they wired it to the underside of the limb. After descending from the bait tree, they smeared the trunk with the warthog's blood and offal to disguise the human smells and to lure *Nyalubwe* from the bush.

Building a good leopard hide is an art, and the professional hunter was an artist. It's got to fit in perfectly. It's got to be constructed entirely of materials native to the area, but you can't cut nearby or *Nyalubwe* will smell the sap or see the fresh cuttings and be scared away. Bark and leaves and sticks and grass must be laced together and arranged so cunningly that if you walk away from it and then turn around to look for it, you won't be able to distinguish it from the rest of the terrain. Inside, you set up a camp stool in front of an inconspicuous hole in the side of the hide. The rifle is propped up on forked sticks so that it is aimed at precisely where *Nyalubwe* will be when he's flattened on that limb tearing away at the bait. When it's set up right, the client has only to squeeze the trigger.

They hunted elephants forty miles away for the next five days. Then on the sixth day one of the trackers, who checked the bait each day, reported that a leopard had come to feed. The client sighted in his Remington .375, loaded with three-hundred-grain Silvertips, for forty-six paces—the forty-three they had measured from the hide to the base of the bait tree, and three more to account for the height of the bait, twenty feet above the ground.

At four in the afternoon, while the sun was still hot and high in the sky, the professional hunter and his client and seven natives piled into the Land-Rover and drove to the hide. While hunter and client installed themselves inside, the seven others milled around the area, talking and laughing and in general making their presence obvious.

They knew *Nyalubwe* was there, somewhere, watching, guarding his bait. They knew they couldn't sneak into the hide without being seen. So after the two of them got settled, the others created noise and confusion before they drove off. Leopards are poor mathematicians.

The client set his .375 into the forked sticks and tapped it this way and that while he peered through the scope until the crosshairs settled on a spot a foot above the limb to which the rancid warthog was wired. Through the scope he could clearly see the claw marks on the bark and the flies swarming over the bait and the strings of freshly ripped flesh where *Nyalubwe* had already feasted.

The hunter had insisted they leave their wristwatches back in the Rover. Leopards can hear the ticking of miniature gears and the humming of tiny batteries.

They sat still and silent. And waited.

The professional hunter tapped his client's knee and held a cigarette pack to him. The client arched his eyebrows in question. But they had already accounted for the direction of the breeze. The smell of smoke wouldn't drive the leopard away. If he could smell the smoke, he could smell the men. Might as well smoke. Something for the nerves. Just don't scratch the match. *Nyalubwe* could hear that.

After what seemed like hours, a large bird flapped squawking out of a distant tree. A moment later they heard the sudden, nervous chatter of a monkey somewhere off in the jungle. The hunter stiffened, and the client lifted his eyebrows. The hunter shrugged. Then an entire neighborhood of monkeys began to shriek. The hunter turned and nodded to his client.

Nyalubwe was coming.

The sun sank toward the horizon. The hide lay in deep shadows. They waited. It seemed like hours.

Suddenly the hunter tapped his client on the leg.

The client peered through the scope. A mottled expanse of gold, black, and amber filled the sight. *Nyalubwe*'s coat. The leopard seemed to have materialized out of the humid jungle air. He was in the rifle's sights at the warthog carcass.

He was a big one, close to a hundred and fifty pounds, nearly seven feet from tip of nose to tip of tail. A real trophy. And a man-killer. All leopards are man-killers. This was not a comforting thought to either man.

The client took a deep breath. He felt the trembling in his hands and shoulders. A dribble of sweat ran down his side. His palms were wet. He wiped them on his pants. Then he touched the rough surface of the trigger with the ball of his forefinger. He braced the rifle in its rest with his left hand, adjusting it so that the crosshairs intersected the shoulder of the cat.

Another breath. He let it half out, squinted, tried to hold steady on the center of the black spot just behind the cat's shoulder, and squeezed.

The sudden roar of the rifle inside the hide sounded like an exploding bomb. All around them birds and monkeys began to scream.

"Shit!" muttered the professional hunter.

"What?" said the client. "What happened?"

"He moved. He started to go just as you shot. You got him in the gut. He's down in the grass."

"Is he dead?"

"I don't know. He's wounded bad. He could be stone dead. He could live for a long time."

"So what do we do? Do we wait for him to die?"

"No," said the professional hunter. "We can't let him get away. He's suffering, and he might start killing people. Anyway, it's the law. I've got to go dig him out."

"But it's almost dark."

"So I've got to go now."

"I'll go with you."

"The hell you will. You wait right here. Don't move."

When a man goes into the grass after a leopard, he hopes the cat's already dead. Usually it is. The hunter knew better than to count on it. He carried a cut-down old Winchester twelve-gauge pump. Six shells in the magazine and one in the chamber. Double-ought buckshot. A man never has time to raise a gun and aim when *Nyalubwe* comes after him. He only hopes for the chance to get the muzzle up. Then he'll depress the trigger and hold it there and pump those shells back against the firing pin as fast as he can and hope to hell he can blow away the cat's face before it can rip off his.

The hunter found gouts of fresh blood beneath the bait tree. He followed the spoor into a sea of head-high grass. He moved slowly, a cautious toe-to-heel step at a time, hoping he'd come upon a dead carcass, but knowing that a wounded leopard could be waiting. If he was lucky, he might hear the rustle of brittle grass the instant before the cat leaped. Otherwise, he would have to match his human reflexes against the jungle speed and single-minded intent of the desperate animal.

He went perhaps forty yards into the bush. It took fifteen minutes, one agonizing step at a time, every sense raw and alert.

The man's sudden scream came from behind him, and close. It started low and gurgling in his throat, rose to a high-pitched agonizing cry, more animal than human, and then, abruptly, died.

The hunter pivoted and pushed quickly back through the bush. He found his client on his back, his gun thrown aside. The leopard was on him, his teeth sunk deep into the side of the man's neck, all four paws swiping and swirling. The hunter raised his shotgun but dared not shoot. He raced forward and swung the gun butt at the leopard.

Instantly the cat was on him. Its forepaws smashed against the hunter's chest and knocked him backward to the ground. He felt the searing pain as the cat's teeth sank into his shoulder and its claws raked his face and back and belly and thighs. He had managed to cling to his weapon, and he brought it back so that he could shove the business end against the side of the cat. He pulled the trigger and began pumping . . .

ONE

• • • • • • •

SOMETIMES I drive to Cape Cod voluntarily. In May, when the dimples of rising trout pock the surfaces of the little ponds in Nickerson State Park, for example. Or in early October, when they're harvesting cranberries and the bluefish are schooling up in preparation for their southward migration and you need to wear a sweatshirt to walk the beaches.

I love Cape Cod in the winter, when it's bleak and cold the way it was when the Pilgrims first saw it.

I despise the Cape in the summer. Maybe it's because everyone else seems to love it so much then.

I never voluntarily drive down to the Cape on a Friday afternoon in July.

This trip was not voluntary. My secretary made me do it.

This was one time I shouldn't have listened to her. I should have stayed home that weekend. I could have slept late, watched the ball game, tied some flies, watched the late movie. Maybe I could've gone bass fishing with Charlie or invited Sylvie over for gin and tonics and a steak grilled on the hibachi on my balcony and a sleepover.

If I'd stayed home, instead of listening to Julie, none of it would have happened.

* * *

"Jeff Newton keeps calling," she told me on a muggy Wednesday while we shared a mid-morning coffee break in my office in Copley Square.

"Tell him I've gone fishin'."

"That's what I've been doing. He's not easily put off."

"What's the old shit want?"

"He wants you to go down there."

"Christ. Why?"

She shrugged. "Doesn't matter. You gotta go."

"I don't wanna," I said.

"That doesn't matter, either. It's your job. So you gotta do it."

"Aw, nuts," I said. I pounded my fist on my desk and scrunched up my face as if I was about to bawl. "He's my client, and if I don't wanna visit him I don't hafta."

There are times when a man has to assert himself.

Green eyes, black hair, fair skin, freckles lightly sprinkled across the bridge of her nose. Julie, my secretary. The Irish beauty. The Boss.

She folded her arms. She was trying not to smile. She succeeded. She looked as if she might rap my knuckles with a ruler.

"He called twice on Monday," she said. "Once yesterday. And again this morning. I don't feel like lying to him anymore. So get it out of the way, huh?"

I shrugged. "There's no point to it. We've got no business. He's practically broke."

"He's a lonely old man. For some obscure reason, he likes you. That's point enough."

"He's a grouchy man is what he is," I said. "And not that old. He just looks it. Jeff Newton is a broken, defeated excuse for a human being, with nothing to live for except the arrival of the guy with the big sickle. He's no fun. He's a pain in the ass."

Julie glared at me. She looks especially beautiful when she glares. Something about how her skin stretches across those great cheekbones of hers. "He still pays you a retainer," she said, sensing it was time to close in for the kill, knowing she was right, that she had me. "Besides, it's what you do best. Visiting your clients, making them feel worthwhile. Invent some business for him. Tell him about the new tax law or something."

"This is not what I envisioned my legal practice would be when I went to law school. Inventing business for clients. Paying house calls. Keeping them company. Letting them beat me at checkers. Wiping away their drool."

"Jeez, Brady," she said. "Visiting your clients, making them feel worthwhile, is the main thing you do. It's what you're good at. Whether you like it or not, it's your niche. So you better get on with it."

"Do I really hafta?"

She grinned away the glare. "You hafta, pal."

So I returned Jeff's call. Julie was right. He wanted me to visit him. "I need to talk to you," he said.

"Can't do it on the phone, huh?"

"Nope."

"Gimme a hint."

"The will. Some other stuff."

I sighed. "Yeah, well let me check my schedule."

"Screw your schedule. This weekend. I know you don't do anything on weekends. Any reason you can't make it Friday suppertime?"

I told him the truth. Telling the truth is one of my weaknesses. It's the reason I have Julie screen my calls. She lies better than I do. So I told Jeff yeah, okay, he was right, I had no weekend plans, as usual, and there was no reason—aside from the fact that I loathed the thought of it—that I couldn't drive down and spend the weekend with him. I told him part of the deal was that I'd take his canoe onto his pond in the evening to see if I could catch some of those big rainbows that sipped tiny insects off the surface after the sun sank behind the hill. Jeff said he didn't give a shit one way or the other, which, from him, constituted unbounded enthusiasm.

The last time Joey, my younger son, borrowed my car, he left a collection of his tapes in it. I fumbled in the glove compartment while I drove, looking for my Mozart and Beethoven. All I came up with was something by a group called ZZ Top, which I unexpectedly liked, and then one by Van Halen, which I didn't. Then a treasure—Jimi Hendrix. And then The Who and Chicago and Three Dog Night and Janis Joplin and, mercy me, Chuck Berry.

I revised my opinion of the next generation's taste in music. They liked my old stuff. Good kids. Smart. There was hope.

And I got to play it all as I sat in a great cloud of automobile exhaust, bumping and stopping in first gear on Route 3 all the way from Marshfield to the Sagamore Bridge.

Cape Cod in the summer. Humbug.

Grinding along in that traffic gave me time to ponder the message I'd found on the answering machine in my apartment before I'd left. It was from Joey. He said: "Dad. It's Joey. Give me a call." That was all.

When I listened to it, I got a vaguely uneasy sense that I couldn't pinpoint. There was nothing in his tone, nothing in the content of his message, that seemed disturbing. I'd tried calling him back, of course. But all I got was Gloria's businesslike message. "You've reached the Coyne residence. Please leave your number and we'll get right back to you." I told her machine that I was returning Joey's call, that I'd be away for the weekend, and that I'd call again when I got back. Then I loaded up my car and pointed it toward Orleans on the Cape.

But after Joey's message had a chance to rattle around in my head during that slow drive down Route 3, I recognized what it was that bothered me.

Dad. Joey never called me "Dad." It was always Pop, or Old Man. And he'd called himself Joey, too. He hadn't done that since he turned twelve. That's when he became Joe. Joe Coyne. Tough, grown-up Joe Coyne. Gloria and I still called him Joey, of course, and he tolerated it. But to his friends and teachers—and especially to himself—it was Joe.

Another thing about that brief phone message. No joke, no wisecrack, not even a hint about what he wanted. That, too, was uncharacteristic.

I concluded that something was wrong, and a small wart of fear took up residence in my stomach. If something was wrong with my son, then something was wrong with me. Maybe I'd have a chance to call him from Jeff's place. I expected to have plenty of loose time. It promised to be a long, boring weekend.

There's a big sign where you swing around the rotary onto the bridge. It says, "Desperate? Call the Samaritans." For all the weekend commuters, I guessed. I suspected the Samaritans did a big business in the summer, what with desperate traffic-jammed vacationers trying to drive off the bridge into the canal.

I hooked onto Route 6A after the bridge, and it went faster, through salt marshes and over tidal creeks and past all the neat little authentic silver-shingled Cape Cod houses and antique shops.

It took me three and a quarter hours that Friday afternoon in July to drive from my apartment off Atlantic Avenue on the Boston Harbor to Jeff Newton's place on Quashnet Lane in Orleans, down at the narrow bend of the Cape's elbow. I figured I averaged thirty miles an hour.

I wound up the long driveway past several "Beware of Dogs" signs and tucked my BMW under the canopied branches of a wind-twisted Cape Cod pine tree. The other car there was a white Cherokee four-wheel drive. It belonged to Lily Robbins, Jeff Newton's full-time housekeeper. Jeff didn't drive anymore.

I grabbed my overnight bag from the backseat and stepped out. Even on the hilltop, no sea breeze stirred the humid summer air. Somewhere in the shimmering afternoon heat a bobwhite whistled. In the distance off to my left stretched a silvery ribbon of the Atlantic Ocean, blurred in the afternoon haze so that the line between ocean and sky was fuzzy. Down the hill to my right huddled Thomas Jefferson Newton's trout pond.

Jeff's little compound lay ahead of me, at the top of the hill at the end of a wide pathway. I clunked the car door shut, giving it plenty of emphasis. I didn't want to take the dogs by surprise.

I approached the gate, ten feet of heavy-gauge one-inch chain link wired onto steel crosspieces. The fence enclosed Jeff's rambling unstained cedar-shingled bungalow and the three or four acres of grounds, the retreat from which he rarely ventured since he returned there, six years earlier, mangled in body and spirit.

The two Dobermans crouched inside the gate waiting for me. They were sleek and black and thoroughly malign, with narrowed hate-filled eyes. When they spotted me, their lips curled back from their fangs. The muscles along their shoulders rippled with nervous anticipation. They wanted to rip flesh from my bones. Good clean doggie fun. It's what they lived for.

I reached for the pull rope and clanged the big brass bell to announce my arrival. That's when the dogs began to leap. They hurled themselves against the fence. They didn't bark or growl. They whined high in their throats, as if I was withholding their dinner from them, which I suppose is how they saw it. Savage, stupid, single-minded, again and again they attacked the fence, throat-high on a man, the claws of all four of their feet clinging momentarily to the mesh at each onslaught before they fell back, only to leap again. Their teeth snapped at the fence as they would have preferred to snap at my face.

"Come on, guys," I said. "It's me, your old pal, Brady. Cut it out."

The sound of my voice intensified their mindless efforts. The two of them crashed against the chain link, one after the other. Saliva dripped from their flashing teeth. I would have felt better if they had barked or at least growled.

I approached to within a foot of the fence. "Tondo," I said softly.

The first dog sat instantly, cocked his head at me, lolled out his tongue, and began to pant.

"Ngwenya," I said to the other dog, slurring the consonants the way Jeff had taught me. The second dog, too, sat.

Jeff had named his twin Dobermans after the African game he used to kill. He had patiently taught me how to pronounce their names, which served as passwords with the dogs. If you knew their names, you were their friends, and therefore immune from attack. Few people knew the dogs' names. Few people entered Jeff Newton's compound.

Tondo was the African word for an old tuskless elephant, a fiercer, more aggressive critter than his ivoried counterpart.

Tondo would not bluff. Tondo was grouchy, quick-tempered, ruthless.

Ngwenya was the croc. Jeff once told me that crocodiles polished off an average of ten human beings a day in Africa, making them the most prolific mankillers on the dark continent. When a croc's jaws glom onto an animal, human or otherwise, it drags it to the bottom of the river and rams it into the mud under a log until the victim's flesh ages to suit the croc's palate. Jeff says he once saw a twelve-foot crocodile grab a two-ton hippo by the nose and haul it under water until the big stupid herbivore drowned.

Jeff hated crocodiles. And he had no particular love for tuskless elephants, either. They had personalities to match his Dobermans. Jeff Newton did love his dogs. They were about the only living creatures he did love. Perhaps, in his own way, he loved Lily. He claimed to like me.

Jeff despised himself.

I yanked the pull rope again. The bell bonged. A minute later Lily came down the path. She unlocked the gate, pulled it open, smiled, and held her hand to me.

"Ah, Brady," she said. "Boy, is it good to see you."

I gripped her hand. She pecked a kiss onto my cheek. "Himself's been looking forward to seeing you," she said. She had a musky smell, a complex compound of clean sweat, salt air, and flower blossoms.

"Can't honestly say it's mutual," I said, returning her chaste kiss. "But you are looking absolutely great."

She wore blue jogging shorts and the flowered bikini top of a bathing suit. Lily was a big girl, only a couple inches shorter than I, and meaty. But her meat was firm muscle, so that she gave the illusion of slenderness, especially in shorts. She had long legs, still shapely, and a heavy but solid bosom. Creases along the sides of her mouth and streaks of gray in her black hair betrayed her age. Fortyish, I guessed. She had been with Jeff for nearly fifteen years.

A red bandana was wrapped around her forehead. She was, as usual, barefoot. Beads of perspiration stood out on her chest and forehead. "Oh, hell, I'm a mess," she said. "I was pulling some weeds from the rock garden out back when I heard the bell." She tucked a wisp of hair back under the bandana. "Well, come on in."

She took my overnight bag and grabbed my arm. We went through the gate. "Down," said Lily to the dogs.

The two dogs stretched out their forelegs and lay down. They flattened their chins onto their knees and followed us with their eyes. I reached down and scratched the muzzles of each of them, muttering their names again. "Tondo. Ngwenya," I said, using my best "nice puppy" tone. "You nasty sons of bitches. You should both be shot." They jiggled their little stub tails in appreciation.

Lily laughed. "Did they behave themselves for you?"

"Impeccably, as usual. They wanted to tear my throat out."

She grinned. "You spoke their names."

"Yes. Magic words. Where's Jeff?"

She jerked her head toward the house. "On the terrace. Staring off toward the ocean, as usual. As if he could see Africa if he looked hard and long enough."

"How is he?"

She shrugged. "No better than last time you were here. No worse, either, I suppose. Up and down, as usual. He sleeps. He stares at the sea. Sometimes manic, usually depressive. He looks forward to his doctor's visit. The highlight of his week. Except, of course, when you come to call." She hugged my arm against her breast. She was strong. I couldn't have resisted if I'd wanted to. Which I didn't. "Come on," she said. "You always cheer him up. And the martinis are all mixed."

She led me into the cool interior of the house. Floor-to-ceiling windows gave a long view of the ocean. I paused by the series of glass cases that were lined up on the table beside the fireplace.

"The jaguars," I said. "God, they're beautiful."

Lily, standing beside me still holding my arm, nodded. "I never tire of looking at them."

There were seven of them, each under its own glass dome. Solid gold jaguars with oval emerald eyes, fashioned centuries earlier in the crude impressionistic style of Mayan artisans. Each was sixteen or eighteen inches long from tip of nose to tip of tail. They had been molded in different positions—some crouched, some caught in mid running stride, some standing with their heads held high, as if they were sniffing the jungle breezes. I had hefted one of them once, and its weight had surprised me.

But mainly it was the eyes, those opaque, pale green eyes without pupils, that fascinated me. Primitive, deadly fire seemed to glow inside those eyes.

My friend Daniel LaBreque from the Museum of Fine Arts brought down his assistant, Marla Conway, who specialized in Mayan and Aztec artifacts, to appraise those seven cats soon after Jeff brought them home. They agreed that the fourteen emerald eyes alone put the value of the collection in the early six figures. Then there was the gold, primitively smelted yet as pure as the ingots that theoretically backed American currency. Nearly one hundred pounds of gold. "Fort Knox," Dan had said. "By God, this is Fort Knox gold."

Dan estimated their worth at one-point-two million dollars. Marla put it nearer one-point-seven.

The value of the seven jaguars derived more from their

provenance than from the gold and emeralds, however. They were pre-Columbian—fourteenth century, according to Marla —from the Mayan civilization of southeastern Mexico near the border of Belize, which was still called British Honduras when Jeff hunted real jaguars in the Yucatan. The seven gold jaguars had been gifts from a grateful Mayan Indian chief to Jeff Newton, then an apprentice professional hunter, who had slain the cat that had eaten away the face and throat of the chief's eldest son while he was urinating against a tree in the jungle. The gold jaguars had lived with the old patriarch's tribe for uncounted generations. The tribesmen worshipped them, as they worshipped the living cats themselves. They were the ultimate reward for the man who had avenged the death of the heir to the tribal throne.

Although they were freely given to him, technically the jaguars did not belong to Jeff. They belonged to the government of Mexico. No pre-Columbian artifacts could legally leave the country after 1971. The United States government supported the Mexican law.

Jeff Newton didn't care. He didn't care what those jaguars were worth, and he didn't care about the Mexican law. Had he wanted to sell them, he would've had a problem. But he didn't intend to sell them. Jeff, I knew, loved those seven golden jaguars perhaps as much as he loved his dogs. Probably more than he loved any human being.

Dan LaBreque did care. He called Jeff a thief. Insofar as a law was being violated, I cared, too. But there wasn't anything either of us could do about it.

Lily tugged at my arm. "Come on," she said. "The great hunter is waiting. He heard the bell. He'll be wondering what we're up to."

She led me through double glass doors onto the fieldstone patio behind the house. Thomas Jefferson Newton lay on a chaise longue facing off to the east, his back to me. His thinning white hair grew close to his scalp. Pale urine-yellow streaks stained it. The back of his neck was thin. The two cords stood out in sharp relief. Even in the muggy Cape Cod summer heat, he had a blanket spread over his legs. His crutch was propped on the wrought-iron table beside him. The promised pitcher of martinis and two glasses sat on the table.

I turned to Lily and arched my brows at her.

"Go ahead," she said softly. "I got some things to do in the kitchen."

I shrugged and stepped out onto the terrace.

"Jeff," I said.

He waved his hand without turning around. "Come sit down, Brady," he said.

I went over and perched on the edge of the chair beside his chaise. He turned his head slowly and peered at me through watery blue eyes. I was startled at his appearance. I had seen him dozens of times since he got out of the hospital six years earlier, but I still remembered him as the dark, powerful man who had gone to Africa. He was, I knew, barely fifty. He looked twenty years older. His skin glowed with the papery translucence of old age. It was patched with pink blotches as if disease was showing itself, except along the three parallel scars that began in front of his left ear and angled across his cheek, through his lips, and across his chin. The scars shone stark white.

He reached toward me. "Shitty weather," he said.

I squeezed his bony hand. "Summer on the Cape," I said. "It's what you get."

"Traffic bad?"

"As always. Route 3 was backed up to Marshfield."

"Cape's going to hell," he said. "Just like the rest of the

world. Pour us a martini. And fill the damn glass all the way up. Lily doesn't know how to fill a glass with a martini."

I poured from the pitcher into the glasses and handed one to Jeff. He took it and brought it to his lips. I noticed that his hand trembled, and when he sipped, some of the drink dribbled from the corner of his mouth. He swallowed, cleared his throat, and took another, longer swallow.

He cocked his head and narrowed his eyes to look at me. "You gaining weight?" he said.

I shrugged. "I don't know. I never bother weighing myself."

"Fatter in the jowls," he said.

"Thanks." I lit a cigarette.

"Those things'll kill you."

"Something's got to," I said.

"Stupid habit."

I nodded and sipped my martini. "How are you feeling, other than mean-spirited and nasty?" I said.

"Piss poor. As usual. Nice of you to ask, as if you couldn't see for yourself."

He stared down at his legs, twin lumps under the blanket. One of them, I knew, was half the diameter of the other. Most of the thigh muscle had been torn away from the bone by the windmilling hind legs of the same leopard that had gouged his face and clomped its teeth through his shoulder and ripped at his abdomen. "The body's as good as it's going to get. I still dream about that hospital, those doctors mumbling in their deep voices, a dialect I didn't know. They all looked like Magic Johnson."

He smiled quickly at me, then drank again, emptying his glass. Without speaking he handed it to me. I refilled it and gave it back. He sipped, more slowly this time, and stared out toward the ocean.

"I been thinking," he said. "When Jack Kennedy was my age, he was already dead."

I smiled. "That doesn't necessarily make you old."

"No. Other things make you old besides the passage of the years. You have any idea what it's like to feel absolutely powerless? To have no control, to know what you want, to know it's right, and to realize that there's not a damn thing you can do except wait, even then knowing that it probably won't happen the way you want it to?"

I shrugged.

He snorted a mirthless laugh through his nose. "No," he said, "I didn't figure you'd understand. The only thing worse is to look back and see your mistake and know you blew it, and know what you should've done, and know you can't ever go back and try it again, do it right, make it right, and you've just got to live with it, and you don't know how you can, but you do, day to day, hour to hour, churning it around and around in your head."

I looked out toward the ocean and said nothing.

"So," he continued in his weak, moist, old man's voice, "I screwed up the past and I can't do a goddam thing about the future. So here sits Jeff Newton, professional hunter, twisted and broken inside and out. A poor excuse for a human being."

"Stop feeling sorry for yourself," I said. "You're alive."

"More's the pity."

"Jeff, for Christ sake," I said, "it's been six years."

"The man died," he said softly. "His name was Walter McIntyre and he was a chemical engineer from Teaneck, New Jersey. It was his first trip to Africa. He was my client and *Nyalubwe* got him. I killed him."

TWO

• • • • • • •

JEFF REACHED OVER and put his hand on my leg. "I don't usually talk about it," he said quietly. "But I think about it all the time. That instant in my life. It changed everything."

"Jeff, you don't have to . . ."

He shook his head. "I remember that leopard's breath. It was hot and rotten on my face. And the red. I saw red. Blood in my eyes. And the pain and the rush of adrenaline. The pain was only for an instant, and it seemed to be everywhere. But all that was the same instant of memory as the business I had to do, getting the muzzle of my gun against that cat's belly and blowing him away. I wasn't thinking of dying. Not then. I was thinking of killing. And I wasn't thinking of Walter McIntyre, the poor silly son of a bitch. If he'd stayed in the hide he would've been fine. And so would I. I would've found that cat and killed him. He followed me into the tall grass after I told him not to." Jeff arched his eyebrows. "I keep telling myself it was his fault. And it was. But I was responsible for him."

"Can't you just let it go?" I said.

He gazed out toward the ocean. "No," he said after a long pause. "No, I guess I can't. See, there was something else that happened. Another series of thoughts on a different, deeper, more abstract level. I was thinking that finally, this was it,

what I had been waiting for. This was the moment I had
wanted. Hand to hand with a leopard. Equal terms. His teeth
and claws, my shotgun, strength against strength on the terrain that we both knew. This was why I had come to Africa.
To kill or be killed. Before I went unconscious, when I still
didn't know which of us was the winner, I experienced this
odd, wonderful sense of fulfillment, a kind of peace, as if it had
all, finally, come together for me. At that instant I think I
believed I was dead. And right then it was okay."

He turned his head and stared at me. "See," he said, "it
isn't really guilt over Walter McIntyre. That would be simple.
And it wasn't death. I didn't fear death itself. But it was death
in that tall grass. When I was in the hospital I dreamed about
it. I still do. Weird, terrifying dreams. In the hospital I think I
would've welcomed a peaceful death, numbed by drugs and
fever and pain. I hallucinated on images of all the animals I'd
ever killed coming after me, goring me and trampling me and
ripping at me with their teeth and tusks and claws. It was
them that I feared, not death itself. So I knew. I couldn't go
back. A lot of hunters get hurt. They go back. I knew I
couldn't. That's what's so hard to live with."

Jeff closed his eyes.

"Is that why you wanted me to come?" I said. "To share
this with me?"

He turned his head slowly and opened one eye. He gave
me a quick, ironic smile, then closed his eye. "Ignore me," he
mumbled.

Jeff's body healed as much as it was going to after he
killed his last African leopard. The razor claws of that gutshot
leopard had permanently reduced the big muscles of his left
thigh to strings, but with the support of a crutch he was able to

dodder around the bungalow. He had lost one testicle. His shoulder and his face healed. His soul never did.

He lived on the royalties from the books he had written about Africa and the films he had made. It was a living for him. Barely. But then, Jeff Newton himself was barely living.

On my rare trips to Orleans to visit him, I tried to persuade him to go out onto the pond with me in his canoe, or take a stroll through the wooded gardens inside the fence, or climb into my car for a drive to the ocean.

"Another time, maybe," was his standard reply.

Once I suggested he write another book.

"Can't even begin to think of it," he said.

He read a little, watched some television. According to Lily, he mostly lay around with his eyes closed listening to Mozart tapes, and on especially nice days he let her persuade him to sit out on the patio to look at the flowers she was cultivating in the terraced rock gardens and watch the hummingbirds and sniff the salty breezes. He received company infrequently and unenthusiastically.

He still slept away more than half of each day. He continued to require medication for the residual infections and chronic pain. A local doctor visited him weekly.

At first, Lily had cooked elaborate meals for him. But Jeff showed no enthusiasm for her efforts and only picked at them, so after a while she gave it up. She fed him canned soup and sandwiches. He grew thinner and softer and more wrinkled.

Life, it seemed, was a condition to be endured until something better came along.

Now we were sipping martinis at the end of this Friday in July.

After a while, I said, "Did you want to talk business?"

He opened his eyes. "Why the hell else would I ask you to come down here?"

I smiled.

"I want to rethink my will."

"Not much to think about, Jeff. You haven't got a helluva lot to leave behind."

"I got this place. I got the movies and books. I got the jaguars."

I shrugged. The place was mortgaged, the movies and books weren't worth much, and I had long ago persuaded him to will the jaguars to the Museum of Fine Arts, knowing that they'd return them to the Mexican government.

"I want to take care of things," he said. "Set things right."

"How?" Jeff had a simple will. Jeff's wife divorced him when he took off for Africa. Everything except the jaguars was going to his kids fifty-fifty.

He closed his eyes again. "We'll discuss it later."

A few minutes later Lily came out onto the patio. She carried a glass, which she filled from the martini pitcher. She pulled a chair close to mine. Jeff opened his eyes, glanced at her, and closed them again.

She had brushed back her hair and tied it into a ponytail with a yellow ribbon. She had done something to her eyes. She wore a white sleeveless blouse, knotted at her stomach, over her bikini top.

"How's fresh lobster salad sound?" she said.

"Terrific," I said.

Jeff mumbled, "Mmm."

Lily stuck out her tongue at him. "You can have a peanut butter sandwich, you old shit."

"Good."

"It's Friday, don't forget. Dr. Sauerman'll be here after supper. Think you can stay awake that long?"

"Mmm."

She looked at me. "Brilliant conversationalist." She took a big gulp of her drink. "Come on, Brady. See what I've done with the gardens."

She took my hand and led me down the path that zig-zagged among the terraces on the hillside behind the house. She had planted them with exotic Japanese irises and gladioli. The irises had finished blooming, but the glads spread great washes of color against all the greenery, oranges and pinks, reds and whites, and Lily told me the names of all of them. Over the years, she had set out azaleas and rhododendrons and lilacs, ground covers of myrtle and pachysandra, wildflowers and herbs, and here and there, where a column of sunshine angled between the trees, a cluster of annuals made a brilliant splash. There were three or four acres in all, amidst a forest of gnarled pine and pin oak and Volkswagen-sized boulders, all enclosed by the ten-foot chain link fence where the patrols of Tondo and Ngwenya had worn paths.

At the foot of the hill a little rock-paved pool caught a trickle from a hidden spring. It tinkled and gurgled over a miniature waterfall. A jumble of boulders made natural seats beside it, and Lily and I sat down. A screen of giant rhododendrons and tall pines shaded the place. It smelled cool and moist.

"The whole place was supposed to be a sort of benign jungle," said Lily. "A place for the professional hunter to come, acclimate himself, watch the little animals and birds. When he was still hunting, it was a place to meditate, and he used to wander around a lot. After he came back for good, I thought it would be a place where he could heal." She placed her hands beside her to brace herself on the rock where she sat. She arched her back. "It hasn't worked," she said. "He doesn't come down here anymore. Says the hill is too much for him. Which is total bullshit. He can get around fine. Oh, he likes to hobble on his crutch and piss and moan, but I've seen him when he thinks I'm not looking. He's got a limp is all. Sometimes he plays with the dogs, and he forgets himself, I guess, and he bounds around like a kid."

I lit a cigarette. "What about you?"

She smiled. "Me? What about me?"

"What's in it for you?"

She shifted on the rock so that she was sitting cross-legged facing me. She propped her elbows on her knees, rested her chin on her folded hands, and frowned. "Once upon a time there was this young woman whose man dumped her. He told her it wasn't working. That was his only explanation. It wasn't satisfactory. She"—Lily peered up at me—"I, that is—I didn't understand. I was unprepared."

I nodded. "I've been through something like that," I said.

Lily smiled and shrugged. "I guess lots of people have. It's new to everyone, though, when it happens. Anyway, the young woman was shattered. She moped around for a year. She thought she'd blown her only chance at happiness. With no hope or enthusiasm for it, but because she was broke and didn't know what else to do, she took a job keeping house for a fascinating, colorful man, an older man who had, coincidentally, abandoned his wife. She must've been as baffled as me. Now this young woman had no particular skills, if you exclude certain man-catching tricks that came pretty naturally and didn't seem to work for very long. But the pay was good, considering the work was pretty menial, and the demands were few. The man was around only enough to continue to seem fascinating and colorful. The woman's tricks worked because about the time they might begin to wear thin the man was off to another exotic jungle. Mostly, she was alone, which was okay by her. She kept the house clean, dusted the glass cases where the pretty jaguars lived, took care of the stupid dogs, and planted elaborate gardens. She waited for the hunter to come home to admire everything she had done. And when he did she loved him. She didn't assume he loved her. It wasn't part of the bargain, and it wasn't necessary. She always knew he'd leave, and she knew he'd always come back to her, and that was enough."

"You've been with him a long time," I said.

She nodded. "Yes. I was young when I came here. Now I'm not young anymore. It doesn't bother me. I have no regrets. Oh, I assumed when Jeff got old he'd retire from his hunting and then we'd be together, and it would be glamorous. Well, it's all happened. It just didn't turn out very glamorous, did it?"

"You could quit."

"And what would happen to him?"

"He could hire someone else."

"Know something? I don't think he would. I think he'd just lie around until he died."

"Or maybe he'd gather himself together and start to live."

She cocked her head and looked at me. "You think I'm holding him back?"

"I think," I said slowly, "he may be playing the invalid role to the hilt, and that he needs an audience for it."

"And without me for an audience he'd do better?"

"He couldn't do worse, could he?"

Lily's eyes brimmed. "Aw, shit," she said.

I reached to her and touched her arm. "I'm sorry," I said. "I didn't mean it the way it sounded."

"Yeah," she said. "Yeah, you did. I've thought of that. You're probably right. I try to see myself as some kind of

Florence Nightingale, sacrificing myself for the sake of this broken and twisted old man. But I'm really doing it for me, aren't I?"

I shrugged. "What do I know about it?"

She took my hand and squeezed it quickly. "Nothing." She tried to smile. "Can I tell you something?"

"If you want to. And if you're prepared to put up with a tactless reply, which I seem to be especially good at."

She nodded. "You are. Good at tactlessness, I mean." She let go of my hand and stared off into the woods. "We were lovers, of course. I assume everybody knew that. We were probably never exactly in love. But we loved each other, in our ways. And it was good, Brady. It was good enough for me, at least. The boundaries were clear, and that may be as good as it ever gets for anybody."

"No argument there."

"Since he came back—since his, the whatchacallit—the accident—he can't, or he won't, he doesn't want to . . ."

I nodded.

"He's like a baby," she said softly. "Once in a while, usually when he has his bad dreams, he wants to be held, rocked, cuddled. Mostly, though, he's cruel to me. This man was a powerful lover. Tender, strong. Sometimes almost brutal, but . . ." She smiled at the memory. "Oh, he was something. Now?" She shook her head quickly. "I shouldn't be talking about it." She stood up. "Come on. Let's go back."

I held out my hands to her and she took them and I helped her climb down from the rock. She kept hold of one of my hands as we followed the pathway back to the bungalow.

Jeff hadn't moved from the chaise. He appeared to be asleep. The martini pitcher looked emptier than it had when we left. I sat beside him while Lily continued into the house. I lit a cigarette and stared up into the darkening sky.

"You and her gettin' it on in the woods?" Jeff said after a few minutes.

"For Christ sake," I said.

"She's a helluva lay. Shame for something nice like that to go to waste."

"You're drunk. Shut up."

"Can't service her properly anymore. Half a man. Half my quota of testicles."

"A matter of looking at your scrotum as half full or half empty, I guess," I said.

"Funny."

I shrugged.

He stared off toward the ocean. "She finds me repulsive," he said.

"You ever consider the possibility that the only one who finds you repulsive is you?"

He glanced sideways at me. "Thank you, Dr. Freud."

"You're welcome."

"She throws a good fuck, though, I'll tell you that."

"Don't be an asshole, Jeff."

"Hey, I see how you two look at each other. So go ahead. Climb between those sweet thighs. You two deserve each other."

I sighed. "Grow up, Jeff. It's time you grew up. Your hunting days are over."

"I am some kind of asshole, ain't I?" he said.

"Yes," I said.

Lily came out and stood beside us. "Chow time," she said brightly. "Hobble on in here, men."

"Help me up, Brady," said Jeff.

I held my hands to him and he heaved himself into a sitting position on the chaise. He disentangled his legs from the blanket and swiveled them over the side. Lily handed him his crutch and he used it to brace himself so he could stand. Then without looking at us he stumped into the house.

Lily and I watched him go. She touched my arm. "What were you two talking about?"

"The fact that he's an asshole," I said.

Big chunks of lobster claw and tail and bits of onion and celery, mixed in a homemade mayonnaise lightly spiced with dill, mounded on leaves of Bibb lettuce, with slices of early local tomatoes and cucumbers and hot rolls on the side. Lily had decanted a Riesling for the occasion. She declared it "piquant" and I countered with "foxy." "Gnomical," she said. "Canny," I retorted.

"Bullshit," said Jeff.

He ate little. His fork vibrated in his hand and his lips quivered. Once or twice during the meal his eyelids drooped, but he caught himself with a jerk.

"What time is that doctor supposed to come?" he growled at Lily.

"Nine-thirty, as always."

"Nine-thirty, as always." He mimicked her in a high-pitched, querulous voice. He shoved back his chair, fumbled for his crutch leaning on the wall beside him, and staggered to a standing position. "I'll be in my bedroom. You two can play word games to your hearts' content, or grapple around in each other's crotches, for all I care."

After he left the room, Lily looked at me. Tears glittered in her eyes. "He's not always like this," she said. She tried to smile. "Sometimes he gets kind of grouchy."

"You don't need to tolerate it."

She shrugged. "I can. I suppose I will continue to."

I helped her clear the table. Then I went into the living

room and sat in the darkness looking out at the purple summer sky while she loaded the dishwasher.

A few minutes later she came in and sat beside me. Her leg pressed against mine and her cheek rested against my shoulder. "Maybe we should," she said softly.

"Should what?"

"What he said." She chuckled quickly. "You know. Grapple around in each other's crotches."

I kissed the top of her head. "No we shouldn't."

"No discussion?"

"No discussion."

She squirmed against me. "Why not?"

"You know why."

"What if I left him?"

"That would be different."

"Would it really?"

"Yes."

"Does that mean . . . ?"

"That I find you attractive, yes."

I felt her take a deep breath and let it out. "That's something, I guess."

We sat in silence. After a while, she said, "I'm not going to, though."

"Not going to what?"

"Leave him."

"No, I suppose you're not."

Sometime later I heard the clang of the bell. Lily stood up. "He's here."

"The doctor?"

"No one else comes here." She went toward the door.

"Can't he pronounce the dogs' names?"

"Oh, heavens, no. You're the only one."

She turned on some lights before she went outside. I

heard her speak to the dogs, and a minute later she returned, leading a tall, stooped man wearing rimless glasses. He had a smooth round face and a smooth round head fringed on the sides with reddish-brown hair. He appeared to be not much older than thirty. He actually carried a black bag.

I stood up and went to him.

"Dr. Sauerman, this is Brady Coyne, Jeff's lawyer," said Lily.

We shook hands. His grip was firm and he peered solemnly into my eyes. "Pleasure, sir," he said.

"He seems eager to see you," I said.

He nodded.

"The highlight of his week," said Lily.

"He is not a well man," said Sauerman.

"So he insists," I said.

The doctor frowned for an instant, then turned to Lily. "Well, I better go in."

Lily did not follow him. We stood in the middle of the living room for a moment. "More wine?" she said.

"Bourbon, I think."

"Sounds good."

She was back a minute later with two short glasses tinkling with ice. We took separate seats. "I'm sorry," she said.

"For what?"

"That previous conversation. I know you're his friend and a loyal person."

I shrugged. "I'm his lawyer, that's all."

"But a loyal person."

"Something like that, I suppose."

After a while the doctor came out. "Well, that's that, then," he said.

"How is he?" I said.

"Sleeping."

"No, I mean . . ."

Sauerman shrugged. "Nothing changes. Physically, he'll always have pain. And without his medication, any one of those dozen or so infections could crop up again. The antibiotics seem to keep them down, whatever they are. Otherwise, he's fine."

"And mentally?"

"What you see is what you get. That's not my field. I take his temperature and BP, poke around at his body, listen to his heart and lungs, leave a week's supply of medication. He's an unhappy man. Doesn't take a doctor to diagnose that." To Lily he said, "Let me out of here, please. I don't like those dogs."

"No one likes those dogs. Except Jeff. You don't want to stay for a drink?"

He shook his head. "The wife's at a party in Chatham. I better get there before Harry Carter drags her upstairs."

"I didn't know you guys did house calls anymore," I said.

Sauerman shrugged. "He refuses to leave the house. He needs medical attention. What's the choice?"

"Hippocrates lives," I said.

He frowned for an instant. Lily took his arm. "Come on, then. Tondo and Ngwenya are out there slobbering. Let's disappoint them."

While Lily was showing Dr. Sauerman out, I took my empty glass into the kitchen, rinsed it out, and set it beside the sink. I remembered Joey's disturbing message, so I picked up the kitchen phone and pecked out the familiar number in Wellesley. It was the same phone number Gloria and I were given when we bought the place all those lifetimes ago. The line was busy. I listened to the monotonous beep for several seconds before I hung up. Then I wandered out onto the patio. I lit a cigarette and waved ineffectually at the mosquitoes that came swarming. I smoked half of it and flicked it off into the darkness, then retreated back inside.

Lily was in the kitchen loading the coffeepot. "Your bed's all made up," she said.

I nodded. "How long has that doctor been treating Jeff?"

"Around two years. He went through about half a dozen before he found one he liked. Dr. Sauerman doesn't mind coming to the house. He kids around with Jeff. Doesn't mind spending a little time with him. The others were always looking at their watches, reminding everybody how dedicated they were."

"But Jeff doesn't seem to get better."

Lily shrugged. "I guess he's as well as he'll ever get." She rinsed her hands in the sink and turned to face me. "Aren't all of us, though?"

I smiled. "Probably." I stretched elaborately and yawned. "Well, I'm off to bed."

She tiptoed up and kissed my cheek. "Night, Brady. Sleep well."

Ten minutes later I was lying there reading a new book on Western fly fishing, waiting for my eyelids to clang shut. I heard something scratching softly at my door.

"Do not enter," I said.

The door pushed open and Lily came in. She was wearing a long nightgown, pale blue and sheer so that her nipples were clearly visible under it.

"Depart," I said.

"Old poop," she said. She sat on the side of my bed.

"Really," I said. "Please."

She touched the side of my face. "You sure?"

"Positive." I closed my book and put it on the floor.

She bent down and kissed my cheek. "Absolutely positive?" she whispered against the side of my face.

I grasped her shoulders and pushed her gently away. "For Christ sake, no, of course I'm not. So please go."

She smiled and stood up. She put her hands on her hips. "Who's teasing who here?"

"Whom," I said.

"Right."

She turned and padded out of the room. She latched the door quietly behind her.

I sighed and turned off the light. My eyelids then did clang shut.

It seemed that I had been sleeping for a long time when my eyes popped open. Through the bedroom window, I could see the sky. It was dark and starry. I lay there, tense and alert. Something had awakened me. I heard nothing.

A night bird, maybe. Or maybe it was the country silence, a kind of booming absence of sound compared to the city noises that normally lulled me to sleep.

Then I heard it. A muffled footfall outside my door, a rustle of fabric. The latch clicked. Slowly the door opened, emitting a faint light from the hallway. A figure appeared silhouetted against it.

Lily. She had come back. I started to speak to her but, for some reason, weakness, probably, or curiosity, I didn't. I closed my eyes and pretended to sleep and waited for her to come to me.

The hand on my mouth was hard and callused. A light shone in my eyes. I closed them against it. I felt an elbow on my chest and I could smell harsh breath. I tried to gather my knees to shove at this weight on me, but he was strong and he had me pinned.

I tried to yell, but his hand covered my mouth.

"Keep quiet or I'll kill you," said a deep muffled voice.

I squinted against the blinding light. There were two of

them, I realized. One holding a flashlight, the other pressing his weight on me. They wore something over their heads. Ski masks. I felt something sharp pressed against the side of my neck, and it took no imagination to know it was the point of a knife. I closed my eyes again, waiting.

"Say a word and this goes in to the hilt." He took the knifepoint away from my chin and pressed its sharp edge against my collarbone. "I mean it, pal," said the man. Then the blade broke the skin, a sudden, hot, tugging pain. I felt blood ooze and begin to dribble down my chest.

He removed his hand from my mouth. He moved the point of the knife into my nostril. "Should I rip off his nose?" the man said to his companion. The other guy laughed. I remembered what had happened to Jack Nicholson in the movie *Chinatown.*

"Just don't move," he said.

"Okay," I managed to say. I hated the fear I heard in my voice. I hated the man for creating my fear.

He wrapped a wide strip of tape over my mouth and completely around my head. He taped my wrists to the bedposts. I twisted and tugged at them, but the tape was too strong. Duct tape, I thought vaguely. That's what I'd use.

"I think I'll kill him anyway," said the voice conversationally.

"Why not?" said the other man, the first time he had spoken.

I felt the knife edge across my Adam's apple. He moved it a millimeter and again my skin split open. The blade was as sharp as razors I had cut myself with shaving, and the sensation was the same. Except I could picture the glittering blade and how easily it could slice through tendons and muscles and cartilage.

My heart pounded. I felt an almost irrepressible urge to

urinate. I swallowed against my gag reflex. I couldn't seem to get enough air through my nose. With the tape over my mouth, I thought I would suffocate. Never had I felt such fear. I stared wildly into the darkness, but outside the cone of light from the flashlight all I could make out were the intruders' fuzzy gray shapes.

I waited for that blade to slice across my throat, to sever all those tubes and tendons that connected me to my body, so that my life would spill out onto my pillow. I expected to die, and the thing that made me angriest was that if I died, I'd lose the chance to rip the eyeballs out of the heads of those two men.

When one of them slugged me on the side of my head with something hard and heavy, I saw lights for an instant, brilliant, exploding flashes like a silent fireworks display, reds and yellows and greens bursting and cascading inside my head.

They faded as quickly as they had appeared. Then the darkness became absolute.

THREE

• • • • • • •

I DON'T KNOW how long I was out. When I opened my eyes, the sky outside the bedroom window looked the same as it had before. The only thing different was the sharp pain in my head and the dried blood that I could feel caked on my chest from the wound on my collarbone.

I twisted my wrists against the tape that bound them to the bedposts. Both of my arms had gone tingly and numb and weak, and I was unable to get them loose. I felt a moment of panic. Suppose Jeff and Lily were similarly immobilized. All three of us might just lie there in our beds until we died. Nobody but Dr. Sauerman ever came to the place, and he wouldn't be back for a week. Besides, he couldn't get past the dogs.

These kinds of thoughts accelerated my pulse so that it thudded in my chest and throbbed in the wound on the side of my head, and I gasped against the band of tape over my mouth. I couldn't seem to get enough breath through my nose.

Calm down, Coyne, I told myself. Relax. Think.

Easier said than done. I realized that I was terribly thirsty. My throat was raspy and constricted, as if blood had dribbled back there and dried. I thought about water. It was impossible not to think about water.

The back of my neck itched. I wanted to rub away the aching tingle in my arms.

I hitched myself backward in my bed until my shoulders were propped against the headboard. That eased some of the tension in my arms, and I felt the blood gush through previously constricted arteries. It was terribly painful.

I twisted and yanked at the restraints around my wrists. The effort only made them tighter. I tried to bite at the tape across my mouth, to no effect. Every muscle in my body hurt. Every organ complained.

Okay, then. Don't think. Squeeze thoughts out of your mind, Coyne. Find an empty black hole in there and focus on it until it becomes larger and larger and blots out the rest. Sylvie Szabo had once told me how she prepared herself for meditation. She had called it a sort of conscious effort toward unconsciousness, an orderly progression toward relaxation. Begin with the body. The mind follows.

Slow, deep breaths. Relax toes, then arches, ankles, and knees. Left leg first. Then the right one. Concentrate on each muscle, one at a time. Let them go.

I remember working up my body as far as my chest before I went back to sleep.

When I awakened, sunlight was streaming through the window and Lily was bent over me, her breasts pendulous under her nightgown. My arms were completely numb. My head ached wickedly. But there I lay, admiring Lily's breasts. I took that as a good sign.

Her eyes were wide. "Brady, what has happened?"

I made noises in my throat.

"The place has been ransacked. Oh, look at you." She picked at the tape on my mouth with her fingernails. "It won't come. Wait. Let me get scissors."

She left and returned a minute later with a pair of long

shears. She sliced through the tape on the back of my head and began to peel it off. I squeezed my eyes shut against the sharp pain of my hair being uprooted. She did it slowly, so that each hair was dragged out one at a time, each a separate dart of pain. I wanted to tell her just to give the tape a good yank. But, of course, I couldn't speak, because there was tape over my mouth. If there hadn't been tape over my mouth, I wouldn't have needed to speak.

Irrelevantly, it reminded me of the old childhood joke:

"Hey, you've got a banana in your ear."

"Sorry. I can't hear you. I've got this banana in my ear."

As she dragged the tape away from my cheeks and mouth, it seemed as if several layers of skin came off with it. Tears welled up in my eyes.

When it was off, I whooshed out a great breath. "Man!" I said. "You should've just given it a big quick yank." My voice was a croak.

She smiled. "Sorry."

"Are you all right?" I said through stiff and swollen lips.

"Me?" She nodded. "Sure. I'm fine."

"What about Jeff?"

"Still asleep, I suppose."

"Go see."

"Your hands . . ."

"Lily, for Christ sake, go check on Jeff, will you?"

She stared at me for an instant, then nodded.

She was back a minute later. Her eyes were wide. "He's not there. He's gone."

"Get my hands. Quick."

She worked at the tape with her scissors and soon she had them free. My arms fell beside me, dead senseless weights. I tried to lift them. It was as if they were not attached to my body. I couldn't even wiggle a finger.

"My arms won't move," I told her. "Help me get my clothes on."

She tugged my pants up onto my legs. "Brady, the jaguars are gone."

"Sure," I said. "That's what they were after." I arched my back so she could yank my pants up around my waist.

"Jeff . . . ?" she said.

"Lily, my sweatshirt."

She started to jam my limp arms into my sweatshirt.

"Was anything else missing?" I said, groaning as she maneuvered my numb limbs.

"I don't know," she said, frowning as she worked on my clothing. "The furniture's all shoved around and cabinets and drawers are open. I haven't really had a chance to check. I noticed the cats were gone. Then I came in to get you." She tugged the bottom of my sweatshirt down over my stomach.

Sensation was returning to my arms as blood began to course through the constricted veins and arteries. The pain was exquisite. I whooshed out a deep breath.

"It must hurt," said Lily. She began to massage my shoulders.

"It hurts like hell. Rubbing me doesn't help."

She jerked her hands away. "Sorry."

I pivoted around awkwardly so that I was sitting on the edge of the bed beside her. Lily was still wearing her slinky nightgown. "Will you for Christ sake get some clothes on," I said. "We've got to see what Jeff's up to."

She nodded and left the room.

I lurched to my feet and staggered into the living room. The big glass cases where the jaguars used to live sat on the long table beside the fireplace where they always did. But the cats had escaped. The sofa had been shoved aside so that the carpet was wrinkled, and one of the big chairs lay on its back.

One drawer from Jeff's desk had been pulled out and tipped upside down onto the floor. The others hung open. Papers were scattered everywhere.

I yelled for Jeff.

No answer.

I went out onto the patio and yelled again. Jeff did not answer. I called for the dogs. They did not come bounding up to me.

I had started down the path toward the gate when Lily caught up to me. She had donned denim overalls over a pink sleeveless T-shirt. She had wrapped a blue bandana around her hair. Bare feet. Daisy Mae Yokum. Fetching.

Lily was hugging herself. "Brady, where is he?"

"I don't know."

"Jeff!" It was a scream, sudden and full of terror, and then she screamed again. Her voice echoed emptily back to us.

She stared wild-eyed at me and began to shake her head violently from side to side. She opened her mouth again. I went quickly to her. I put both of my arms around her and held her tightly. "Hey," I whispered into her hair. "He's probably out there in the yard somewhere, stomping around, too mad to answer. Pissing and moaning as usual, right?"

She clung to me. Her nails dug into my back. I murmured to her, "It's all right. He's okay, now. Take it easy." I hugged her against me. Gradually I felt her relax.

After a minute she tilted her chin up to look at me. She tried to smile. "Okay," she said. "I'm all right now."

"Yes," I said. "You're fine." I stepped away from her and took her hand. "Come on. Let's find him."

We moved down the path, Lily gripping my hand hard and leading me along behind her. Abruptly she stopped short, took a step backward, and I bumped into her. "It's Tondo," she said. I gripped her shoulders and looked past her.

He was lying on his side just off the path. I squatted beside the Doberman. His eyes were glazed open. Tiny black insects crawled over them. The dog's tongue lolled out of his half-open mouth. It was pink and waxy. Under its head a puddle of black blood had soaked into the pine needles and congealed. It looked like an oil spill.

Tondo's throat had been slashed.

I looked up at Lily. "Dead," I said.

She nodded. "Ngwenya," she called. "Where are you, dog?" She whistled once.

I stood up and continued along the path to the gate. Lily followed behind me. Twenty feet farther along I saw dark stains in the sand. I followed them. I found Ngwenya under a bush. It looked as if he had crawled there to die. He was lying in his own pool of clotted blood. Large, shiny green-eyed flies sipped at it. "He's here," I said to Lily. "Dead, too."

She didn't answer. I turned. She had moved past me toward the gate.

She didn't scream. Her voice was almost conversational. "Brady," she said, "come here."

She was kneeling beside Jeff. Her head was bent close to his face. I scooched down beside her. "Is he . . . ?"

"No. He's breathing. Very slowly. He's—oh, Jesus."

He was lying fetally on his right side, wearing his cotton pajamas. A dark wet patch stained the white hair over his left ear. There was a great deal of black blood on his pajamas. More blood had pooled and congealed on the ground under his head.

"Don't move him," I said to Lily. "Stay here. I'll get an ambulance."

I sprinted up the path to the house. I went to the telephone on the kitchen wall and tapped out the 911 emergency number.

"Orleans 911." Professional, efficient, bored, female. "Can I help you?"

"I need help. There's been an assault. A man is seriously injured."

"What sort of injury?"

"Head. He's been hit on the head. He's unconscious."

"Breathing?"

"Yes."

"Where are you?"

"Quashnet Lane. Jeff Newton's home. I don't know the street number."

"Hold the line, please."

After perhaps thirty seconds of static, she came back on the line. "Okay, sir. The EMTs are on the way. Don't touch the injured man or try to move him. Put a blanket over him. Okay?"

"Yes."

"Who is this, please."

"Coyne. My name is Brady Coyne."

"And the victim?"

"It's Jeff Newton. I'm his lawyer."

"Was this an accident, or—?"

"I told you, he was hit on the head. It was an assault."

"Yes, I'm sorry. You did say that. When did it happen?"

"I don't know. Last night sometime. There was a burglary, too."

"Okay. I'll inform the police. Try not to touch anything."

I said, "Thank you," but she had already hung up.

I went into my bedroom and ripped the blanket off my bed. I jogged back to where Lily was crouched beside Jeff. I folded the blanket over his inert body. Lily patted it smooth and tucked the edges around him.

"Any change?" I said.

She shook her head. "He's breathing. Real slow. He—he doesn't move. Brady, the blood . . ."

"The ambulance is on its way."

At that moment we heard the siren, and a minute later the emergency vehicle slammed up to the gate, its high beams flashing. Its siren growled, then stopped. Three men leaped out. One was black and skinny. One was beefy and blond. The third could have been the second's brother after a rigorous diet. All seemed very young. They wore white short-sleeved shirts with patches on the left shoulders. I went to the gate. It was ajar. The three men came in. The black one said, "Where is he?"

I nodded backward. "There."

The thinner of the two blond men slid a wooden plank from the back of the van. It was about six and a half feet long and three feet wide, narrowed down to a foot at one end. The three of them hurried over to where Jeff lay. Lily, who was still crouched beside Jeff, stood up and backed out of their way. I moved beside her and hugged her against me. She put her arm around my waist.

The EMTs squatted beside Jeff. The black guy, who seemed to be in charge, shone a penlight into Jeff's eyes while one of the others strapped a blood pressure cuff around his arm. The way they had clustered around him, it was difficult to see clearly all that they did, and I couldn't make out what they were saying to each other.

After a minute or two the black man stood up. I could see that Jeff had been strapped onto the wooden board. His neck was immobilized in a rigid collar, and a strap around his forehead kept his head from moving. A green oxygen mask, with a white plastic inflated bag beneath it, covered his mouth and nose. They had put a gauze dressing on Jeff's head. Dark blood stained it.

The black EMT jogged back to the van. I hurried along behind him.

"How is he?" I said.

Without turning around, he said, "He's alive." I deduced he wasn't interested in a conversation.

He reached into the front of the van and pulled out the radio. "This is Orleans Car Nine," he said.

"This is Cape Cod Hospital," came a fuzzy voice from inside the van. "The time is oh-seven thirty-six. Go ahead, Orleans."

"We have a white male, sixty—" He glanced at me, his eyebrows raised.

"Fifty," I said.

"Fifty," he said. "Head trauma. He's comatose. Vital signs as follows: BP 180 over 110. Respirations twelve and shallow. Pulse ninety. Physical examination shows major depressed skull fracture, left temporal area, with bony fragments. Pupils dilated, gaze fixed to the left."

I glanced back to where Jeff had fallen. The other two EMTs had lifted him, board and all, onto a stretcher and were lugging him toward the van at a trot. Lily straggled along behind them.

"He's boarded. Full C-spine precautions have been taken."

The EMTs slid Jeff into the back of the ambulance. Then they jumped in behind him. The doors slammed.

"We're initiating an IV line of Ringer's Lactate. Preparing to intubate. ETA nineteen minutes. Suggest neurosurgery be ready."

Their radio crackled. A voice said. "We copy, Car Nine. We'll be expecting you."

"Here we come," said the black man. He leaped into the van.

"Where are you taking him?" I said.

"Hyannis. Cape Cod Hospital."

He slammed the door. The siren grumbled, then screamed. Gravel spewed from the tires.

We stood there for a few moments, staring down the driveway, listening to the wail of the siren grow dimmer. When the sound died, the silence seemed vast.

Lily had her arm around my waist. She was leaning against me. I felt that if I moved, she'd topple over. After a while she sighed. "Well . . ."

"That was impressive," I said.

"They came and went. It seemed like just an instant." She shuddered.

"Are you all right?"

I sensed her nodding. "Yes." Her voice was soft but firm. "I'm okay. He's going to die."

"They'll take care of him."

"Don't patronize me, Brady. Did you see his head?"

"I saw it. It was bad."

"I've been waiting for him to get sick and die. So has he. I just didn't think it would be this way. It's too sudden. I'm not ready for it."

"We don't know that he's going to die, Lily."

She gave me a quick hug and stood away from me. "Sure. Right."

I took her hand. "Nothing we can do. The police will be here. We'll have to answer a lot of questions. Let's go have some coffee. I want to grab a quick shower."

FOUR

• • • • • •

LILY AND I sat at the kitchen table sipping coffee. We talked about Jeff and the jaguars. We tried to figure out what had happened. Who came for the cats? Why was Jeff out at the gate? If he had suspected a break-in, Jeff would have brought a gun with him, and he wouldn't have hesitated to use it, we agreed.

Lily was calm and steady. I did all right, too. But when the bell at the gate bonged, both of us spasmed. Then we smiled at each other.

"I'll get it," said Lily. "It must be the police."

"I'm with you."

We went down the path, past Tondo's and Ngwenya's carcasses, past the place where Jeff had lain, past the black stains in the sand, to the gate. Two uniformed policemen waited on the other side of the fence. Lily unlocked the gate and swung it open.

The older of the two cops—he might've been thirty-two or -three—looked at me. "My name is Coyne," I said to him. "Mr. Newton's lawyer."

"You got here fast, sir."

"I was spending the night."

He shrugged. "Officer Maroney," he said, not offering his hand. "This is Officer Kinney."

Maroney was short, slim, quick, deeply tanned. Kinney was a bigger guy, mid-twenties, with small pink eyes and a roll of pink flab bulging over his shirt collar. Neither of the two struck me as particularly affable.

Maroney arched his eyebrows at Lily. "Lillian Robbins," she said. Maroney nodded. "I'm Mr. Newton's housekeeper," she added. Maroney shrugged, as if he didn't believe it but didn't care.

"You'll want to know," he said, looking at Lily, "that they got Mr. Newton to the hospital in Hyannis okay. I got it over the radio. He's holding his own."

"Thank you," she said.

"Hey, look," said Kinney to his partner. He was pointing down at Ngwenya's corpse under the bush beside the path. "A dead dog."

"Good," said Maroney. "We'll make a detective out of you yet." To me he said, "This supposed to be a watchdog?"

I nodded.

"Did a helluva job, didn't he?"

"Actually," I said, "there were two of them. They were both killed trying to do their job."

"Probably some kind of crime, killing dogs." Maroney glanced at Lily, then back to me. "What about Mr. Newton? You found him out here?"

Lily nodded. "Here. By the gate." She gestured to one of the bloodstains on the sandy path.

Maroney barely glanced at where she pointed. "Okay. Let's go inside. You can tell us what happened, first. Then we'll have a look around."

On the way up the path Kinney paused beside Tondo, opened his mouth, and then closed it. Maroney glanced at me. I couldn't read his expression.

We sat in the living room. Maroney and Kinney looked around without apparent interest at the disarray.

"Coffee?" said Lily.

Maroney declined with a wave of his hand. Kinney did not respond at all. Maroney seemed to speak for both of them.

Maroney took a notebook and a ballpoint pen from his shirt pocket. He clicked the button on the pen and licked the tip. "Okay, then," he said. "Let me have your names again, first, please."

We told him our names. We had to spell them for him.

"And you were all here last night?"

We nodded.

"On business, Mr. Coyne?"

"Partially."

"Huh?"

"Partially a visit, partially to clean up routine things. Mr. Newton is an invalid, so whenever I have business with him I come here."

"An invalid, huh?"

"Yes."

"But he was down there by the gate in the nighttime."

"He could get around. He wasn't bedridden. He used a crutch."

"Was his crutch down there with his body?"

"I didn't notice it," I said. I glanced at Lily. She shook her head.

"So you were spending the weekend?" said Maroney to me.

"Yes."

"Okay." He shrugged. "What happened last night, then? Any idea who hit Mr. Newton?"

"No. We were both sleeping."

"Miss?" said Maroney to Lily.

She nodded. "I was asleep."

Maroney sighed. "So much for the assault." He looked over at Kinney, who had one fat leg crossed over the other. "Hopefully we'll get to talk to Mr. Newton," he said to his partner. "He obviously saw who it was. That's why they hit him." He turned back to me. "Why don't you just tell me what you know, then, Mr. Coyne."

"I was awakened by two men in my bedroom. One of them—"

"What time was this?"

"I have no idea. Before daybreak."

"Two men, you said?"

"Yes. One held a flashlight. The other had a knife. They taped my wrists to the bedposts and they taped my mouth shut. They pretended they were going to kill me. They seemed to find this amusing for a while." I touched the scratch on my throat and the bigger wound on my collarbone. Lily had put Band-Aids on them. "They finally got tired of that game. So they hit me on the head and I went unconscious."

"What'd they hit you with?"

"I'm not sure. A gun, maybe. It looked like they hit Jeff with something bigger, blunter. His wound was . . ." I glanced at Lily. She was watching me, nodding.

"We'll get a report on Mr. Newton," said Maroney, tapping his teeth with his pen. "Describe these two men, please."

I shrugged. "It was dark. I think they had ski masks or hoods or something over their faces. They were shining a flashlight in my eyes. All I can tell you was that there were two of them, both male."

"Did they speak?"

"One of them did most of the talking. Sadistic bastard. The other one mostly laughed."

"What about their voices? Any accent?"

I shrugged. "Their voices were muffled. No accent that I noticed."

Maroney gazed placidly at me. "Well, did they sound educated? Did they use proper English and all?"

"I can't remember being struck by anything they said. Just the content of it. How much fun it might be to sever my head from my body."

"Had they been drinking, could you tell? Drugged up? Anything like that?"

"No. Well, maybe something. The guy who taped me up had bad breath."

"Booze, maybe?"

"More like garlic, or old tobacco."

"Big or small? Black or white? Come on, Mr. Coyne."

"I'm sorry," I said. "They seemed big to me. Otherwise, I don't know."

Maroney nodded. "Okay. Fine. So then what happened?"

"Well, when we got up this morning, we found the jaguars missing and the dogs with their throats cut. Then we found Jeff. We called 911. The EMTs came." I shrugged. "That's what happened."

"Jaguars? What about jaguars?"

I gestured across the room at the seven empty glass cases. "Mr. Newton owned these seven statues—sculptures—solid gold, Mayan works of art. Very valuable. Very old. They're gone."

Maroney glanced at the glass cases, as if to verify that they were indeed empty. "What else did they get?"

"Nothing," said Lily, speaking for the first time. "Just the cats."

"As if that's what they came for," said Maroney, allowing himself a faint smile. He turned to Lily. "You live here, right?"

"Yes."

"What was Mr. Newton doing outside last night?"

"I don't know," she said. "He usually sleeps soundly. He takes pills."

"Pills?"

"Sleeping pills. And other pills. He's not well."

"Where's his bedroom?"

"In the back of the house. Next to mine."

"You didn't hear anything last night?"

"No."

"These two men, they didn't come into your room?"

"No."

"Did you hear Mr. Newton get up?"

"No."

"Noises?"

"I didn't hear anything. I didn't wake up."

"Did Mr. Newton take his pills last night?"

She shrugged. "I suppose so. I left them for him."

"Are you a sound sleeper, miss?"

She nodded. "Average, I guess."

"Does Mr. Newton get up in the night? To go to the bathroom, for example? When the pills wear off?"

"I don't really know," said Lily. "I don't think so. Sometimes he has bad dreams. I hear him when he cries out. But he doesn't usually get up."

"But he did last night."

She shrugged. "Obviously," she said.

Maroney peered at his notebook for a moment. Then he looked up at me. "The dogs were supposed to guard the place, then," he said. "Right?"

"Right," I said. "They were trained killers. You had to know their names, to be able to say them properly, to get by them."

"Explain." Maroney's eyebrows furrowed.

"Tondo and Ngwenya," I said, pronouncing them carefully. "Their names. African words. He—Jeff—he used to be a professional hunter in Africa. You can't pronounce the dogs' names unless Jeff taught you. If you couldn't say them right, the dogs would bite off your leg."

"So the bad guys knew their names, then, huh?"

"No," said Lily. "Only we three could say their names."

Maroney turned to look at her. "And you were sleeping, Miss Robbins, when Mr. Coyne here was being taped to his bed and Mr. Newton was outside getting hit on the head and the dogs were getting their throats cut?"

"Miz," she said.

Maroney rolled his eyes. "Miz. Sorry."

"I was sleeping, yes," she said. "I told you that. I didn't hear anything."

"So," said Maroney, glancing at Kinney, who was sitting back in a soft chair, his little pig eyes darting from one to the other of us as we spoke, "they came into your room, Mr. Coyne, tied you up, scratched you with a knife, and hit you, but they didn't go near Miz Robbins here. What do you make of that?"

I shrugged. "I don't know," I said. But, of course, I did. Lily could have been in on it. I doubted it. But it was possible.

"Miss?" he said to Lily. "I mean, miz?"

"I don't know." She sat forward and jutted her chin at Maroney. "My bedroom's in the back. Brady was in the guest room, right off the living room. Maybe that's why they went in there."

Maroney nodded.

"Why are you asking a question like that?" said Lily.

He stared at her for a moment. She returned his gaze levelly.

"It's a logical question," he said finally. "Did they take a blanket or a pillowcase or a slipcover from the sofa or some-thing?"

My estimate of his competence clicked up a notch. He was asking if the thieves brought something with them to carry the jaguars in, meaning they knew exactly what they were after, or did they break in, see the golden cats and decide they were valuable, and then look around for something to lug them away in.

"Nothing," said Lily. "Nothing else is missing."

"You're sure?"

She shrugged. "Nothing that I noticed, anyway."

Maroney jerked his head toward the scattering of papers on the floor by the desk. "Have you looked through all that stuff?"

"No," said Lily. "We didn't think we should touch any-thing."

Maroney nodded and glanced again at Kinney. Kinney nodded. It was hard to tell if the younger cop was following this.

"Back to those dogs," said Maroney. "You said if some-one knew their names—"

"The dogs would lie down," I said. "Friendly as cocker spaniels. You could kick them and they wouldn't do any-thing."

"But—"

"Otherwise, they were vicious, monomaniacal killers."

"So our burglars—"

"Either knew their names, or—"

"Or tranquilized them or something," finished Maroney. "Otherwise they couldn't have gotten close enough to them to cut their throats."

I nodded. "That's what I've been thinking."

Maroney stared out the wall of windows. A brilliant,

cloudless Cape Cod Saturday. The beaches would be mobbed, as would the pizza and ice cream and T-shirt emporiums that lined Route 28 on the ocean side of the Cape. A fun place.

"I suppose we could have somebody do an autopsy on the dogs," he said. "Don't know what it would tell us."

"Shit," said Kinney. "Never heard of that."

"Me neither," said Maroney. He shrugged. "Are those jaguars insured, do you know?" he said.

I nodded. "Sure."

"A good thing. Someone best call Mr. Newton's adjuster. Describe the missing pieces for me."

"They were solid gold," I said. "Emerald eyes. Each weighed about twenty pounds. The smallest was fifteen and a half inches long. The biggest was nineteen and a quarter. They looked—like cats, you know? Jaguars, of course, are spotted. Like leopards. These gold ones weren't spotted. Just burnished gold. Quite beautiful, in their fashion. A little crude, representative. Primitive. Jaguars were kind of gods to the Mayans."

"So the seven of them—they'd weigh well over a hundred pounds."

I nodded. "Closer to one-fifty." Maroney was taking notes.

"What's their value?"

"They're insured for seven hundred seventy thousand. One-ten each. They were appraised for about double that. That was a number of years ago."

Maroney whistled softly between his front teeth. "You have photographs of the cats?"

"Yes," said Lily. "Want to see them?"

Maroney nodded.

She stood up. "I'll get them."

She left the room. Maroney watched her go. "We'll circulate the pictures," he said, still staring at the doorway through which Lily had disappeared. "Local art dealers, junk stores, and so forth. If we're lucky, your burglars'll turn out to be kids looking for crack money, have no idea what they've got for themselves, and your cats'll turn up. I'm guessing that won't happen, though."

"Because they brought sacks to carry them out in," I said.

"I'm guessing that's what they did," said the cop. "That plus the way they handled the dogs."

"What do you make of their slugging Jeff?" I said.

Maroney shrugged. "Your guess is as good as mine right now. Maybe after we look around something'll suggest itself. On the surface, it looks as if he heard something, maybe the dogs barking or something, and went outside to see what was going on—"

"Those dogs didn't bark," I said. "All they'd do was whine. You couldn't hear them from inside the house."

He shrugged again.

"And anyway, Jeff's room's in the back, and he doesn't get around very well, and he takes sleeping pills. And if he did hear something, he'd most likely call for Lily."

Maroney cocked his head. "If she was there."

I shrugged.

He glanced at Kinney, who was watching me.

"Well," I said, "they weren't kids. They were adults. Judging by their voices, anyway."

"Some kids on crack are pretty old," said Maroney.

Lily came back and handed Maroney a large manila envelope. Maroney reached into it and took out a sheaf of eight-by-ten color photographs. He shuffled through them. "Seven of them, right?"

"Yes," said Lily.

"Mind if I keep these?"

She nodded. "We've got duplicates."

"Lily," I said, "were the papers there?"

"Papers?"

"The papers on the jaguars. The appraisal that Dan LaBreque and Marla Conway did, the import papers, insurance policies?"

She nodded. "Yes. Right with the photos. The file cabinet's in Jeff's bedroom." She gestured at the mess of papers on the floor. "They must've been looking for them, huh?"

"Looks like it," I said.

Maroney tucked the photos back into the envelope and glanced at his notebook. "Well," he said. "I need some names."

"Names?" said Lily.

"Who knew about the jaguars. Who knew the dogs' names. You know. Suspects. People who visit Mr. Newton. Who could've done this. We'll have to talk to Mr. Newton when he's able, but for now, what can you come up with?"

Lily stared at him blankly. "No one. No one I know would do this."

"Well," said Maroney placidly, "someone did. Think, please."

She shrugged. "His children. They visit him. I don't think they stole the jaguars."

"He's—"

"Divorced," said Lily. "For about fifteen years."

"Names?"

"James and Ellen."

He wrote them down. "How old are they?"

"Jimmy's twenty and Ellen's twenty-two."

"How does he get along with them?"

She shrugged. "Okay, as far as I know. I'm usually on vacation when they're here."

"When were they here last?"

"Last August. They come every August." She hesitated. "Come to think of it, last summer Jimmy didn't make it. He was working up in New Hampshire and couldn't get away."

"So he didn't see his son all year?"

Lily shrugged. "I guess not."

"But you say he gets along okay with his kids?"

"Ellen, anyway. I think there's some tension between him and Jimmy. He doesn't talk much about it."

"What about Mr. Newton's wife?"

"I told you. He's divorced."

Maroney looked up. "Right." He nodded. "His ex-wife, then. Does she visit him?"

"No."

"But she probably knows about the jaguars. From the children."

Lily rolled her eyes. "I doubt that Sheila came down, hit Jeff on the head, tied up Brady, and stole the jaguars."

"It was two men," I said.

"Okay," said the cop. "Who else?"

"Well," said Lily, "his insurance person. She comes by now and then. She certainly knows about the jaguars, what they're worth. At least as likely a suspect as his children."

"Name?"

"Miss Kline," she said. "Jeff calls her Tory. For Victoria. Tory Kline. She's with the Seacoast Agency in Hyannis. They broker all his insurance, and she's the agent he deals with. She arranged the policy for the jaguars. Also the homeowner's policy, life insurance, my automobile, and so forth. She helped Jeff get his claim for disability."

"You know a lot about Mr. Newton's business," said Maroney mildly.

"Yes," said Lily. "I do. I take care of him."

Maroney was writing into his notebook. "Hyannis, you said?"

Lily nodded. "The Seacoast Agency."

"When was she here?"

"She's been here several times."

"Most recently?"

She gazed up at the ceiling. "I don't know. Last winter sometime, I guess. Periodically she calls, wants to come over to sell Jeff more insurance. He generally lets her come."

"What'd you say those cats are insured for?"

"Seven hundred seventy thousand," I said.

"Good thing," said Maroney. "Anybody else you can think of?" He looked from Lily to me.

"Well, Dr. Sauerman," I said. "He comes every week to examine Mr. Newton."

"And what exactly is the matter with Mr. Newton?" Maroney arched his eyebrows.

"He was mauled by an African leopard," I said. "He spent six months in a Nairobi hospital. Bad infection, serious wounds. He still needs medical treatment. He used to be a professional hunter."

"The Great White Hunter, huh?" said Kinney, smirking so that his fat cheeks bunched up and his eyes became slits.

"They're called professional hunters," said Lily. "Sometimes professional white hunters. Never great white hunters, except maybe in movies. To call a professional hunter a great white hunter is to reveal ignorance."

Kinney squinted at her for a minute, then shrugged.

"He's really got a thing for cats, though, huh?" said Maroney.

"I suppose so," said Lily.

"Alan Sauerman," said Maroney, looking sideways at Kinney.

Kinney nodded. "Sure. The Doc."

"He was here last evening," I said. "He knows about the cats. He knew about the dogs, too."

"Good," said Maroney, again writing in his notebook. He looked at Lily. "Miss? Miz? Anybody else? How about you? Boyfriend?"

She shook her head.

"There must be other people who come here. To visit, to make deliveries. Relatives?"

Lily shrugged. "Sure," she said. "The usual meter readers, oil delivery men. We had an exterminator last May. Carpenter ants. Does that help?"

"Sure," said the policeman. "Everything helps."

"I can't think of anybody particular," said Lily. "We don't have a great deal of company. Occasionally one of Jeff's old friends will drop in. I mean, how can we tell you every single person who's ever been here, who might've known about the jaguars?"

Maroney shrugged. "Sure. Right." He turned to Kinney. "Anything else?" This struck me as a courtesy to his partner, who had not seemed interested in any of the interrogation, and who did not appear to have a question—or, for that matter, much of anything else—in his head.

Kinney shrugged.

"Well," said Maroney, pushing himself to his feet with a sigh, "we better have a look around, then."

He flipped his notebook shut and jammed it into his shirt pocket. "That gate have a lock on it?" he said.

"Of course," said Lily.

"That fence, it goes all around the property?"

"Yes."

"So someone could sneak over anywhere."

"The dogs would get him," she said. "No matter where they came over."

"Wait a minute," I said.

They all looked at me.

"The gate was unlocked."

"When?" said Maroney.

"When we went down there this morning. When the EMTs came, it was ajar. I didn't think about it at the time."

"Is it always locked?"

"Yes," said Lily.

"Did you lock it after Sauerman left last night?" I said to her.

She nodded slowly. "Sure." She paused, frowning. "At least, I think so."

"You could have forgotten to lock it?" said Maroney.

She shrugged. "I could have, I guess. I don't think I forgot. I mean, I always lock it, but I can't specifically remember . . ."

"Mr. Newton had a key, right?"

Lily nodded. "Sure."

"Who else?"

"Just me," she said.

Maroney and Kinney exchanged glances. Then Maroney stood up. "You folks just sit tight," said Maroney to us. "We'll have a look outside. We'll be back in a few minutes, see what we can see in here."

After the cops left the room, Lily said, "Do you think Jeff let them in?"

"Maybe he did," I said.

She shook her head. "Sure. So they could bash in his skull."

I shrugged.

She stared out the window for a minute. "That Maroney," she said. "He suspects me."

"I don't think so. I told him it was two men."

"He thinks I left the gate unlocked for them. He thinks I set it up."

"He might think that," I said.

She turned to me. "I didn't, you know."

"I know."

"Professionals," said Lily. "It was professionals. They were prepared for the dogs. They came for the jaguars. They had it planned."

"I agree," I said. "Could somebody else have a key?"

"Jeff could've given somebody a key, I don't know." She shrugged. "I don't know what to think. To tell the truth, I don't much care about figuring it out. Figuring it out isn't going to change anything."

"I'm pretty interested in revenge, myself," I said.

Lily and I remained in the living room while the policemen prowled around outside. We had more coffee. We didn't talk. There wasn't much to say.

Maroney and Kinney came back in about fifteen minutes later. "We found the crutch," Maroney said. "It was fifteen or twenty feet away from where it looked like his body was."

"As if he threw it or something," added Kinney.

"Don't you folks touch those glass cases," Maroney said. "We'll get some forensics guys over here. Maybe we'll get lucky."

"What else did you find out there?" I said.

Maroney shrugged. "A couple dead Dobermans. I'll give the dog officer a call, have him come by to pick them up. We'll see if there's some way they can be tested for a drug."

"Why is that important?" said Lily.

Maroney sighed. "If they were drugged, it tells us your

burglars didn't know how to talk to them. It also tells us the bad guys came prepared, knew what they were after, what they were doing, had the whole thing planned out, that they weren't just beered-up kids on a lark, which I seriously doubt anyway."

After the cops left Lily called the hospital. I stood beside her while she nodded wordlessly at the telephone. When she hung up she turned to face me. I couldn't read her expression.

"Well?" I said.

She shook her head. "He's in the operating room. They wouldn't tell me anything else. It seems I'm not next of kin or something. He's alive, I got that much out of them."

I nodded. I reached for her hand. She allowed me to squeeze it, then she moved away from me.

"I'm going to go change," she said. "I'm going to the hospital."

"It won't do Jeff any good."

"It'll do me some good."

About an hour later we were out back on the patio sipping coffee. Lily had changed into a narrow gray skirt and a yellow blouse. She was wearing heels. I had never seen her in heels before. She was attempting to summon up the courage to drive to Hyannis. When we heard the bell by the gate bong, she stood up and said, "I'll get it," and I also stood and said, "I'll go with you."

We walked through the house and down the path. In her heels, Lily was as tall as me. Two men stood outside the gate, one a portly guy with a bald head and round wire-rimmed glasses and the other a teenage boy who reminded me of Tom Cruise with acne. The older of the two blinked at us and said, "Dog officer. Francis Filmore."

Lily unlocked the gate and they came in. Francis Filmore spotted Ngwenya's body sprawled by the path. He went to it and squatted down. "Aw, jeez," he said softly. He touched the dog's black fur, already dulled by death.

"Its throat was cut," I said.

Filmore peered up at me. "Why do people do things like this?"

I shrugged. "It was a robbery."

"So I heard. There's another one?"

I nodded and jerked my head in the direction of Tondo's corpse up the path. Filmore stood up slowly. "Dobermans are nice dogs," he said to me.

"I guess that depends on your definition."

"Smart, loyal, dependable."

"By that definition, I agree."

At that moment, a dark blue sedan pulled up beside Filmore's wagon, and two men in suits got out. Lily went to the gate. One of them flipped a leather case open, showing her a shield. "Forensics," he said.

She jerked her head up the path in the direction of the bungalow. "Up there."

The detective nodded, and he and his partner moved toward the house. Lily came back and stood beside me and the dog officer. The detectives exchanged hellos with Francis Filmore on their way by.

"Road pizzas," said Filmore, after the forensics cops had disappeared into the house.

I frowned at him. "Huh?"

"Some people try to run dogs over," he said. "Also squirrels, coons, possums, housecats. Turtles and snakes and frogs, too. They think it's sport. The kids around here, they like to cruise at night, see what they can run over. Dogs get them the most points. They have contests. Half a dozen kids in cars. End of the evening, they tote up their points. Loser buys a case of beer for all of 'em. They guzzle it down, then, lots of times, they end up as road pizzas themselves. Great sport."

"Some people deserve to have their throats cut," I said.

Filmore nodded and sighed. To the boy he said, "Well, come on, Jackie. Let's lug 'em out."

Jackie took Ngwenya's front end and Filmore lifted the dog by its hind legs. Ngwenya's body had already stiffened. They carried him to their van, laid him gently in the back, and returned for Tondo. Lily stood close beside me, watching.

When the two were done, Filmore slammed the back door shut. "Sorry about your dogs," he said to us with a wave.

"Thanks," I said.

"Why people think they have to kill dogs," he said, shaking his head.

We watched as the van turned around and bumped down the dusty road. Then Lily took my hand and we went back into the house.

FIVE

• • • • • •

AFTER Francis Filmore carted away the dogs and the forensics detectives finished snooping around the house and grounds, Lily said, "I'm going to the hospital."

"Want company?"

She touched my face with her fingertips. "I don't think so. Do you understand?"

I nodded. "Sure."

"I'll be back for dinner. You'll be here?"

"If you want."

"I want. I'll cook something fancy."

I walked down the path with her to her Cherokee. She opened the door, then turned to face me. She leaned against me and kissed my mouth. It was a sweet, quick kiss. All affection, no passion. "I'm sure glad you were here, Brady Coyne," she said.

I fingered the Band-Aid on my throat. "Yeah, me too."

I wandered back to the house. I made myself a sandwich from the leftover lobster salad I found in the refrigerator. There was a bottle of Grolsch beer in there, too. I ate at the kitchen table. Then I went back into the living room.

The contents of the desk still littered the floor. Maybe the forensics guys had looked over everything. But they didn't clean up.

I decided to save Lily the trouble. I knelt down and began to gather everything into a pile. There were bills waiting to be paid, some correspondence, assorted pieces of junk mail. I couldn't help glancing at it all as I picked it up. I told myself I was Jeff's lawyer. His business was my business.

A letter from James, Jeff's son. News from school and a carefully worded request for money, dated back in April.

A note from Sheila, Jeff's former wife, June 6. Civil, formal, short. Her check hadn't arrived.

There was an insurance policy and an accompanying bill. The policy was a standard homeowner's. The bill noted a health policy, the homeowner's, and the separate policy for the jaguars. Jaguar insurance was costly, but now it looked like a shrewd investment.

I stacked everything up after glancing at it. There was an electric bill, a bill from the exterminator, a property tax bill. There was a phone bill which listed about a dozen long-distance calls. Three I recognized as my office number. There was one to Rutland, Vermont—that, I figured, was Sheila, who lived in Rutland—two to Saratoga Springs, New York, where Ellen attended Skidmore, and one, collect from Lewiston, Maine. James went to Bates.

There were also four collect calls from the same number in West Yellowstone, Montana, all on consecutive days at the end of May. They caught my eye, because it just happens that West Yellowstone, Montana, is one of my favorite places in the entire world. Aside from being the gateway to Yellowstone Park, West Yellowstone is the fly-fishing center of the universe. I've spent lots of time there. I have many friends in West Yellowstone.

As far as I knew, Jeff Newton had no interest in fly fishing.

I stared at the phone bill. Then I went to the kitchen phone and pecked out the West Yellowstone number. It rang four times before a man's voice said, "The Totem."

"Who is this, please?"

"Gleason. Buddy Gleason. Can I do somethin' for you?"

I hesitated. "I'm calling from Massachusetts. I'm a friend of Jeff Newton?"

"Who?"

"Jeff Newton. You don't know him?"

"I don't think so. What's up?"

"Somebody there called him collect. My name is Coyne, and I'm Mr. Newton's lawyer. I'm checking his phone bill for him, and he's got several collect calls on it from this number."

The guy called Gleason chuckled. "This is a bar, Mr. Coyne. The Totem Café? This here is our pay phone. All sorts of people use it."

"The Totem," I said. "I've been there. A guy named Fred used to tend bar there."

"Fred took a job up to Great Falls sometime last summer. Nice fella, Fred."

"Any idea who might've called Jeff Newton here in Massachusetts?"

"Nope. Coulda been anybody."

"These calls were on May 20, 21, 22, and 23. One call each day. Evening, actually. All were around eight in the evening."

"Shit, that was two months ago. Sorry I can't help you."

"Well, I appreciate it, anyway. Next time I'm out there I'll drop in."

"Do that. Be nice to see you."

I hung up. All Westerners were friendly. That had been my experience.

I found another Grolsch in the refrigerator and went back into the living room. I finished stacking the papers on the desk. I moved the furniture back to where it belonged. I didn't touch the glass cases.

After I got the place cleaned up, I took my Grolsch into the kitchen. I sat at the table and lit a cigarette. Then I picked up the phone and tried the Wellesley number again.

Gloria answered on the second ring. "Yes? Hello?"

Oh, oh. I could read volumes in the way Gloria answered the phone. Or at least I imagined I could. Today she was busy, distracted, unsettled. "Hi, hon," I said.

"Oh, Brady." Pause. "Where are you?"

"At Jeff Newton's in Orleans. Everything okay?"

"Sure. Fine."

Everything was not fine, she meant.

"Well, uh, Joey called me yesterday. I'm returning his call. Is he around?"

"Nope."

"Oh. Well, um . . ."

"Your son is gone for the weekend. Where? I don't know. With whom? None of my business." She laughed quickly. "Sorry. Joseph and I have had a few issues recently, that's all."

"What kind of issues?"

"It doesn't matter, Brady. Not your problem."

"Is that why he called? These issues?"

"I don't know why he called. We're not, um, communicating very well lately."

"Gloria," I said, "what's going on?"

"I suppose," she said slowly, "you've got a right to know. I just—hell, Brady. He's not doing his part. It's as if I was his servant. He's got a few chores, you know? Things that need to be done. No reason he can't help out. But will he go to the dump, like I ask him to? Hell, no. Not without a big scene. Does he pick up the Coke cans and empty potato chip bags from the TV room after he and that little Debbie finish watching movies and making out in there? Shit, no." I heard her take a deep breath and let it out. Its accusation hissed into the telephone. "I'm sorry. You asked."

"Look . . ."

"I don't know why I'm telling you this. He and I will work it out. Listen, if you want to talk to him, I assume he'll wander back tomorrow night sometime. Want me to tell him you called?"

"Sure. Thanks." I hesitated. "I'll try to talk to him, hon."

"Don't bother. This is our problem. I can handle it."

"I'll talk to him. He's got to contribute."

"Yeah," she said. "Yeah, well maybe you could. Because I don't seem to be getting very far. Billy was never like this."

"Billy was himself. This is Joey."

"Hey, wow. Thanks for the philosophy. Brady, you're always so damned good at analyzing other people's problems. We clients really appreciate all your wisdom."

I tried to ignore her sudden burst of sarcasm. "He's my son, too," I said. "That makes it my problem."

She snorted a short, ironic laugh. "Hardly."

"I'll talk to him," I repeated.

"That should be interesting," she said. "You should have great perspective on it."

Which meant that Joey, in Gloria's mind, was becoming just like me. This did not bode well for either of them.

"I've gotta go," I said, after taking in and letting out a deep breath. "Have a nice weekend, Gloria. I'll try Joey again."

"Okay. 'Bye."

I hung up the phone gently. I sat there for a minute while I finished my cigarette. Perspective was the word Gloria had used. I never had perspective when it came to my family. And even though Gloria and I had been divorced for more than a decade, which was almost as long as we'd been married, I still couldn't stop thinking of her as my family.

Nothing I could do about it now, I told myself.

Which didn't make me feel any better about it.

I wandered back into the living room and snapped on the television. Red Sox versus Kansas City, fourth inning. We were losing, five to two.

An inning later I went back into the kitchen for another Grolsch.

The place seemed to echo. It was empty. Before Lily had left, it hadn't seemed that way. I settled onto the sofa with my beer and my Red Sox.

Sometime later the phone rang. I had been dozing.

I went to the kitchen and picked it up. "Yes?"

"This Mr. Coyne?"

"Yes."

"This is Officer Maroney. Is Miz Robbins there?"

"No. She went to the hospital to see how Jeff's doing."

"Right," he said, as if he already knew it. "Can you come to the station?"

"Now?"

"Yes."

"Me?"

"Yes."

"Why?"

"If I wanted to talk about it on the phone, I wouldn't've asked you to come to the station, Mr. Coyne."

"Sure. How stupid of me."

"Know where it is?"

"I've seen it."

"Okay. You'll be here, then?"

"Give me half an hour."

I went back into the living room in time to hear the announcers award the Star of the Game to Bo Jackson. I deduced that Kansas City had won. I snapped off the set.

Before I climbed into my car, I showered and changed. It didn't help much. The beers and the interrupted nap, combined with a less than restful night's sleep and the trapped heat in my car and the poison of fear that still lingered in my gut, all made me feel sluggish and queasy, and I drove the back roads to the police station slowly. Just about the time I pulled into the parking area alongside the square brick building, the cranky air-conditioning in my BMW kicked in, so I sat there for a few minutes to savor it.

I entered into a narrow corridor. The police station was air-conditioned, too. On the right was a glass window, shoulder-high, and behind it, like a ticket seller at a movie theater, sat a uniformed cop. His amplified and distorted voice came through a little metal vent at the bottom of the window. "Help you, sir?"

"Maroney," I said. "He's expecting me."

"Your name?"

"Coyne. Brady Coyne."

"Just a moment, please."

I waited while he spoke into a little microphone, and then the door behind me buzzed. "Go ahead in," he said.

I tried the knob on the door and pushed it open. I entered into a small sitting area, not unlike a doctor's waiting room except for the heavy wire mesh that covered the windows. I took a contoured plastic chair. The chair's contour did not match mine.

I looked for a No Smoking sign, but all I saw were a half

dozen ashtrays on pedestals, all overflowing with butts. I lit a Winston.

I was halfway through it when Maroney opened a door and beckoned to me with a jerk of his head. "Come on in here, Mr. Coyne," he said.

I stubbed out my cigarette in the ashtray, igniting the filter of an old butt in the process, and followed him. He led me to a glass-partitioned cubicle and gestured to one of the two chairs. The other was behind a littered desk. Maroney sat in that one. He picked up a pencil and began to tap his front teeth with the eraser end. He pretended to study me. His intention, I guessed, was to make me feel uncomfortable.

After a minute or two of this game, I said, "Well?"

He smiled without humor. "I've talked to the hospital. Mr. Newton's out of surgery. He's still alive."

"Good."

"They don't know if he'll be able to tell us anything."

I nodded.

"They're not sure how much damage was done. Whether he'll regain consciousness."

"I see." I found myself nodding. "Thank you."

He let his pencil fall onto the papers on his desk. "What do you know about Lillian Robbins?" he said.

I shrugged. "What do I know about her? Nothing, really. Why?"

"How long has she worked for Newton?"

"Twelve, fourteen years, I'd say. Look, do you—?"

"Can I ask the questions, please?"

I shrugged. "Sure."

He narrowed his eyes for an instant. "You had nothing to do with Newton hiring her, then."

"No." I fished out a cigarette and lit it.

"I thought maybe the guy's lawyer would've checked her out."

"You think Lily . . . ?"

He shrugged. "It's a thought." He cocked his head at me. "I understand you killed a man a few years ago."

"You've been busy."

"I had to report this thing to the state cops. Ended up talking with a detective named Horowitz. He recognized your name."

"I killed a man in self-defense," I said. "With a properly registered handgun. I was never arrested or indicted for a crime. I assume Horowitz told you that. Maybe you could tell me—"

"This is a pretty serious crime here, Mr. Coyne."

"It's not at all clear what you're asking me."

"Okay," he said. "Here's what I'm asking." He leaned toward me on his forearms. "I'm asking if you and the lady set up the theft last night. I'm asking if you and her got up, went outside and killed the dogs, and started piling the jaguars into one of your cars, thinking Mr. Newton was dead to the world, loaded up with sleeping pills, in his back bedroom. And when he came out and surprised you, you slugged him on the head. And then you took the jaguars somewhere for safekeeping. I'm asking if when you got back you went to bed and she taped you up and cut you a little and whacked you alongside the head, to make it look good, and then went to bed herself."

"You're asking me this?"

He nodded.

I shrugged. "No. We didn't."

He smiled without showing his teeth. "Somehow, I thought you'd say that."

"No," I said. "You thought I would protest my innocence loudly. You thought I would be angry. You thought I would be self-righteous, remind you that I'm an officer of the court and a respected Boston lawyer. Because you thought maybe Lily and I did it, and if we did, you thought that would be my guilty reaction. Listen. If I did it, I would've said the same thing the same way. Okay?"

He held up both hands, a gesture of surrender. "Okay. Fine. No offense intended." He cocked his head. "Odd, though, that it would just happen to occur while you were visiting."

"Sure. Just the way I'd do it. Make sure I was there so it'd go down right. Good way to allay suspicion, being there. It'd really call attention to myself if I was in Boston at the time, or in Idaho fly fishing, or something. Hell, I'd be the first one you'd think of if I was in Idaho."

"You couldn't've done it if you were in Idaho, Mr. Coyne."

"Right. Best way is to spend the night. Jesus!"

He shrugged. "I just said it was odd."

"I didn't do it," I said.

"We'll see."

"This is why you asked me to come down here?"

"You gotta admit," he said, grinning, "it's an interesting scenario."

I denied him the satisfaction of a reply.

Maroney laced his fingers together behind his neck and arched his back. He groaned softly. "You wouldn't believe the paperwork on something like this," he mumbled. He leaned forward. "Let me level with you, Mr. Coyne."

"I wish you would."

"I think the lady's involved."

"Why?"

He shrugged. "Think about it. If what you tell me is true—"

"It is."

"Sure. If it's true, she could've gone down to unlock that gate, let the bad guys in, right?"

He was right, of course. Lily could have purposefully left the gate unlocked when she let Dr. Sauerman out. But I didn't believe it.

"She knew about the jaguars," continued Maroney. "She knew about the dogs. Hell, Mr. Coyne. She's a big, strong lady. She could've hit Mr. Newton herself."

"It wasn't Lily who came into my room," I said. "It was two men."

"Maybe," he said. He cocked his head and looked at me. "This thing absolutely stinks of an inside job."

"I didn't know cops really talked like that."

"What, inside job?"

"Yes."

"Sure we do. We watch TV just like anybody else."

I shook my head. "I don't think Lily had anything to do with it."

"How well do you know her?"

"Not that well, really."

"So give me a hand."

"Why?"

"The man was your client. I assume you care about him. And you got yourself scraped up a bit. Anyhow, there's a question of justice here. You're a lawyer. It's your duty." He grinned broadly.

"What do you want me to do?"

Maroney picked up his pencil. This time he rolled it in his fingers. "I don't know, exactly. Watch her. See what she says, where she goes. See what you can get out of her."

"Right now she's at the hospital checking on Jeff. Does that help?"

"Sure. You already told me that. Okay? Will you do it?"

"I'm leaving soon. Tomorrow, probably. Monday, the latest, depending on Jeff. I've got a business in Boston."

"So that gives you a little time. I tried to check up on her, too."

"What'd you learn?"

He shook his head. "Nothing." He peered at me.

"You think I have better sources than you?"

"Lawyers are supposed to be resourceful. You probably know Mr. Newton's business better than anybody. That's a place to start."

"Oh, we are resourceful as hell." I thought of those collect calls from the Totem Café in West Yellowstone. I wondered if tracking down that number qualified me as being resourceful. I studied the ceiling for a minute. I remembered how Jeff looked, crumpled there on the path, a sickening bloody dent above his ear. I remembered the red smiles on the throats of Tondo and Ngwenya. I remembered the metallic taste of fear in my mouth when I thought I was going to die.

I remembered that of all of us who were there, dogs and people, only Lily had been untouched.

I looked up at him and nodded. "Okay," I said. "I'll see what I can do."

He returned my nod, one quick jerk of his chin. "Good."

"I hope you're not laying your whole wad on her. Or me."

"I've already put out the word on the jaguars. But you and I know that they're not likely to turn up on the Cape. New York, maybe. Or L.A. Hell, it's basically a theft with assault. Not like it was a homicide. Not yet."

"You're saying that this gets treated like any other housebreak, unless . . ."

"Oh, it's a heavy felony, Mr. Coyne, and the state cops

will be involved for sure. Burglary, grand larceny, assault. If Mr. Newton dies, sure, it'll be heavier. But you've got to remember. There's lots of things happening on Cape Cod in the summer. We have to hire a bunch of auxiliaries just to direct traffic, patrol the parking lots, check out the nightspots. Million things. Fights, fires on the beaches, underage kids buying booze, head-ons on 6A, drownings, shoplifting. Not to mention your routine cocaine busts, bales of marijuana coming on pleasure boats into any one of two hundred Cape Cod harbors, several of which are right here in sleepy little Orleans."

"Road pizzas," I added. "Don't forget road pizzas."

He shrugged. "Hell, you look at it one way, this is like any other housebreak. Only difference is, what they got is worth more than most of 'em and somebody was injured."

"Injured badly."

"Injured is injured."

"And what they got is worth a lot more, probably."

He nodded. "No doubt."

"And they killed two dogs."

He shrugged. "That's probably some kind of crime, too. Cruelty to animals or something. We don't exactly call it murder."

"And you need all the help you can get."

He nodded.

"Fine," I said. "I'll see what I can do."

"Good. Thanks." He stood up and reached his hand across his desk to shake mine. I took it.

I moved toward the door. "Oh, Mr. Coyne. One other thing."

I stopped and turned. "What's that?"

"The dogs?"

"Yes?"

"They were shot before their throats were cut."

"I didn't hear any shots."

"Twenty-two shorts. One each in the chest."

"Even so . . ."

"Ever hear a twenty-two short from a rifle?"

"Sure."

"Sounds like an elastic snapping," said Maroney.

"I'm impressed," I said. "They did an autopsy on the dogs, huh?"

"Not exactly an autopsy," he said. "The dog officer took 'em to his kennel and called me down. Showed me the bullet holes. He dug out the slugs with a penknife and forceps. I showed 'em to a couple of the guys. They agreed with me. Twenty-two shorts."

"What do you make of that?" I said.

"Whoever broke in last night didn't need to know those dogs' names. They could've stood outside the fence and shot 'em, then come in and finished 'em off with a knife."

"How, then," I asked, "does that implicate Lily? Or me?"

"Somebody unlocked that gate."

I nodded.

"And think about this," he said.

"What?"

"If you wanted to make it look like outsiders—"

"You'd shoot the dogs even if you did know their names," I said. "True. But if it really was outsiders—"

He shrugged. "How'd they get in?"

I drove back to Quashnet Lane slowly. Maroney wanted me to play detective for him. I had no stomach for trying to lure Lily into a contradiction. On the other hand, I had plenty of incentive for nailing the bastards who had stolen Jeff's jaguars and smashed in his skull. For one thing, they'd made me believe I was about to die. I could forgive no one for that.

The parking area at the end of the driveway was empty.

Lily wasn't back yet. I pushed open the gate. We had left it unlocked. I followed the path to the house, skirting the dark places where Jeff and the dogs had lain. There was no yellow crime scene barricade tape or signs. I supposed if Jeff had been murdered it might have been different.

I got the last Grolsch from the refrigerator and took it out onto the patio.

The sun settled beneath the tall trees behind me while I gazed easterly. There were still several hours of daylight left, but the shadows in the hollows below Jeff's hill grew long and dark.

I wondered if he was going to make it.

Lily. I knew nothing about her. It would be easy to create a scenario of the crime with her at the center of it. I could see how Maroney could do it. He had the advantage on me there. I knew her, or thought I did. What I knew didn't fit. It skewed my perception, fuzzed the picture. She was beautiful, sexy, sensitive, loving, loyal. None of those was a criminal trait.

But aside from the beautiful and sexy parts, it all could be pretense. That plus my own predisposition to project a certain repertoire of feminine qualities onto beautiful women.

I wondered about those phone calls from the Totem Café in West Yellowstone, Montana. They could have been for Lily, not Jeff.

I sipped my beer slowly. Swallows soared and swooped against the afternoon sky, waiting for the mosquitoes to come out. I waited for them, too.

I had begun to slap at their scouts when I heard a car engine whine up the driveway. Then it stopped. A door chunked shut. I got up and went into the house. The rooms were growing dark. I switched on some lights.

Lily came in. I studied her face. It showed me nothing. She gave me a quick, weary smile. "Hi."

"Hi."

She dropped her purse on the table next to the empty glass cases and plopped onto the sofa. "I'm beat," she said.

"Beer or something?"

She shook her head. "Nothing." She looked around. "You cleaned up."

"Yes. It was a mess."

"Thanks."

I sat beside her. She reached for my hand and pulled it into her lap. She laid her head back on the sofa and closed her eyes. I waited for her to tell me that Jeff had died.

It was several minutes before she spoke. "They wouldn't even let me see him," she finally said, her voice soft and vague. "They had him in surgery for like three hours, and I just waited, and finally a nurse came out, and I could tell by the way she looked at me that he was dead. And, Brady, I had this feeling—I'm ashamed, but I couldn't help it—I was relieved. Just in that moment between the time I saw her face and she spoke to me, it was like a big rock fell out of my stomach. And it wasn't that I was relieved on Jeff's account, either. Not as if I was happy that his misery had ended, or that it was better that he wouldn't live like a vegetable or something. I was relieved on my own account. I felt free, finally, and I realized in that instant that I hadn't been free for a long time and that I had resented the hell out of Jeff, that he had kept me imprisoned all those years."

She squeezed my hand tightly with both of hers. I turned to look at her face, expecting, from the tone of her voice, to see tears. But she wasn't crying. Her forehead was furrowed, her eyes squeezed shut, her lips taut, and I read more anger than sadness there.

"He's not dead," she said after a long pause. "Holding his own, was how the nurse put it. Stable, she said. I asked for details. How badly hurt is he, I said. What will happen? Will he be okay? Stable, she repeated. That's all she could tell me. I got—I got a little loud, I guess. I had been sitting there for a long time, waiting, trying to figure out how I felt about it, what I wanted to happen, and it was like something snapped. So a doctor came out. He put his hands on my shoulders and kind of sat me down. So I asked him the same questions. Know what he said?"

"What?" I said.

"He asked me if I was next of kin. I said I was his goddamned housekeeper, that's all I was, but I was there and I was all he had just then. And this doctor—he couldn't have been thirty years old, with a dippy little blond mustache and these round wire-rimmed glasses down on his nose—he gives me this bullshit smile they probably teach them in medical school, and he tells me Jeff's stable, he's holding his own, the surgery was successful. So I asked him what the fuck that was supposed to mean, what was going to happen, and he told the nurse to bring me a glass of water, for Christ sake. I stood up. I told him I didn't want water. I wanted to know about Jeff, and since they didn't seem like they wanted to tell me, I was gonna get a lawyer."

"You are a piece of work," I said.

She moved her head and looked at me. "I am, aren't I?" She sighed deeply. "Anyhow, was that okay?"

"Was what okay?"

"About you going there tomorrow and demanding to know about him?"

I smiled. "Oh, sure. Badgering doctors is one of the main things lawyers do."

She rested her cheek against my shoulder. "Good. I think I'll have that beer now."

"Sorry," I said. "I just finished the last one."

SIX

• • • • • • •

L ILY AND I arrived at the Cape Cod Hospital in Hyannis a little after noon on Sunday. The day had dawned drizzly. The roads were clogged with traffic, vacationers aimlessly seeking alternative time-killers to lying on the beach. It took nearly an hour to get there.

At the main desk we got directions to the ICU. We found the waiting room, so named, I supposed, because people waited there for other people to die. No one happened to be waiting there this time.

I told the secretary behind the chest-high counter that I was Thomas Jefferson Newton's attorney—sometimes I use the word "attorney" rather than "lawyer" because laypeople seem to respond more quickly to it—and that I wanted to talk to the doctor in charge.

She had hair like Brillo and a quick sympathetic smile that wrinkled her face like a gust of wind across a pond. She squinted at me for a moment, then nodded. "Okay. Have a seat, please. The doctor will be with you." I waited at the counter until she picked up a phone and spoke into it. Then I went back and sat beside Lily.

Fifteen or twenty minutes passed before a man wearing pale green hospital scrubs came into the room. He was probably forty, although the bags under his eyes made him look older. His skin was pale and his shoulders sagged. He looked overworked, underpaid, strung out on too much stress and too little sleep. He looked at me and Lily, hesitated, then came over.

"You're here about Mr. Newton?" he said, aiming his question at the space between me and Lily.

I stood up. "Yes. I'm Mr. Newton's lawyer. Brady Coyne. This is Miz Robbins."

"I'm Dr. Rodman." He shook my hand and nodded toward Lily. There was a bloodstain the size of a dime on the sleeve of his smock. It was as perfectly round as a button. "Mr. Newton's holding his own. He's had quite a bad accident."

"Holding his own," I repeated. "What does that mean?"

"He's stable. All his vital signs are stable. He's unconscious, of course, but—"

"Why 'of course'?"

The doctor gave us a tired smile. "His injury was potentially . . ." He let his voice trail off.

"Fatal?" I said.

He nodded. "Yes. Fatal."

"Doctor," I said, "would you mind sitting with us for a minute?"

He shrugged. "Sure." He pulled a chair around and sat facing me and Lily.

Lily reached for my hand and pulled it into her lap.

Dr. Rodman took a deep breath, expanded his cheeks, and let it out in a long, slow sigh. "When Mr. Newton arrived, his vital signs were poor. The EMTs probably saved his life. We suspected an epidural bleed." He looked at Lily. "Bleeding in the brain. Visually examining the wound, we were worried about bone fragments. We gave him a CAT scan then took him into surgery. We evacuated the blood and bone, but he herniated before we could—"

"Herniated?" I said.

He nodded. "The brain swells and bulges out. A bad sign." He leaned toward us. "A lot of the cortex on the left side of the brain was disrupted. The left hemisphere of the brain, you know, controls speech, plus the entire right side of the body and the face."

Lily's grip on my hand tightened. "So what's the prognosis?" I said.

The doctor shook his head. "I wish I could be more optimistic."

"What's that mean?" said Lily.

"We haven't done an EEG yet."

"Therefore?"

"Therefore, I'm reluctant to say."

"You're familiar with head wounds?" I said.

He nodded.

"We'd like to know what to expect."

He narrowed his eyes and studied me, then Lily. Then he nodded. "Okay. Here's what I expect. Should Mr. Newton regain consciousness, at the very least he will be nonverbal and paralyzed, or virtually so."

"But," I said, "you don't expect him to regain consciousness."

His mouth smiled. His eyes did not. "I expect Mr. Newton to remain comatose," he said.

"For how long?" said Lily.

The doctor looked at me as if he wanted help.

"Until he dies," I said.

The doctor shrugged. "That, I'm afraid, would be my expectation. We'll know better in a couple days. That's as candid as I can be with you. Things happen we don't expect.

Right now Mr. Newton is on a ventilator. His intercerebral pressure is being monitored. Sometimes . . ." He shrugged, then smiled quickly. "There's a lot we don't know," he said. "Injuries like this, people often survive for a long time."

"On machines," said Lily.

"Yes. Sometimes independent of machines. Sometimes they even regain consciousness. But not often. You shouldn't get your hopes up. There is no question whatsoever that Mr. Newton has suffered severe, irreversible brain trauma." He looked at me and narrowed his eyes, as if he had just thought of something. "I think you will find that we did everything we could. He's lucky to still be alive."

I smiled. He was worried about a lawsuit. I couldn't blame him. I figured, for Jeff's sake, it was just as well that he was worried.

"You can see him if you want," said the doctor.

Lily looked at me. "You go ahead," I said.

She shook her head. "I don't think so."

Dr. Rodman stood up. He shook hands with both of us. "If there's any change, we'll let you know," he said.

I took back roads from Hyannis to Orleans. Although they were a little less congested than Route 6 had been in the morning, I found myself stuck behind a Dodge wagon trailing a big powerboat in Dennis. He kept the needle on 20.

"Who does Jeff know in Montana?" I asked Lily as we crept past a miniature golf plaza in Harwich.

"Montana?"

"Yesterday when I was picking up the living room I saw his phone bill. There were four collect calls on four consecutive days, all from the same number in West Yellowstone, Montana."

I glanced sideways at her. She was frowning at me. "I don't know," she said. "Why?"

"Just curious, I guess."

"So he's got a friend in Montana," she said.

"He doesn't have many friends."

"Well, he used to."

"What about you?"

"What about me?"

"Know anybody in Montana?"

"What are you getting at, Brady?"

I reached over and touched her leg. "Nothing. Sorry. I'm nosy. After the other night . . ."

"Yeah, well, me too, you know."

I squeezed her knee. "I know. Accept my apology?"

"Sure." She didn't sound especially enthusiastic.

Lily and I didn't talk much the rest of the way back. There didn't seem to be much to say. Lily stared out the side window. I repressed urges to curse the traffic.

When I finally pulled in beside her Cherokee, I turned to her and said, "I guess I'll head back tonight, okay?"

She turned in her seat to face me. "No."

"No?"

"No. It's not all right. I don't want you to go."

"Lily—"

She smiled quickly. "Yeah, I know. You've got to get back to your office. I understand that. But it's not all right with me. I don't want to be alone here. Not yet. Do what you feel you have to do. But don't ask me what I want."

"I can't stay with you here forever."

"I know. One more night would be nice, though."

"I'd have to take off early in the morning."

She nodded. "That'd be great." She reached over and placed the palm of her hand on my cheek. Then she tilted toward me and kissed me there. "I'll take you fishing tonight, how'd that be?" She kept her mouth against my face. "Jeff's pond is full of nice rainbow trout. I'll paddle."

"The way to a man's heart," I said. The dewy touch of her lips remained long after she had pulled away from me.

Lily broiled T-bone steaks for dinner. Baked potato, salad of mixed greens, a musky red wine. We ate in the kitchen.

While she was cleaning up I retrieved my fly-fishing gear and went out back to the toolshed to hunt up the paddles and cushions for our canoe excursion. The sun had already dipped behind the trees, and the shed had no windows. The only light came through the open doorway. Everything in there was a shadow.

I squeezed around a lawn mower and a wheelbarrow. I spotted a pair of paddles propped up in the corner behind a large object shrouded under a canvas cover. As I leaned over it to reach the paddles I realized the object was a motorcycle. Seeing it saddened me somehow. The bike was a relic, I guessed, from Jeff's vigorous youth. Before the leopard got him. And now he was lying in a hospital, more dead than alive.

Lily was waiting for me on the dock. She had the canoe drawn up alongside. I held it for her while she stepped in. I handed her the paddles and cushions. Then I took the bow seat. Lily shoved us off. I stripped line from my reel and began fly casting.

A furry blanket of mist skimmed the inky surface of the pond. An orange wedge of moon hung low in the eastern sky, and toward the western horizon the brilliant gold of an hour earlier had faded to yellowish pewter. Aside from the close-up hum and zizz of swarming mosquitoes and the rhythmic, dis-

tant swish of the traffic on Route 6, out there in the canoe Lily
and I seemed cocooned in the liquid silence of the evening.

She had been right about the trout. The rings of surface-
feeding fish caught wiggly reflections from the night sky, expanded them outward, broke the fragile light into pieces, and
scattered them until they seemed to sink into the depths of the
pond. They were fat, healthy rainbows, averaging a foot or so
in length, and they sucked in the little white-winged dry fly I
cast to their swirls.

I released the first few I caught without boating them by
tracing the leader down to the fly in their mouths with my
fingers and twisting the tiny hook free. Finally, Lily said,
"Hey, that could be our breakfast," so I lifted the next two
into the canoe and snapped their necks.

She had changed into snug-fitting white jeans and a rust-
colored flannel shirt. She had the sleeves rolled up to her
elbows and had left several buttons on the front undone. She
was adept with the paddle, although once she had pushed us
up into the cove across the pond she barely had to paddle at
all. Down there in the bowl formed by the hills on all sides,
there was no breeze to ruffle the surface of the water, and we
drifted slowly on unfelt currents of moving air, just fast
enough to give me new fish to cast to.

We hardly spoke. When we did, it was in whispers. "See
that one over there?" she'd say, or "Damn. Missed him," from
me. The quiet of the place commanded respect.

There was a hypnotic rhythm to it—false cast once, twice,
shoot out the line, watch it settle like a silvery snake onto the
black skin of the water, squint at the barely visible white wings
of the little fly, twitch it once, pause, then the swirl, the lift of
the rod tip, the pulse at the end of the line, a leap or two, quick
bursts of shimmering light against the darkness, then the

thrumming resistance as I stripped in the line with a rainbow trout hooked on the end of it.

I sat up in the bow with my back to Lily, surrounded by the place, my head empty of all else, intent only on the fishing and the silence and the pond. No thoughts of Jeff, being kept alive by machines in Hyannis, of myself, waking up with an elbow digging into my chest and a knife at my throat, of stolen Mayan jaguars, road pizzas, murdered watchdogs. In that canoe, it was mindlessly sensual, and I was cleansed and filled and satisfied with the delicate organic smell of night air and water and coolness, the sounds of tiny wavelets slapping against the sides of the aluminum canoe, the feel of the dampness of the air as it gathered into droplets in the hairs on my arms, the silhouettes of shadowy night birds and bats swooping and darting over the pond and now and then brushing its skin with their wingtips.

And I was aware of Lily. I remembered the feathery kiss she had brushed onto my cheek, and her scent, flowers and perspiration.

I also remembered Maroney's suspicions. She could have planned it. He was right. She could have.

Out on that pond, I didn't believe it. Nobody who handled a canoe so effortlessly, who honored so fully the silence of the place and the gentle art of fly casting for evening trout, could be a criminal.

So we drifted and I cast and I let the darkness absorb me until, inevitably, I struck too hard at a trout that might have been bigger than the others, and the frail leader snapped. I sat there for a moment, letting the limp line trail out on the pond. Then I reeled in.

"Had enough?" said Lily softly.

"I never get enough of this. Busted off my fly. Too dark to tie another one on."

I lit a Winston—my first since I had stepped into the canoe. I always suspected that if I could do nothing but fish I would quit the cigarette habit instantly. I hoped someday to test my theory.

Lily paddled us slowly back to the dock at the foot of Jeff Newton's hill. Trout continued to break the surface ahead of us, some of them almost close enough to touch with my rod tip. Occasionally one would burst completely out of water, and the sound of the splash would ride across the water toward us.

She eased the canoe alongside the dock. I climbed out and snugged the painter to a ring. Then I held down my hand to Lily. She took it, braced one knee on the dock, and hauled herself out of the canoe. She didn't let go of my hand. Instead, she tiptoed up and kissed me beside my ear. "That was the most fun I've had in years," she said quietly. "For a while out there, I didn't think of anything except being there. Thank you."

"They say fishing is the most fun a man can have standing up. I guess that goes for a woman, too." I gave her an awkward one-armed hug. "You're an accomplished guide," I added. "Thanks."

She turned and relaxed against me, and I could feel the fronts of her thighs pressing against mine and her breasts soft against my chest. She burrowed her face into the hollow of my throat and muttered something I couldn't understand. I felt her mouth against my skin. I leaned back and nudged her chin with the crook of my forefinger. She looked up at me. "I couldn't understand what you said," I said.

I heard her chuckle. "I said, you really love fishing, don't you?"

"Yes," I said. "It's my passion."

"I like that. A man with a passion. Most people don't have a passion."

I hugged her. "Fishing helps me see things straight. It works as a kind of a metaphor for me. A metaphor for life."

Her lips pressed against my throat.

"Actually," I said, "I think it's the other way around. Life is a metaphor for fishing."

"Oh, sure," she whispered. "I understand perfectly."

She touched the back of my head with the fingers of one hand, and then her other hand reached up to my neck and she moved against me.

"Hey," I said.

She tilted back her face and smiled at me and then angled her head so our mouths would meet. I stroked her hair. Her hips pressed against me.

After a long moment she twisted her mouth away from mine and ducked her head. "Oh, boy," she whispered into my throat.

I held her against me, gazing up at the dark sky, suddenly feeling awkward. "Oh, boy?"

She looked up at me. "Yeah. Oh, boy. Something wrong with oh, boy?"

"No. Oh, boy is perfect." I kissed her again. We dragged it out, improvised a little. I moved my hand up and down her back. I could feel the tenseness of her muscles.

Standing on a dock by a little Cape Cod kettle pond, holding a woman seemed the natural way to end an evening of fly fishing for trout. But after a few minutes, one either proceeds to the next step or else breaks the embrace. Lily seemed inclined to do neither, so it was I who gently held her by the upper arms and pushed her away from me.

She looked at me with her head cocked to the side, smiling. Then she shrugged. She picked up the two trout and the paddle and I gathered up the fly-fishing gear and we trudged up the path to the house. We were careful that no parts of our bodies touched along the way.

When we got back to the house, she disappeared in the direction of her room. When she came back, I was cleaning the trout in the sink. Her face shone as if she had just scrubbed it. She had brushed her hair. The top of her shirt was still unbuttoned. She stood close to me, her hip firm against mine.

"Hi," she said softly.

I nodded. "Look at this."

I slit the belly of one of the fish from anus to pectorals, hooked out the entrails with my forefinger, and then pricked the stomach with the tip of the knife. I sorted out the bits of matter that burst out and showed them to her. "Damselfly nymphs," I said. "They were gorging."

Women, in my experience, have stronger stomachs than men, but the residual chauvinist in me still assumes that when they are shown the entrails of a fresh-caught trout they will avert their eyes, perhaps gag, or at least say, "Yuck! Gross!"

Lily reached into the sink and poked at the gunk with her forefinger. "There's other stuff in here, too," she said.

"Sure. A few mayflies. Lots of midges. *Diptera,* to us entomologists. Mainly, though, these big things. The damselflies. That dry fly I was using they must've mistaken for emerging adults."

She looked up at me and grinned. "Whatever you say."

"We anglers like to understand what's going on."

"It seems like magic to me."

"Juju," I said. It was the African word Jeff often used. "All fishermen believe in *juju.*"

"Lots of *juju* out there tonight," she said.

"Look, Lily—"

She smiled. Sadly, I thought. "For a while there I didn't

even think about Jeff, or the jaguars, or anything. Except . . ."

"There's all kinds of magic," I said. She frowned, so I added, "Once I found the filter from a cigarette in a trout's stomach. A Parliament, it was. I caught him on a Red Quill. Looks nothing like a cigarette filter. After that, I had to believe in *juju*. Skill just wouldn't explain it."

She shrugged and nodded. We weren't talking about the same thing at all. I rinsed out the belly cavities of the two fish, dabbed them dry with paper towels, wrapped them in sticky plastic paper, and put them into the refrigerator. Then I washed my hands.

"Nightcap?" said Lily.

"Sure."

We took our glasses of Old Grand-dad and ice onto the patio. Somehow, on top of the hill far from the water, it seemed different. The mosquitoes still zizzed and the night birds swooped and the traffic swished in the distance. But the stars looked dimmer than they had from the pond, and up there on the hilltop a breeze sifted through the pines, bearing on its currents the aroma of salt fog from the sea.

It was different. Different *juju*.

We sat apart and stared up at the sky and didn't talk. I smoked. Once in a while Lily slapped at a mosquito.

I heard ice cubes click against her teeth. She sighed and stood up. "Bed for me."

"I guess I'll sit awhile longer," I said.

She bent and kissed my forehead. "Night," she murmured.

"Good night."

"I had fun."

"Me, too. Thanks."

I lit another cigarette, telling myself it would be my last of the day. I watched a cloud drift across the face of the moon. I thought about the theft of the jaguars. It could not have been a random housebreak. It must have been what Maroney had called an inside job. But who? Lily? The doctor, Sauerman? Jeff himself? There were no other candidates that I knew of. Except me.

None of them, I concluded. Everybody on the Cape probably knew about the jaguars. Word gets around. Dr. Sauerman, or the meter reader, or the exterminator, one of them would mention it to a stranger at a party in Sandwich, who'd tell the guy who replaced his muffler in Barnstable, who'd pass the story of the golden jaguars and the vicious Dobermans and the old invalid and the sexy housekeeper on to the boys on the bowling team in Falmouth.

It could have been anybody. To suspect Sauerman himself, or Lily, or me—that was naive and simplistic.

But somebody had smashed in Jeff's skull, and someone had held a knife to my throat, and the fear I had felt remained with me. I realized it was mingling with anger, and I knew that was a dangerous sign.

Let go of it, Coyne, I told myself. Chalk it up.

Good advice, I replied. But hard to follow.

I crunched what was left of the ice in my drink between my molars and went into the house. Lily had left the lights on for me. I put the glass in the sink, brushed my teeth in the bathroom, shut off the lights, and went to bed. I closed my eyes and drifted on thoughts of rainbow trout sucking in white-winged dry flies and Lily's soft, eager mouth and the way the canoe rode on the pond's liquid surface and the smooth curve of her back, and I began to float, only it seemed as if it were on her liquid skin . . .

The click of the doorlatch sounded like a gunshot. It yanked me up from the beginning of my descent into sleep, reminding me all at once of a knife at my throat and the taste of fear. "Who is it?" I said loudly.

The door cracked open. I saw her shape against the dim light in the hallway. She was still wearing her jeans and flannel shirt.

"Lily. For Christ sake."

The door opened wider. Her shadowy form entered. The door closed. I sensed rather than saw her move toward me.

"Go away," I said.

"Shut up," she said. I felt her rump hard against my hip when she sat beside me. Her hand touched my face, and she bent and kissed me softly on the mouth. Then she stood up.

"What are you doing?"

"Look," she said. "I just want to be held. Do you mind?"

"I suppose I could handle that."

"Then for Christ sake don't talk anymore."

She unbuttoned her shirt and dropped it onto the floor. Then she sat beside me and shucked off her pants. She stood up again. She was still wearing her bra and panties. She fumbled for the covers. Her skin slicked against mine as she slid in beside me.

She burrowed against me, one arm over my hip. I kissed her throat.

"Just hold me is all," she said.

"I'll try," I said.

She burrowed and squirmed against me. I trailed my hand down her back, over her rump. I could feel her muscles tense as I touched them.

She moved her head. Her mouth was soft against my jaw. She kissed my mouth and pushed against me. Her nails dug into my shoulders. My hand moved along her back. "When I was a kid," I said into her hair, "I could unsnap these things one-handed."

"I'll do it," she said.

Afterward, we held each other for a long time, until I felt myself twitch and I knew I had been drifting into sleep.

"I'm sorry," I mumbled. "Did I kick you?"

She kissed my throat. "It's okay. Sleep."

I hitched myself into a half-sitting position with the pillow bunched under my neck. "I think I was dreaming," I said. "Someone was coming at me with a knife."

"Aw," she said. She rubbed my chest.

"I didn't know Jeff rode bikes," I said.

"Bikes?"

"Motorcycles."

"Me neither," she said.

"He did. There's one in the shed."

"Must've been a long time ago."

She adjusted herself against me. She was making a purring sound against my shoulder. I stroked her back.

"Tell me about your husband, Lily."

"It doesn't matter."

"What was his name? What did he do? What happened?"

"It wasn't a husband," she murmured. "It was just a man. His name was Martin Lodi and he wasn't very good for me and it was a long time ago. He's all gone now."

"Dumb guy."

"Dumb lady," she said.

I woke up suddenly and all at once. Lily was gone and gray light suffused the room. Just outside my window a bobwhite whistled, a human sound, easily imitated. I got up and went to the window. Fog blurred the trees. It was hard to guess what time it was. The bobwhite sat under a pine outside, strutting and pecking among the needles. I whistled to him once through the screen. He lifted his head quickly and peered around. Then he resumed strutting and pecking. I watched him until he wandered out of sight among the trees. Then I went back to bed.

I lay there, cradling my head in my hands, staring at the ceiling. I thought about making love to Lily. I couldn't remember when we stopped and when I had gone to sleep. Then I remembered Jeff and the stolen jaguars, and how those two men had come into my bedroom and pricked my throat and sliced my collarbone with their knife and taped my hands to the bed and slapped that big band of tape across my mouth and frightened the piss out of me before they gratuitously smashed the side of my head.

And all the anger and indignation that had been simmering in me for two days bubbled over.

You see things with particular clarity in the very early morning when you first wake up after having made love to a beautiful woman.

Jeff was going to die.

Tondo and Ngwenya, nasty animals that they were, didn't deserve to be murdered.

Maroney and the Orleans police and perhaps the state police would all go through their motions. When Jeff died, they'd approach it differently, but that would probably take a while. By then it would be too late. The trail would be too fuzzy to follow. Crimes like this, I knew, were rarely solved, except by luck.

And Lily—maybe Maroney was right. Maybe she had set up the burglary. Maybe she had left the gate unlocked, and maybe it was she who advised the two intruders to shoot Tondo and Ngwenya and slit their throats and then tape me up and scare me with a knife and hit me on the head. And, if necessary, to hit Jeff hard enough that he'd never be able to tell what he had seen.

Maybe she thought if she came to me in the night I would

not pursue it. If she could make me love her, I would not suspect her.

The longer I lay there thinking about it, the angrier I became. I wanted to pursue it. Not for Jeff. For me. Somehow, it had become personal.

I recognized it as a decision, and that recognition allowed the anger to metamorphose into its mature form—something like stubbornness, or commitment, or resolution. I still visualized holding a knife at a man's throat until he wet his pants. That was the anger in its immature stage. But it was a vision I wanted to hang on to. I didn't think that would be a problem.

I would find out all I could about Lily.

Finally I padded into the bathroom and took a long hot shower. Then I shut off the hot faucet and forced myself to stay under the water for a full count of sixty, going one-thousand-one, one-thousand-two . . . This was my daily—and, on a good day, my only—exercise of willpower.

I shaved and dressed. Then I packed up my stuff and lugged it out into the kitchen. It was twenty minutes after five. I switched on the coffee machine. I found a piece of paper and a pencil and sat at the table.

"Lily," I wrote. "I'm going to practice doing it one-handed. I'm heading back. Keep me posted on the Hunter. I'm borrowing a coffee mug. You get to eat both trout. Be well. Brady."

I put the note in the middle of the table. The coffee machine had finished chugging. I poured a mugful and, balancing it carefully in one hand, gathered up my fishing gear and overnight bag in the other and left the house.

The paddles and cushions were still on the porch where we had left them in the dark. I put my stuff down and gathered up the boating gear. I could save Lily one chore, anyway.

I took them around back to the shed. When I opened the

door, I could see more clearly than I had the previous night. I wedged myself between the lawn mower and the wheelbarrow and leaned over the motorcycle to return the paddles and cushions to their places.

Out of curiosity I folded the canvas off the motorcycle. It was a big Harley. Powerful and fast. Just like Jeff, I thought. He'd want a big hog between his legs.

As I tugged the canvas back down over the rear of the bike, I noticed the license plate. Montana.

SEVEN

• • • • • • •

COLLECT PHONE CALLS from Montana. Now Jeff's motorcycle. It probably had no bearing on what had happened to Jeff and his jaguars. But it made me realize I knew less about my old client than I had thought.

I headed out on 6A. The traffic wasn't bad on the way back to the city. I listened to Beethoven and tried to ponder the questions of wills and estates I would face at the office. The more miles I put between myself and Quashnet Lane, the easier it became.

I pulled into the parking garage under my apartment a little before seven-thirty. I changed my clothes and made it to the office by eight-thirty.

Monday morning. Another week.

I was on my second mug of coffee when Julie came in. Nine o'clock on the button, as usual. She glowered at me. Her morning face. I poured coffee for her, stirred in one sugar, no cream, and placed it on her desk. She sat down, wrapped both hands around her mug, lifted it about an inch off her desktop, and lowered her face to it. She alternated blowing and sipping for several minutes. When she looked up at me she was no longer glowering. But she did frown. There's a difference, at least when Julie does it.

"What happened to you?" she said.

"Why?"

"Your mirror must've been all steamed up this morning. You nicked yourself."

I touched my throat. "Oh, that's a knife wound."

"Always the joker. Even first thing in the morning." She grinned. "You got a nasty shaving rash, too."

"I was bound and gagged. Tape across my face."

She cocked her head at me, nodded once, and dipped back to her coffee.

"I got a big bump where I got slugged, too," I volunteered. "Also a worse gash here on my collarbone."

"Right." Julie smiled into her mug. Then she looked up at me. "So," she said. "Truthfully. How was the big weekend on the Cape?"

I wiggled my hand back and forth.

"Boring, huh? Well, I never promised you excitement. I just said you had to go and sit with Mr. Newton." She slurped, then looked up again. "Come on, Brady. Something worth reporting must've happened. I thirst for gossip. How's Mr. Newton, anyway?"

"He's in the hospital," I said.

She peered at me over the rim of her mug. "Poor man," she said. "He's been sick for a long time."

"And," I continued, "really, nothing much happened. We were burglarized. A million and a half dollars' worth of pre-Columbian artifacts were stolen. The cops think I might have masterminded it. I was pistol-whipped, sliced with a knife, and tied up in bed. Two security personnel were shot and had their throats slashed. I caught seventeen rainbow trout on dry flies. The housekeeper seduced me. Your basic boring weekend."

She arched her eyebrows. Her head still hovered over her coffee mug. She grinned. "Sure," she said.

"Okay, so maybe it was only twelve trout."

"Twelve?"

"At least twelve. We kept two. I caught them on Royal Wulffs."

"That's more like it." She swiveled around and whisked the dust cover off her word processor. I was dismissed.

I went into my office. My desktop was clean, the way I like to see it. I tapped out the number for my friend Dan LaBreque over at the Museum of Fine Arts. Two or three times every summer Dan took me and Charlie McDevitt out on his boat to catch bluefish. It was Dan who had appraised Jeff Newton's seven gold jaguars when he brought them home from Mexico.

Dan answered the phone himself.

"It's Brady," I said.

"Oh, hi. To answer your question, yes, the blues are running, and sure, anytime. They were hitting Rapalas the other night, but I imagine those fancy poppers you throw with your fly rod would work. Actually, I was going to call you this week. So when?"

"I'd love to go fishing. But that's not why I called." I hesitated. He waited. "You remember Jeff Newton?"

"The guy with those gorgeous Mayan jaguars? I don't remember him particularly well, but I sure remember the artifacts. Gorgeous. Also unquestionably imported illegally."

"The jaguars were stolen Friday night."

"Yeah? Really?"

"Yeah. Really. And Jeff had his skull smashed in."

"Was he . . . ?"

"He's alive. Irreversible coma, it looks like."

"Jesus," he said. "So tell me about it, for Christ sake."

I told Dan what had happened over the weekend. I included the part about the trout fishing. Dan liked fishing stories. I used the figure seventeen with him, pausing to give him a chance to express his doubts. Bless him, he didn't. I left out the part about Lily, even though Dan didn't mind that sort of story, either. He didn't seem to notice anything was missing from my recitation.

He listened without interrupting. When I was done, he said, "I'll be damned."

"What's the market for pre-Columbian artifacts?" I said.

"Depends."

"On what?"

"Whether they're authentic, with papers to prove it. Whether they were brought in legally before 1971, and there are papers to show that, too." He paused. "Look, Brady. The truth is, any museum would pay top dollar for those seven jaguars, provided the seller's got the papers."

"Even if they had been stolen?"

"Not if they knew they were stolen, of course. But frankly, there are some museum purchasers who wouldn't look real close at bills of sale. What they'd really scrutinize is the original import papers."

"Why's that?"

"Because without them, the Mexican government could reclaim the pieces and the museum'd be out a million or so bucks."

"None of the papers on the jaguars were taken," I said.

"Wouldn't matter," said Dan.

"Why not?"

"Because Newton's papers, as I seem to recall, were phony."

"You weren't particularly sure of that at the time."

"I suspected it. I don't know enough about those kinds of papers. But I'd bet anything your friend smuggled in those pieces."

"Those papers passed muster with the insurance agency."

"They wouldn't pass muster with a museum purchaser. Not if they were fake."

"Here's my question, then," I said.

"Who'd steal them? Who'd buy them from the thief? Right?"

"Right."

I heard him clear his throat. "You want me to name names, I can't. There are collectors in this country who would buy those jaguars, no questions asked, if the price was right, and some who might even set up a theft. They have the money to pay cash. They have the resources to hang on to the pieces for a long time, let the hubbub die down, let them appreciate. They have the contacts to assemble papers that would be hard to prove were fake. Lots of these collectors just really love the stuff. They like to own it, look at it. They're genuine art lovers. They just happen to be crooks."

"But you can't name names."

"No."

"Who could?"

He hesitated for a minute. "Marla Conway," he said. "She might be able to. Probably wouldn't. But she could."

"Why wouldn't she?"

"Hell, Brady. There's confidentiality in our business just like there is in yours."

"What if she knew one of these so-called art lovers stole the pieces, or bought them from whoever did?"

"I can't speak for Marla. But, yeah, that would make a difference."

"Does Marla still work there with you?"

"No. She's curator for a museum in Phoenix. Has been for five or six years. I still talk to her now and then."

"How do I reach her?"

"I'll give you her number. Hang on a minute."

I waited. He came back on the line and gave me the phone number of Marla Conway's museum in Phoenix.

"Listen, Brady," he said. "The way these things usually work, whoever whacked Newton and took those gorgeous pieces had a purchaser all lined up. The crooks probably got fifty, maybe a hundred grand for their night's work. They probably dumped them the next day. In quick, out quick. From what you said, they were pros."

"I don't know about that. They were unpleasant fellows."

"Most crooks are."

"Not necessarily," I said.

"It's possible," he said, "that they'll try to ransom them."

"Like a kidnapping, you mean."

"Yeah. It's pretty common with art theft. They try to hold up the owner, or sometimes his insurance company."

"There'd be no sense in holding up Jeff," I said. "He hasn't got much money, and anyway, he's in a coma."

"The insurance company, maybe," said Dan.

"It's Lloyd's."

"Just a thought," he said. "The ransom thing is most common with really valuable stuff, one-of-a-kind things. Paintings by famous masters that the entire world knows about. These cats, there are probably others around. If they were recovered, it'd be hard to prove they were Newton's anyway. Hell, your thieves might just take out the emerald eyes and melt 'em down for the gold. Over a hundred pounds of gold, right? Fourteen big fat emeralds? Plenty of value right there."

"Yeah, I thought of that," I said. "If they do that, we're sunk. Let's go back to these collectors, these unscrupulous rich guys."

"I told you, I don't know any names."

"New York?"

"Some, sure. For stuff like that, Mayan, Aztec, more of

'em are in the West, Southwest, though. Houston, Denver, Salt Lake City, Phoenix, San Diego, L.A. You should talk to Marla. That's her territory. She specializes in that Indian stuff. That's why she's out there. Look. You want to go catch some bluefish, or what?"

"I do. But listen. What're the odds of those jaguars being recovered?"

"Zilch," he said promptly. "Unless they try to ransom them, in which case chances are they still won't be recovered, or if they are they'll be damaged. If they melt 'em down, of course, that's sayonara. But my bet is some collector's got them stashed away. They won't see the light of day for many years. If he tried to resell them through legitimate channels, he'd get nailed. Mexico would take them back."

"What about illegitimate channels? Do these collectors buy and sell among themselves?"

"Probably. We never hear about it, of course."

"What do the police do?"

"The police do what they do with any theft. Which, as far as I know, is diddley squat. The insurance company does a few things."

"Like what?"

"Who'd you say insured Newton? Lloyd's?"

"I think so. He dealt with an agency in Hyannis. I've got to call them."

"Lloyd's probably underwrote the policy. They'll send an adjustor. He'll talk to you."

"Why me?"

"Doesn't sound like they can talk to Newton, and you're his lawyer. Anyhow, you're a witness. You can tell him that there really was a theft, that it's not a fraud. That's what he needs to know. That plus the fact that the security was intact when it happened."

"There was a theft, all right," I said, fingering the scab on my throat. "I can personally vouch for that."

"So if he's satisfied that the pieces were actually stolen, he'll pay off and go through his own motions. If Lloyd's can recover the pieces, they get to keep them. Unless Newton has a buy-back clause. If he does, they get their money back. So they do some standard things. They'll report the theft to the Art Dealers Association of America and the International Foundation for Art Research. These are clearinghouses for information on stolen art. They publish art-theft bulletins. They'll carry photographs and descriptions of the jaguars. Also, the FBI has an Art Squad and a Transportation of Stolen Property desk. And there's Interpol and the Property Recovery Squad of the New York City police. The Lloyd's guy will make his reports to all of them. It's routine. It's about all he can do."

"But this won't do any good, you don't think."

"Like I said, the only ones who've seen those jaguars are the guys who broke into the house and the guy who bought them from the crooks, if somebody did. At least, that's my bet."

"Unless someone catches up with those jaguars, I don't see how they'll figure out who hit Jeff," I said. Or, I thought, who came into my bedroom at night. I lit a cigarette. "Okay," I said, "let's talk bluefish."

"About time," said Dan. There was new animation in his voice. "On the turning tide at the mouth of the Merrimack. Anytime out on Stellwagen. We ran into a huge school of them trolling off Plum Island the other day. Smashing menhaden on the surface. You could smell 'em. You know that smell. Ripe melons. Gulls swooping around everywhere, all we could do to keep the damn birds away from the plugs when we stopped and cast to 'em. The fish were absolutely frenzied. Every damn cast. You would've been proud of us."

"Caught a lot, huh?"

"Yeah. And only kept two. Returned all the rest."

"I am proud."

"Man with a fly rod would've had a blast."

"Okay. I'm hooked. When?"

"Let me check a tide chart. Hang on a minute." I finished my cigarette and stubbed it out. When Dan came back on the line, he said, "What do you say five thirty Wednesday? We should hit 'em off Halibut Point."

"Sure. I can leave the office at four. Be in Gloucester before five thirty, even with the traffic."

He was silent for a moment. Then he said, "Brady?"

"What?"

"You work at night?"

"Of course not."

"I'm talking A.M."

"Like five thirty in the morning?"

"That's what A.M. means. In the morning."

"So I've gotta get up at four."

"About that, I'd say. Four thirty at the latest."

"Fine. No problem. Actually, I love that time of day."

"You just love fishing."

"Naw. I like everything about it. When everyone else is asleep, and the sky is just starting to turn silver, and the ocean from my window looks like burnished pewter, and—"

"Hey, shit," said Dan. "Can the poetry, huh?"

"Yeah, well I do love fishing. I'll see you at the marina at five thirty Wednesday."

"I'll bring a thermos of coffee," he said. "Why don't you see if Charlie can join us."

"Sure. I was going to call him anyway."

"Charlie's really big on crack of dawn stuff." Dan paused. "Hey, Brady?"

"What?"

"They have any suspects on that theft?"

"They think they do."

"Yeah?"

"Yeah. Me, for one."

I replaced the phone on its cradle and wrote a note on a piece of yellow legal paper. "Bluefish, Wed. 5:30 A.M., " it said. I folded the paper three times and stuffed it into the pants pocket where I kept my car keys. Not that I was likely to forget.

I buzzed Julie. "What?" she grumbled.

"Hey. Have another cup of coffee."

"I'm working on it. What do you want?"

"Seacoast Agency. Hyannis. Victoria Kline."

"Ten-four."

I hung up. A minute later my console buzzed. I pushed the blinking button and picked up the phone. Victoria Kline had a Lauren Bacall voice. I told her what had happened to the jaguars. She neither interrupted nor asked me to repeat myself. When I finished, she told me that an adjuster from Lloyd's would be in touch with me. I congratulated her on her efficiency.

I lit a cigarette and had tapped out half of Charlie McDevitt's phone number when Julie scratched at my door. I replaced the receiver on its cradle. "Do enter," I called.

Julie came in. She strode purposefully to me and placed the palms of both of her hands on my desk. She bent toward me and said, "I want to know the truth about your weekend, Brady Coyne."

"Truth?"

"Not your childish fairy tales."

"Okay," I said. "Sit down."

She remained standing, her eyebrows arched.

I waved my hand at her. "Please sit?" I said.

She sat. "So tell me. And no bullshit this time."

"What I told you is true."

"About Mr. Newton being in the hospital?"

"Yes."

"His sickness?"

"He was hit on the head."

"Are you serious?"

I nodded.

"Then the burglary, it really happened?"

I nodded again.

"And those marks on your face?"

"Knife wounds."

"Mr. Newton—will he die?"

I shrugged. "The surgeon wasn't optimistic."

"Oh, wow." She sighed deeply and shook her head. "I don't care about the housekeeper or the fishing."

"You don't care about the fishing?"

"You said two people were killed. You were kidding about that, right?"

"I believe I said security personnel."

"You did. What—?"

"Dogs, Julie. Two guard dogs."

"Are you really some kind of suspect in this?"

I spread my hands. "Probably not a serious one. The local cops are fishing around, trying to make it understandable. I could have had something to do with it. I mean, I was there. I could've arranged it, let the bad guys in."

"And hurt yourself like that?"

I shrugged. "I could've had them do it. To take the heat off myself."

"Cops think that way, huh?"

"Sure. Anybody would."

She shook her head. "Not me. I know you. You're a baby. You'd never agree to get hurt like that."

I patted her arm. "Thank you for your continued support."

"So what are you going to do?"

"Me? I'm just a lawyer, Julie. This is a police matter."

She grimaced. "Right. And I'm Joan of Arc."

"I hope I haven't got anything important for Wednesday morning."

"Would it make a difference?"

"It'd just have to be changed."

"Fishing, huh?"

"Matter of fact, yes," I said. I don't know why I felt defensive saying it.

She shrugged. "I will, of course, work it out for you. That's what you pay me these big bucks for." She got up and went to the door. She paused there with her hand on the knob, staring thoughtfully at me. Then she came back and sat beside me. She frowned. "It must have been an awful experience for you."

I nodded. "It was. It was scary. The whole thing. Finding Jeff like that. And what happened to me. Frightening. Except for the trout. And the housekeeper."

"It's all so sad."

I nodded.

She stood up and leaned toward me. She kissed my forehead. "I hope you're not planning on doing anything stupid."

"Not me, babe. I'm going fishing Wednesday, that's all. And that is not stupid."

"That's certainly a matter of opinion." She headed for the door again. After she opened it she looked back at me. "How many trout did you say?"

"I said seventeen. But it was at least twelve. I didn't count. It was good fishing."

She nodded. "I won't even ask about the housekeeper."

"You can't believe everything I say."

"Boy, don't I know it."

She shut the door. I smiled at it. Then I called Charlie. He's a prosecutor for the United States Justice Department. His office is located across town in Government Center on Cambridge Street. Charlie and I went to Yale Law together. He's a good friend and my number one fishing partner. When Shirley, his secretary, answered, I said, "Hello, sexy."

She giggled. "Oh, you silly, Mr. Coyne."

"How are the grandchildren, Shirl?"

"Lorraine had a baby two weeks ago. A beautiful little boy."

"What's that make?"

"Sixteen. And Jimmy's wife is expecting again."

"Marvelous. Congratulations. Hard to believe, a young chick like you with grandchildren."

"Oh, stop," she said. I knew she was smiling. "I hope you're planning on taking himself fishing, Mr. Coyne. He's working so hard. He's just been a bundle of nerves lately."

"Matter of fact, I am. Is he there?"

"I'll get him for you."

A moment later Charlie came on the line. "Hey, Brady," he said. "What's up?"

"Dan LaBreque's boat in Gloucester. Five thirty Wednesday. That's five thirty in the morning. Bring your fly rod."

"Music to my ears. Say no more."

"Charlie, I've got to say one more thing."

"Uh-huh," he grumbled. "I figured as much."

"I need you to check your computers for me."

"Aw, Brady. I thought you'd learned your lesson by now. You're not off detecting again, are you?"

"Naw. Just need some background. It's for a client."

"Oh, sure. I know you, pal."

"Honest."

I heard him expel a loud breath. "You gonna tell me about it?"

"After we catch our fill of blues."

He sighed again. "Okay. What do you want?"

"Three names, for now. Lillian Robbins. Alan Sauerman. Martin Lodi."

"Hang on. One at a time. Spell them."

I spelled Lily's name for him.

"Where's she live?"

"The Cape. Orleans."

"You want criminal records? Tax history?"

"Anything you can get."

"I'll see what I can do," he said. "Next."

"Alan Sauerman," I said. "A doctor. Orleans, also, or someplace nearby." I spelled that for him, too.

"This is gonna cost you, Coyne."

"I'll buy lunch at Gert's after we load the boat with blue-fish."

"Damn tootin' you will," said Charlie. "Sauerman. Robbins. All right. What was the other one?"

"Someone named Martin Lodi," I said. "I've got no idea where he lives."

"And you want this by Wednesday?"

"If possible. Please."

"I'll do my best," said Charlie.

I waited until noon to call Marla Conway in Phoenix. They were two or three hours behind us, I could never remember which.

A secretary put me through to her. When I told her my name, and reminded her of the time she and Dan LaBreque had driven down to Orleans to appraise Jeff Newton's jaguars, she claimed to remember me. "I still see Dan about once a year," she said. "There's an annual convention in Chicago we both attend. We talk on the phone now and then, too. Dan's been a good friend. He helped me find this job. What can I do for you?"

"Dan suggested I call you. Those jaguars were stolen. Dan said you had a handle on the market for Mayan art."

"Not the market for stolen art, Mr. Coyne. Anyway, as I remember it, Mr. Newton brought in those jaguars from Mexico illegally."

"Maybe he did. It's not so much the cats I'm after. It's kind of personal with me. I was there when they were taken. Jeff was seriously injured. I'd really like to track down who did it."

"I can keep my ears open."

"Will you do that?"

"If Dan told you to call, that's good enough for me. I guess I know most of the collectors and museum people in our field. If there's any activity in new Mayan stuff, one of us will hear about it. I'll ask around."

"Well, thanks."

"You know, Mr. Coyne, it's not likely your cats will show up in any legitimate places. I mean, you shouldn't be holding your breath."

"I won't," I said. "I've got some other things to do."

EIGHT

· · · · · · ·

WEDNESDAY the sun rose at four thirty-two. I was waiting for it on my balcony with my second cup of coffee. For half an hour I had watched the painting of the sky over the harbor—gray evolving into the palest yellow and shifting by imperceptible stages through gold into orange. Then, in an instant, the rim of the sun popped out of the ocean.

I had been sitting out there with my early morning thoughts, the kind of clear but untrustworthy insights that seem to come to me first thing in the day before my censoring process kicks in, allowing me to analyze them and reduce them to reason. Usually they take the form of regrets—opportunities unrecognized, mistakes unforgiven, betrayals unavenged, the litany of all our lives. Sometimes they linger with me all day as a vague discomfort in my gut. More often they dissolve like the ocean mists when the sun rises.

My regret on this new day focused on a marriage that had gone sour, on two little boys who had somehow become men, or close to it, while I wasn't looking, on my own independent ways, which struck me, just then, as unbearably selfish and empty, on my isolation from the people who meant the most to me, and on my recognition of the harsh truth that all of that seemed to suit me fine.

I had finally reached Joey on Monday evening. He answered the phone himself, for which I was grateful. I hadn't the courage to talk to Gloria again.

"Yo," he said when he picked it up.

"It's your old man."

"Oh. Hi, Dad." So it was still "Dad."

"Have a good weekend?"

"It was okay."

"That volleyball jock?"

"Debbie? Sure. Mostly me and Cliff hung out. I stayed over at his house. What about you?"

"I was down the Cape. Did some fishing."

"Get some?"

"Yes. It was pretty good. Look, you tried to call me . . ."

"Oh. Right."

"So what's up?"

"It's kinda hard right now . . ."

"Something to do with your mother?"

"You got it."

"She's there?"

"Yep."

"Want to talk?"

"Yes. Can I call you back?"

"Sure."

"Five minutes."

I hung up and waited at my kitchen table, watching the lights wink and flicker over the ocean outside my apartment. It was nearly fifteen minutes later when the phone rang.

"Joey," I answered.

"It's me. Look, Dad, I got a real problem here."

"So I understand."

"You talked to Mom?"

"Yes. She told me her side."

"Yeah, well that's why I didn't get right back to you. I had to take out the trash. She's really on my case."

"Anything wrong with taking out the trash?"

He hesitated. "That's not the point. It's like I've got to ask her permission before I take a leak, practically. She's bitching at me all the time. I never do this, I never do that, I spend too much time with Debbie, there's no way I'm doing my homework, the house is a mess, the lawn needs mowing, I should do my own laundry, she has to do all the vacuuming. She was never like this when Billy was here. I'm going nuts."

"So's she."

"You're not kidding."

"Is she right?"

"What do you mean? Oh. Well, in a way, I guess. But I try, Dad. I mean, sometimes I do things. She never even notices. She only notices when I don't. It's like heads you win, tails I lose. Know what I mean?"

I found myself nodding. I sure did know. "Since Billy went off to school," I said, "it's just the two of you. That's hard for her. She's sad because you'll be gone in a year or so, too."

"She's got a funny way of showing it."

"You've got to try to get along."

"Shit. I am trying. She's not. I can't take it."

"Try harder. It's a big house. You live there, too. She's not your slave, you know. You can make things easy, or you can make things hard. Do things before she has to remind you. She'll notice."

"Yeah, I guess," he said doubtfully. "Look, Dad."

"What, son?"

"Well, I had this idea."

"Yes?"

"Well, I mean, you guys have like joint custody, right?"

"Sure."

"I mean, I could live with you, right?"

"Is that what you want?" I said carefully.

"It'd be great, Pop. Don't you think?"

"I haven't had a chance to think it through." I hesitated. "Have you?"

"Sure I have. That's why I called you."

"You can solve your issue with your mother by running away from it, huh?"

He was quiet for a minute. "You're saying no, right?"

"That's not what I'm saying. I'm saying, you've got to think it all the way through. I'm saying that you can't run away from your problems. I'm saying you've got to think about your mother."

"I think Mom would be thrilled," he said.

"You better think again, then."

I heard him sigh. "I guess I hear you."

"What do you hear?"

"It's a dumb idea."

"It's not that I don't want you," I said, though even as I said it I wondered if I was telling the truth.

"Sure. It's okay. Don't worry about it."

"I am worried about it. Your happiness—and your mother's—is important to me."

"It'll work out," he said. "Look. I gotta go. I'll talk to you later, okay?"

"Sure, son. Talk to your mother."

"Yeah. I'll do that."

And we hung up.

And now I was staring out at the sunrise, awake while the rest of the world still slept, and for some reason that conversation with Joey, with his litany of complaints about Gloria, and hers about him, reminded me of what I have been told more than once and in more than one way by more than one female person: I don't know very much about women. Correct that. I don't know much about intimate and complicated human relationships. Which probably accounts for the fact that I can't seem to sustain many of them, and those that I do manage to hang on to seem to cause me more unhappiness than joy. And which in turn probably accounts for the fact that I live alone and can't imagine living any other way, however lonely and empty it sometimes feels first thing in the morning.

I love my sons beyond all reason. But I couldn't imagine one of them living with me.

I downed the dregs of my coffee and went back inside. I picked up my Winston ten-weight fly rod and saltwater reel, the plastic box of bluefish poppers, and the spool of twenty-pound wire leader from the table where I had assembled them the previous night. Then I elevatored six floors down to the parking garage under my apartment building. I climbed into my car and pointed it north to Gloucester.

Dan and Charlie were waiting for me at the marina. Dan was in the cabin of *Cap'n Hook,* his twenty-two-foot Grady-White, fussing with the controls. Charlie was wrestling aboard a big cooler which, I knew, contained more beer and Pepsi-Cola and ham and Swiss cheese sandwiches on pumpernickel than the three of us could consume in a week. We would be well fortified should *Cap'n Hook*'s engines betray us ten miles out to sea.

Charlie looked up and nodded when I climbed aboard. He was already sweating from his exertions. It was going to be a hot one. I said good morning to Dan, who lifted his hand to me without turning around. He was wearing a long-billed fisherman's cap, a faded T-shirt celebrating Woodstock, stained chinos, and boat shoes without socks. His seagoing uniform.

"Shall I get the lines?" I said.

"We been waitin' on you," he answered in the exaggerated Downeast lobsterman's drawl he unconsciously tended to adopt when he was aboard his boat.

"I'm not late."

"Ain't early, neither."

The twin diesels began to burble. I climbed out, untied the lines, coiled them and passed them in to Charlie, then stepped back into the boat. Dan eased us away from the dock. I unfastened the bumpers and stowed them. Then I ducked into the cabin.

Dan waved at a big thermos. "Java," he said. It was a command, the captain's prerogative. I poured three mugs full, placed one in the spill-proof holder beside Dan where he stood at the wheel, and took two back to where Charlie was rigging a fly rod.

He accepted the mug I handed him and nodded. I grunted. I uncased my rod, screwed on the anodized saltwater reel, threaded the line though the guides, and knotted a foot and a half of wire to the end of the leader. I tied on a red and white popper, hooked it into the keeper ring, and set the rod aside. Then I sprawled into a deck chair with my coffee.

Charlie and I stared at the water as Dan weaved among the boats and buoys of Gloucester Harbor. I took off the thin windbreaker I had worn. Charlie rubbed sun block onto his face and the backs of his hands.

When we cleared the harbor, Dan turned left and we began to follow the shoreline northward. He throttled up and the growl of the engines became a whine. The bow lifted, then settled, and we skimmed across the sea. After ten or fifteen minutes he swung to the starboard. We were heading east, toward the sun, out into the ocean. I lounged back in my chair and closed my eyes, not to sleep but to savor the wash of salt air on my face and the clean smells of the open sea. They soon rinsed from my soul those lingering fragments of doubt and regret.

Joey and Gloria would work things out. She was right. The only thing I could contribute was a little superficial philosophy. It was their problem. It had to be.

The same with Lily Robbins and Alan Sauerman and officers Maroney and Kinney. The hell with them. And the hell with the bastards who had cut me with a knife in the nighttime. For that matter, the hell with Jeff Newton and his Mayan jaguars.

I was going fishing.

Abruptly the pitch of the engines changed. I opened my eyes. Dan was pointing. I looked. A pod of whales. There must have been a dozen or fifteen of them off the port bow, not close, but still huge and majestic, lolling and wallowing on the steely gray surface of the morning sea, surrounded by wheeling gulls. Dan eased us toward them. I saw one of the great mammals spout, a tall fountain of spray that caught the angled sunbeams and scattered them in a million particles of light over the sea. One of the huge beasts slapped his tail against the water like a giant beaver and sounded. A camera with a long lens on it had materialized in Charlie's hands. He was at the side, snapping pictures as if he'd never seen whales before.

Some years they were there, so commonplace that one soon ignored them. Then they would disappear for a year or two, following the erratic migration of the organisms that nourished them. And when they returned, we celebrated it until, once again, they became part of the scenery.

We watched them for a while. I was glad they were back. After a few minutes, Dan gunned the engines and we jumped away, leaving the pod to its piece of ocean. Charlie and I returned to our seats.

I wouldn't ask Charlie about Lily or Alan Sauerman or Lily's old boyfriend, Martin Lodi, nor would he volunteer anything on those subjects. Not out there, not while fishing. We conducted no business while fishing. That was one angling ethic that Charlie and I had never needed to discuss. It was too transparently obvious.

Ten minutes later Dan slowed to trolling speed and we let out jointed lures from the boat rods, one just subsurface, one maybe ten feet down, and one on lead-core line to travel deep. Prospecting, Dan called it. We were looking for a school of blues to cast flies to.

The first one hit fifteen minutes later. Charlie and I were sitting facing the stern, watching the rods fixed in their holders, monitoring the little vibrations at the tips that told us the plugs were still wobbling, that they hadn't snagged seaweed. Abruptly one dipped and the reel began to screech. "Take it," I told Charlie. He grabbed the rod and held it high, while line peeled out. I reeled in the other two lines. Dan threw the engines into neutral.

The bluefish fought doggedly, as they all do. They are strong. They don't leap like tarpon, nor do they cut screaming high-speed runs across the sea like bonefish. But they come to the boat reluctantly, and when they do arrive they thrash and snap with those wicked teeth, and if you aren't careful they'll whip a big plug with three sets of treble hooks into your face.

Charlie managed to get his fish alongside. Dan came back and reached down with a long-handled gaff. He impaled the blue through its lower lip and swung it aboard.

Charlie kneeled beside the fish and gingerly removed the plug from its mouth. "A keeper?" he asked Dan.

Dan shook his head. "Nope. Too big. Ten-pounder, anyway. I don't trust the PCB level of bluefish that big. Toss him back. Let's see if you guys can't snag a few five-pounders on your fly rods."

Charlie dropped his fish overboard. Dan stood at the stern, shading his eyes. After a minute he said, "There."

He pointed. I looked. I saw it, a patch of smooth water like an oil slick surrounded by the natural chop of the sea, and above it the gulls had begun to materialize, seemingly from nowhere. Bluefish sign. They were chasing baitfish toward the surface. I knew that not far beneath that deceptive island of flat ocean a school of blues was chopping and slashing at menhaden or baby eels, and the water was churning with gore and bits of fish meat and guts, and the blues were swirling and snapping frantically, impelled by their primeval appetites.

Dan claims he can smell them. Melons, he says. I've never been able to detect the smell. Probably because I smoke.

Dan eased us over until *Cap'n Hook* sat, her engines idling, on the edge of the slick. I climbed out onto the bow, rod in hand, and stood, legs wide and knees flexed against the rolling of the boat. Charlie was already casting from the stern. Up close, I could see the subsurface flashes of frenzied bluefish. Awkward in my eagerness, I stripped line off my reel and began to cast. In a moment Charlie had one on. Then my rod was nearly wrenched from my grip. My fly rod bent double and the single-action reel screamed as line was ripped off it. I could only hold my rod high and let the fish run against its resistance. I was into a bluefish, and all leftover thoughts of comatose friends and stolen jaguars and invaders of my sleep, both criminal and female, evaporated. I was on the sea with a bluefish on the end of my line and the world was a fine place.

At one thirty that afternoon Charlie and I parked side by side in the gravel lot outside Gert's, my favorite North Shore restaurant. Gert's has thus far miraculously escaped printed evaluation by *Boston* magazine and the *Globe* and other nosy media. It remains a popular secret among local folks and a few others who have, like me, been taken there only after uttering a vow of silence. Those of us who know Gert's want to keep it the way we know it—unpretentious, straightforward, and as honest as the only sign outside, which promises, simply, "Good Food."

The first time I took Charlie to Gert's, I told him, "Pretend this is a trout brook I'm showing you, a place that no one else fishes. It's that kind of secret."

And Charlie had nodded. That analogy he could understand.

We got out of our cars and went inside. The noontime crowd had thinned out. The usual mix of locals lingered, some men in suits and some in work shirts and jeans, women in suits, others in T-shirts and shorts. The tables were covered with red and white checked oilcloths. The flatware came wrapped in an oversized linen napkin. The music over the speakers was Rossini.

Our hostess, a local college girl, I guessed, led us to a table by the window overlooking the parking lot where twin Dumpsters overflowed at the far corner. Gert's lacks the ambiance of the Gloucester restaurants on stilts over the harbor, one of the secrets of the place's continued anonymity. I suppose the *Globe* restaurant critics frown on a view that features Dumpsters.

Charlie and I ordered ale and giant bowls of Gert's fish chowder. We talked about the fishing while we waited the short time it took for our lunches to arrive, complaining with grins about the fish-fighting aches in our arms and the tooth scratches on our hands and the sunburn on our necks.

Only after the big chowder bowls were cleared away and we were sipping coffee did Charlie remove the computer printouts from his pocket. He held the paper against his chest and arched his eyebrows at me.

"Yeah, I said I was paying," I assured him.

He plucked his reading glasses from his shirt pocket, hooked them over his ears, and peered at the paper. "Okay. Lillian Robbins. Nothing from the criminal files. Picked her up from the tax computers. Filed regularly for six or seven years in Connecticut. Occupation listed as a waitress. Nothing amiss. She declared her tips. Then she didn't file for two years. I got her back through her Social Security number, filing separately as a married person. She used the name Lodi."

Charlie arched his eyebrows at me.

"Married, huh?"

"Yes. Married."

I nodded. "Martin Lodi. You looked him up, right?"

"Right," he said. "Anyway, couple years later she began to file as a single in Massachusetts, still using her married name. Occupation housekeeper. That's how she filed last year. You want the dates, list of deductions, and so forth, it's all here," he said, shaking the computer paper. He peered at me over the tops of his glasses. "Really, though, Brady. Nothing of remote interest here that I can see. At least, nothing to ring any alarms for the IRS or the Commonwealth's tax people. You probably ought to tell me what you're after."

I nodded, and proceeded to tell him about my weekend adventures at Jeff Newton's place in Orleans. Charlie is a good listener. He doesn't interrupt, but he watches me closely while I'm talking and he lifts his eyebrows or purses his lips when he needs clarification or elaboration.

When I finished, Charlie said, "How's Newton doing?"

"I talked to the hospital yesterday. They called him stable. Meaning, as near as I can tell, he has neither died nor regained consciousness. The prognosis is pretty straightforward. He'll lie in a coma until something kills him."

"So you've got a potential murder here, not just a theft."

I nodded. "Yeah. Right now, though, it's being treated as a burglary and assault."

"Which means," said Charlie, "that it's not high priority with the cops."

"And by the time Jeff dies, the trail will be cold."

"And you suspect one of these people." He tapped the computer printouts.

"Or all three, for that matter." I shrugged. "It's all I've got right now."

"So you're off sleuthing again."

"Not really. Just banging around."

Charlie gazed out toward the Dumpsters. "Sounds like you had a fun weekend. Did you really catch seventeen rainbows on dry flies?"

I nodded emphatically. "Yes. We counted them."

"Anything you want to add about the lady that might help me understand why you want data on her?"

I had not told Charlie about Lily's visit to my bedroom. Locker-room stuff. I like to think I have outgrown that. "No," I said. "Nothing to add. Just that she could have planned it. What about Sauerman?"

"I found nothing criminal on the doctor. He's gotten two speeding tickets on Route 6 in the last three years. Paid promptly. Never sued for malpractice or anything. His tax reports were all prompt and seemed in order. He doesn't earn that much compared to city doctors, if that's of interest."

I shrugged. "What about Martin Lodi?"

He shuffled the computer printouts, then grinned at me. "I like this one best."

"You gonna drag it out?"

"No. Martin Lodi has filed very few income tax returns. But there's a reason for it." Charlie reached for his coffee cup.

"Come on," I said.

He sipped his coffee, wiped his mouth with the back of his hand, and cleared his throat. "Okay. Martin Lodi. aka Martin Lawrence, Lawrence Martin, Lawrence Martini, Martin Levi, Levi Morton." Charlie arched his eyebrows at me.

"Aha," I said.

Charlie grinned. "Aha, indeed. Eleven arrests. Two convictions. Assault, aggravated assault two times, possession of a controlled substance twice, resisting arrest, assault on a police officer, three B and E's, one battery. First conviction was for the assault on the cop. Served four months of a sixteen-month sentence. That was"—Charlie squinted at the sheet—"fifteen years ago. In Wyoming."

"Fifteen years ago," I mumbled. "That was when Lily went to work for Jeff. When was his second conviction?"

"Last September."

"What happened?"

"Possession of a class I controlled substance with intent to sell. Cocaine. Sentenced to eight years."

"Where'd this happen?"

"Missoula, Montana."

I stared at Charlie. I remembered Jeff's collect phone calls from West Yellowstone, and the motorcycle with the Montana plates. "This Lodi," I said. "You mean he's in prison now?"

Charlie nodded.

"He's not out on parole or something?"

"Nope."

"He didn't escape?"

"No. Why?"

I flapped my hands. "Just something I've got to figure out. So is that it?"

"That's it, friend."

Charlie handed the papers to me. I accepted them, folded them, and stuffed them into my pocket.

Charlie cocked his head and frowned at me. "Brady?" he said.

"Hmm?"

"Want some advice?"

"No, thanks."

He looked at me for a minute, then smiled. "I didn't think so."

"Look," I said. "I am still very angry. I don't like to have my sleep disturbed. I don't like being frightened, made to think I'm going to die. I don't like criminals in general, and ones that tease me with knives in particular. I despise anybody who'd slice open the throat of a dog, even a Doberman. I especially don't like having my clients rendered comatose by blows to the head. I'd sure like to get a line on those jaguars."

He was frowning.

"What's the matter with you?" I said.

"I know you, buddy. You've got that look. I don't like it."

"What look?"

"You're gonna get yourself in trouble again."

NINE

· · · · · · ·

PATIENCE is not one of my virtues. If pressed, I'd probably have a hard time coming up with a virtue, but I know it wouldn't be patience. So that evening, after eating a microwaved beef Stroganoff frozen dinner from its own plastic tray in front of the television, I called Jeff Newton's house in Orleans.

"It's Brady," I said, when Lily answered.

"Oh, gee. How are you?"

"Good, aside from some residual complaints from my shoulder muscles."

"From being tied up like that."

"No, from hauling in bluefish this morning."

I heard her chuckle. "I swear you'd rather fish than . . ."

"It would be a tough choice, if I could only do one." I hesitated. "How's Jeff?"

"He's the same. I saw him yesterday. He's—all hooked up on machines. Tubes going in and out everywhere. It doesn't look like anything's going to change for a while. They're saying they may have to transfer him to Boston."

"Why?"

"I don't know. I guess they're better equipped to handle cases like his up there."

"Probably true." I paused. "You wouldn't like to have dinner with me Saturday, would you?"

"You shouldn't ask negative questions, Brady. But I'll let you off the hook. I'd love to have dinner with you Saturday."

"Sure you're up for it?"

"You kidding? Look, are you positive you want to drive all the way down here just to have dinner with little old me?"

"I thought we could meet halfway, actually."

"Oh. I was hoping you'd say you'd jog to the top of Mount Washington, swim across Cape Cod Bay, something like that, just to see my face. But I guess I'll have to be satisfied with meeting halfway from an out-of-shape and undemonstrative middle-aged lawyer. Like where?"

"How about Scituate? There's a nice restaurant right on the wharf in Scituate Harbor. The Old Mill. Less than an hour for each of us, assuming no traffic on a Saturday evening."

"I'll be there," she said promptly.

"About seven? I'll call for reservations. They'll be in my name if you get there first."

"Oh, I'll get there first, all right. I can't wait."

I lit a cigarette. "So how have you been doing, Lily?"

"Okay, I guess. It's not like I'm not used to being alone here. All those years when he was in Africa. Hell, lately even when he was here it was like being alone. Still, it's kinda weird, knowing he's in the hospital, practically dead. I mean, it feels lonelier, if you know what I mean. I even miss those dumb dogs."

"I know a little about lonely," I said.

"A man was here today," she said. "An insurance adjuster. Name of Patrick Hoskins, a sickly little man who looked as if he had been abused as a child. He tended to cringe. I took him on a tour of the grounds. He examined the fence and the gate. He had a clipboard. Made lots of notes. I had the distinct impression that he was just going through certain motions, but I'm not so sure. He did ask a lot of questions about the dogs, and what happened that night. I gather he had already talked to the police. He wanted to know all about you, although it seemed as if he already knew just about everything. He hinted that there'd be no problem collecting the insurance. Not that it'll do Jeff much good."

"Won't do any harm," I said. "Getting the insurance is a good thing, I guess. But it doesn't exactly nail the bad guys."

"That's not an insurance adjuster's job, is it?"

"No."

"Oh, I get it. It's a lawyer's job, huh?"

I laughed. "No, it's not a lawyer's job, either. Look, I'll see you Saturday."

"I'm looking forward to it."

" 'Bye, Lily."

I hung up.

I wandered out onto my balcony and slouched in one of the aluminum chairs. I lit a cigarette and tilted back until I could rest my heels on the railing. I studied the darkening summer sky. I thought about the feel of Lily's thighs against mine and the smell of her hair. It confused me.

Patrick Hoskins reminded me of a sick fox I once met on a path while walking through the woods to a trout stream in Vermont's Northeast Kingdom. Most of the animal's hair had fallen out, and what was left sprouted randomly in tangled gray tufts on its poor emaciated body. What I remembered about that fox most was its eyes—large, rheumy, and sad. They seemed to beg me to put the poor critter out of its misery.

Unfortunately, I was armed only with a little Orvis two-weight fly rod, a weapon unsuited to the task. So the fox and I studied each other for several minutes before it seemed to shrug. Then it turned and skulked into the brush, its ratty tail dragging along the ground.

Patrick Hoskins had those same eyes. He also sported an untrimmed beard and a head of hair that had once been red, but now was mostly slush gray. He had called Thursday afternoon to set up an appointment for ten Friday morning. He arrived fifteen minutes early, and even though I was free, Julie made him wait, on her unshakable theory that it was always good for people to have to wait for me. It put them on the defensive and made me appear to be busier and more important than I was.

She brought him in at ten after ten, having first buzzed to remind me that Mr. Hoskins was waiting and to inquire if I could see him yet. "I'm twiddling my thumbs in here, Julie," I said to her, "and you don't need to play this game with him. He's not a client."

"I'll remind him he only has half an hour," she said, for the benefit of Mr. Hoskins who, I knew, was sitting across from her listening to her end of the conversation.

He was, like my sick fox, undersized for his eyes, and like the fox, he seemed to slink rather than walk, with his tail, figuratively, dragging behind him, as if he was used to regarding the world as hostile and the people in it as enemies.

I stood behind my desk and, in my best lawyerly manner, extended my hand and said, "Mr. Hoskins, come in."

He took my hand. His grip was surprisingly firm. I nodded to the chair in front of my desk and he sat down primly, back straight, knees together. He was carrying a slender briefcase, which he held with both hands on his lap in the defensive way a matron clings to her purse when seated on a city bus.

"Mr. Coyne, about the Newton theft . . . ."

I waved my hand. "I remember our phone conversation. How can I help you?"

He unzipped his briefcase and extracted a clipboard. I could see a printed form snapped onto it. He studied the form for a moment, shrugged almost imperceptibly, then looked up at me. "I am an independent insurance adjuster, Mr. Coyne. Insurance firms retain me to investigate claims. Mr. Newton filed a claim through his agency with Lloyd's of London, with whom he had insured certain art objects."

"Actually, I filed the claim," I said.

He nodded. "Of course. I understand Mr. Newton has had an accident."

"He was slugged on the head when the jaguars were stolen."

"I'm sorry. Yes." He cleared his throat and peered at me to see if I was finished interrupting. I smiled at him.

"Mr. Newton's claim," he continued, "states that on Friday last those objects were stolen from his home in Orleans, Massachusetts. Lloyd's contacted me on Tuesday to investigate Mr. Newton's claim. My job, sir, is a simple one. My job is to verify that a theft has occurred. You have Mr. Newton's power of attorney, given his, ah, unfortunate condition. And I understand that you were a witness to this theft."

"Yes. I was."

A ballpoint pen had materialized in his hand. He held it poised over the printed form. "Very well, then, Mr. Coyne. As to the events of Friday last—"

"Would you like some coffee, Mr. Hoskins?" I said.

His eyes darted up at me. "What? Oh, coffee. No. No, thank you."

"A Coke or something?"

He frowned.

"Mr. Hoskins," I said. "Relax."

He smiled quickly. "I'm sorry. I'm not much for small talk, I'm afraid. Time is money in my business."

"Mine, too. It's still good to relax." He stared at me, waiting. I shrugged. "I didn't exactly witness the theft," I said. "I was in bed. Two men came into my room. They bound and gagged me, threatened me with a knife, and hit me on the head. The next morning when I was unbound and ungagged, the jaguars were gone, the dogs had been shot and their throats slashed, and we found Jeff Newton outside barely breathing from a blow to the head. My own head continued to hurt."

"The objects were there before you retired that night?"

"Yes."

"And the watchdogs were, ah, on duty?"

"The dogs were always on duty."

"You heard no barking or any unusual noises prior to the appearance of the two men?"

"Those dogs never barked. They whined. And, no, I heard nothing. I didn't hear the gunshots. I was sleeping."

"Why do you suppose the two men came into your room?"

"I have no idea." I lit a cigarette and held my pack to Hoskins. "Smoke?"

He waved his hand. "Oh, no. You go ahead."

"I already did."

"How frequently do you spend the weekend with Mr. Newton, sir?" he said.

"Maybe twice, three times a year."

He peered at me out of those large wet eyes. "Why do you suppose the thieves chose that particular weekend to steal the jaguars, Mr. Coyne?"

I shrugged. "They didn't confide in me."

He smiled.

"Oh," I said. "I get it. You think I—"

He shook his head vigorously. "No, Mr. Coyne. You misunderstand. My job is not to solve any crime. I do not think in those terms. My job is simply to verify that there has been a crime, and to verify that the security systems required in the insurance contract were intact and functional. If, for example, Mr. Newton's dogs had run away the previous week, or if the chain link fence surrounding his property had not been kept in good repair, then Mr. Newton's claim might be denied, even in the presence of a theft. Perhaps, as I have inferred that the police suspect, you or Miz Robbins participated in the theft. I don't particularly care. It is completely immaterial to me whether it was you who arranged the theft or somebody else. No, I don't think about those things. Having satisfied myself that Mr. Newton's dogs and fences were functional, the only thing that concerns me is whether those jaguars were in fact stolen. The police believe they were. Miz Robbins, whom I interviewed, believes they were. And you, sir. Do you believe they were?"

"Hell, of course they were. I had an unpleasant encounter with the guys who did it."

He nodded and began to write on the form on his clipboard. "Well, sir," he said when he finally looked up at me, "I must say, this has been an easier investigation than most."

"Oh?"

"Certainly. Rarely do we have a witness. Typically burglaries occur when no one is home, or, less frequently, when the people are sleeping upstairs. I must make a judgment. Usually I must rely on police reports. Police reports, Mr. Coyne, tend to be slipshod."

"You suspect fraud."

"I always suspect fraud. Actually, my job is to suspect fraud. But I rarely prove fraud. Your testimony makes it much easier for me to discount fraud in the present instance. The police reports make it clear that the security was breached. You had contact with the thieves. I shall recommend that Mr. Newton be awarded his full claim." He slipped his clipboard into his briefcase and stood up. "And I thank you for your time, Mr. Coyne."

I held up both hands. "Mr. Hoskins, for heaven's sake, take it easy. You've been here about five minutes. Can't I get you some coffee?"

"Time is—"

"I know," I said. "Money. Tell me. What happens next?"

"Next?" He hesitated, then sat down again. "Well, next I shall prepare my report and send it to Lloyd's. They will accept it. In due course, Mr. Newton will receive a check." He peered at me dolefully from those sick eyes. "That is, Mr. Newton or his rightful heirs."

"Of course," I said. "What about the crime?"

He shrugged. "The police will attempt to solve it. Should Mr. Newton, ah, expire, of course, they will try harder."

"Don't you attempt to recover the jaguars?"

"Me?" He smiled. "Oh, by all means. Lloyd's will pay a reward for their recovery. Recovering stolen property is not the same thing as solving the crime. I'd love to recover those jaguars, but I don't give a hoot about catching the thieves. To be sure, it would be a feather in my cap—and money in my pocket—were I to recover those objects. I will submit reports to a variety of agencies, hoping the jaguars turn up and someone will be tempted by the reward money. However, I do not traipse around the world like those fictional insurance adjusters in pulp novels, chasing villains, exchanging gunfire, and generally sleuthing about. We don't do that. We investigate, we submit our reports, and we are paid for our work. When stolen objects are recovered, and they rarely are, it's the police who generally do it."

"There is a reward, though?"

"It depends. In the case of these jaguars, almost certainly there will be."

"How much of a reward?"

"Typically ten percent of the value of the policy. In this case, Lloyd's will pay Mr. Newton seven hundred and fifty thousand dollars, so that's, ah, seventy-five thousand for a reward."

"Um," I said. "Whole weeks go by sometimes when I don't make that much money."

He tried another smile. He looked as if he had found half a worm in his apple. "Well, me too. Are you interested in the reward, Mr. Coyne?"

"Time," I said, "is money, Mr. Hoskins."

Lily was gazing out the restaurant window at the boats moored in Scituate Harbor when the hostess led me to our table. She turned quickly when I cleared my throat.

"Oh, Brady," she said. She tilted her cheek to me and I bent and kissed it quickly. I took the seat across from her.

"Your waitress will be right with you," said the hostess.

I nodded to her and she left. I looked at Lily. She was staring at me solemnly. She was wearing a peach-colored blouse, which set off her dark hair and deep tan to good advantage. "How are you, Lily?" I said.

She smiled. "Better now."

"Am I that late?"

"You're on time. I was early. I was afraid you wouldn't come."

"Why wouldn't I?"

She shrugged. "It's been kinda hard, that's all."

I reached across the table and touched her cheek. "Come on. Lighten up. What are you drinking?"

She lifted her glass and looked at it. It was nearly empty. "Vodka tonic."

I glanced around and caught the eye of a waitress, who held up her forefinger to me. I grabbed my throat with both hands, rolled my eyes, and stuck my tongue out of the corner of my mouth. The waitress smiled. A moment later she came to our table. "Are we thirsty, sir?" she said.

"We need a drink. Bourbon old-fashioned. And another vodka tonic for the lady."

"Want to hear our specials for this evening?"

"Anything blackened Cajun-style, forget it," I said.

"Well, so much for the chicken and swordfish. We do have a bouillabaisse which is great. Also unblackened, non-Cajun swordfish broiled with parsley butter. The lobster tonight is your choice of either boiled or split and broiled with herb stuffing. Also fresh yellowfin tuna, broiled with a dill sauce."

"I'll never remember it all," I said.

"I already know what I want," said Lily.

"I'm for the yellowfin," I said.

"Boiled lobster," said Lily.

I nodded. To the waitress I said, "We're easy, huh?"

"Pushovers, both of you."

We made our selection of potato—French fries for both of us—and salad dressings, and our waitress scurried away.

"I'm not sure I trust seafood anymore," said Lily. "Between red tide and PCBs and medical trash washing up on the beaches. But I do love lobster."

"If we worried about what we ate, we'd starve to death," I said. I lit a cigarette. "So how's Jeff doing?"

She shrugged. "Still no change. He coughs now and then. They did an EEG. I guess it doesn't show much going on."

"So if he ever woke up . . ."

She nodded.

"Better if he doesn't," I finished.

She turned her face away from me and looked out at the boats.

Our waitress brought our drinks. "I forgot to ask if you wanted appetizers," she said.

"Lily?" I said.

She shook her head, still staring out the window.

"I guess not," I told the waitress.

"Do you want to wait for a while before I bring your salads?"

"Bring 'em anytime. We're hungry."

We sipped our drinks. I told Lily about my conversation with Patrick Hoskins. She nodded abstractly. I repeated to her what Dan LaBreque had told me about recovering the stolen jaguars. She did not seem interested. I told her that I had talked with Marla Conway in Phoenix. I did not tell her about the computer printouts Charlie had given me.

Our salads arrived, and we ate them without talking. Then our main courses were served. The waitress tied a big bib around Lily's neck. She attacked her lobster with vigor, wielding the shell cracker and pick with the adroitness of a surgeon.

Some people, when they lay siege on a whole lobster, will eat each bite as they extract it. Pick, dip, eat. A little work, and then an immediate little reward. That's my approach. I have no patience for Lily's style of lobster assault, which was to dig out all the meat first, then lay her instruments aside and eat all at once.

You can tell a lot about a woman by how she eats lobster. I figured Lily and I were incompatible.

She broke off the big front claws with her hands, wrenched the segments apart, split them with the cracker, and picked and prodded at the hunks of stringy white meat. Then she ripped off the tail, cracked it lengthwise, and pushed out the big cylinder of meat with her forefinger as if she was goosing it. She peeled the thin strip of meat off the top of it, revealing the black string of intestine. This she pried out and put on her plate. Next she ripped all the legs off the body and then cracked it between her hands. She began to dig into all the bodily crevices with her pick. She looked like a dentist. All the hunks of meat went into the big bowl of drawn butter that had come with the lobster, which soon was overflowing.

When she finished with the body, she picked up the legs and sucked the meat out of them, one by one, and only after she finished with the legs did she wipe her hands on her napkin and arm herself with a fork and a hunk of bread. She had demonstrated incredible restraint. It evaporated once she began to eat.

She ate with vast enthusiasm. It was fun to watch her. Butter dribbled over her chin and little moans of pleasure came from the back of her throat. They were familiar sounds to me.

Once she glanced at me. "What're you staring at?" she mumbled.

I smiled. "You. I like to see a woman being pleasured."

"Eating lobster is the second best way."

After our waitress cleared away our debris and brought coffee, we watched darkness descend over the harbor and the lights on the boats wink on. Once Lily reached across the table and touched my hand. "What is it, Brady?" she said.

"What is what?"

"You are distracted."

I shrugged.

She cocked her head and looked at me for a moment. Then she withdrew her hand.

I paid the bill. We left the restaurant and began to walk along the edge of the wharf. Lily found my hand and held it. Sitting across from her, I had forgotten how tall she was. Her strides were as long as mine.

"I talked with my friend Charlie McDevitt," I said to her.

"Who's that?"

"I went to law school with him. He's a prosecutor with the United States Justice Department."

"Oh?"

"I asked him to see what he could find out about some people."

"Like who?"

"Dr. Sauerman, for one." I hesitated. "And you. And Martin Lodi."

Her hand flinched in mine. "I see," she said. She let go of my hand and began to walk away from me. I hurried to catch up with her.

"I've got to ask you some questions, Lily."

She stopped and peered deeply into my eyes for a long moment. Then she flashed a quick ironic smile. "Fuck you," she said.

"Lily, look. I'm sorry, but—"

She turned and began to walk quickly toward the parking lot. When I caught up to her and reached for her arm, she yanked it away from me.

"Lily, hang on for a minute, will you?"

"That's what this was all about, wasn't it? You wanted to ask me some questions. You think . . ."

"Partly, yes."

"Fuck you, Brady Coyne. Just go fuck yourself."

"Sure. I will. But first you've got to tell me some things."

She turned to face me. Her eyes were brittle. "Fine. Okay. What do you want to know?"

"Why you lied to me."

"About what?"

"About your husband."

"Why should I tell you about Martin?"

"He's a criminal, for Christ sake. Jeff's lying in a hospital and his million-dollar cats are missing because of a crime. I can't think of a better reason."

"Martin didn't do it."

"I know. He's in prison."

She narrowed her eyes. "You've really been busy, haven't you?"

I nodded. "Yes. So I want to know about Martin Lodi. And I want to know why you lied to me."

"Why I lied?" She shook her head slowly. "Remember where we were, what we were doing when you asked me about him? We were lying in bed, and we'd been sleeping because we were tired from making love. So you ask me about another man from fifteen years ago. Jesus."

"You said you hadn't been married to him."

She cocked her head, then nodded. "Right. And I wasn't. Oh, we stood in front of a JP in Reno one night, all right. But we weren't married. Not really. Look. You really want to know about Martin Lodi?"

"Yes. I do."

"Okay. I'll tell you." She took a deep breath and let it out slowly. "He was a poet," she said. "A good one, as a matter of fact. Also an alcoholic and a biker and a man with the most violent temper I've ever known. Imagine Allen Ginsberg and Jack Kerouac as Hell's Angels. That was Martin. I was waitressing this little Mexican restaurant in Hartford and he came in. He wrote me a poem on the napkin. He was waiting for me

TEN

• • • • • • •

JULY PASSED, hot and muggy as usual. The first half of
August was little better. In the middle of the month we
got several days of sullen rain. When the front finally left,
the promise of autumn slid in behind it. The swamp maples
started to turn crimson, the nights were cool, and the days
grew perceptibly shorter. Winter was just around the corner.
The inevitability of winter always ruined New England au-
tumns for me.

Charlie and I drove out to the Deerfield one Saturday to
try the trout and found them uncooperative. Doc Adams and I
trekked to the Farmington River in Connecticut on a Sunday.
We each landed a couple of small ones and tried to convince
each other that we'd had a good day.

I talked with Gloria a few times. Joey had lucked into a
job at a resort in Ogunquit. He'd be there through Labor Day.
She seemed to miss him. I figured they had either resolved
their conflicts or at least achieved a temporary truce. I spoke
with Joey once. He called me Pop. Neither of us mentioned his
moving in with me.

The stock market dipped. Several clients panicked. I had
to make a lot of house calls. On the weekends I even opened
my briefcase.

Jeff Newton's condition hadn't changed. He remained at

the Cape Cod Hospital in Hyannis. Machines did all his living for him.

I hadn't spoken to Lily since our dinner date in Scituate. The knife wounds on my neck and collarbone healed and that searing anger I had felt for the first week or so after the theft of Jeff's jaguars, that thirst for revenge, cooled in me. I called Officer Maroney once in Orleans. He had nothing to report. Jeff's insurance money arrived. I deposited it for him. I talked with Dan LaBreque a few times. Mostly, we discussed bluefish. He said he was keeping his ears open, but had heard no rumors about seven golden Mayan jaguars for sale.

It seemed like a dead issue. I had plenty of other things on my mind.

It was the last Tuesday in August, mid afternoon. I had swiveled around to gaze out at the cityscape, so clear in the pre-autumnal air that it seemed to glitter. The previous Saturday I had, inexplicably, turned down Dan's invitation to go bluefishing. Bluefish weren't what I needed. I didn't know what it was, but it wasn't bluefish.

The buzz of the intercom startled me. I rotated back to my desk, poked the proper button, and picked up the phone. "Hi, Julie," I said.

"Hi, yourself. Daydreaming?"

"Contemplating obscure points of law."

"Sure. You got a call."

"Say I'm not here. I don't want to disturb my train of thought."

"Aquatic insects and whatnot."

I sighed. "Who is it?"

"A woman. Not a client."

A woman who is not a client has to be a lover, past, present, or potential, in Julie's mind. She does not approve of my having lovers of any description. She isn't jealous, at least not on her own behalf. Julie is ecstatically married to her Edward, a young radiologist, and the mother of four-year-old Megan. Julie simply regards me as married, too. The fact that Gloria and I have been divorced for more than a decade has made no impression on Julie.

"What's this woman's name?" I said.

"Conway."

"Marla Conway?"

She hesitated just an instant. "Yes."

"Okay. Good. Put her on."

"I can tell her you're busy, you'll get back to her, if you want."

"I'm not busy, Julie. I'll talk to her."

I heard her sigh. "Fine. Okay."

There was a click in my ear. "Marla?" I said.

"Hi, Mr. Coyne. I promised I'd call you if . . ."

"The jaguars. You've found them?"

She laughed. "Not exactly. This may be nothing, and I really hesitated before calling you. I'm not sure it's precisely ethical, to tell you the truth."

She paused. She wanted me to reassure her.

"I don't want you to violate your ethics, Marla," I said. "But if you've got a line on those jaguars . . ."

"I'm not sure I do. But I was talking with a patron of our museum the other day. It's probably nothing at all, but . . ."

She paused. Finally I said, "Marla?"

"I'm sorry." I heard her laugh quickly. "I guess I'm beating around the bush here because now that I'm trying to tell you, it sounds irrelevant and silly. Okay. This actually happened back in the spring—maybe June, which, as I remember it, was before those jaguars were stolen. Anyway, according to Victor—"

"Victor?"

"Victor Masters. He's a collector who lives in Tempe. Specializes in Latin American stuff. We exhibit his things now and then. He's got some lovely pieces. Very valuable. He's quite well known among people in this field. Anyhow, as I started to say, I happened to mention your phone call to Victor—actually, I didn't mention you, just that I'd heard some pre-Columbian objects had been stolen—and he told me that he'd been approached a couple of months earlier by somebody who claimed to have some Mayan pieces, fourteenth century, that could be purchased."

"This was in June?" I said.

"Late May, early June, something like that."

"These pieces . . . ?"

"They were supposed to be gold jaguars. Victor said he didn't think too much of it at the time. Wealthy collectors get crank calls all the time."

"But it could be the cats."

"Right. So I thought I should call you."

"This Victor Masters. Do you mind if I call him?"

"If I minded, Mr. Coyne, I wouldn't have told you this."

"Does he expect me to call?"

"No. I didn't decide to call you until I actually dialed your number. It still feels like a violation of his privacy. But he's a good man, a gentleman, and I think he'll understand."

"You don't happen to have his number, do you?"

"Sure I do. It's right here on my desk."

She read it off to me. I jotted it down on my yellow legal pad. I thanked Marla Conway, hung up the phone, and swiveled around to resume gazing out my office window. But now I didn't really notice the city out there. Now I was picturing Jeff Newton's dented and bloody skull, and his missing jaguars, and two dead Dobermans, and I once again remembered the feel of a knife blade against my skin.

* * *

I waited until nine that night to call Victor Masters. A woman answered the phone and I asked to speak to Mr. Masters.

"We were just sitting down to dinner," she said. It came out as an apology. "Is it important?"

"I'm calling from Boston. But I—"

"It must be important, then. Just a minute, please."

A moment later a man's voice, soft and cultivated and elderly, said, "Victor Masters. What can I do for you?"

"I don't want to disturb your dinner, sir," I said. "I forgot about the time difference. It's nine o'clock here. We can talk later."

"No problem. My wife said it was long distance. What can I do for you?"

"My name is Coyne, Mr. Masters. Brady Coyne. I'm a lawyer here in Boston." I paused. "Look, it's kind of complicated. Perhaps—"

"Go ahead, Mr. Coyne."

"I understand you collect art."

He hesitated. "Yes, that's right."

"Well, I—"

"Mr. Coyne."

"Sir?"

"What exactly is your business?"

"I'm a lawyer."

"I mean, will you state your business with me, please?"

I cleared my throat. "I started off badly. Marla Conway is a mutual acquaintance of ours, I believe."

"You know Marla?"

"Not well. I haven't seen her for a long time. Several years ago she worked with a friend of mine in the Museum of Fine Arts here in Boston."

"Yes," said Masters thoughtfully. "I knew she once worked in Boston. She is extremely competent. Very knowledgeable. I consult with her frequently. You have dropped a good name, Mr. Coyne."

"I spoke with her today," I said. "She mentioned you, said you were an art collector."

"Not just any art. I collect very old stuff. Central American Indian, mostly. Not to be immodest, but I have quite a valuable collection. Are you selling, Mr. Coyne? Is that why you are calling?"

"No, it's nothing like that. Look. I understand a couple months ago a man approached you, offering to sell a set of Mayan jaguars."

He hesitated. He struck me as a cautious man. "Marla told you that?"

"Yes. She specifically called me to tell me."

"I told that man I wanted nothing to do with his jaguars."

"Did he tell you his name?"

"No. And I didn't ask. I wanted nothing to do with him." I detected a trace of understated anger in his tone. "I suspected he did not own those pieces legally."

"I'm not accusing you of anything, Mr. Masters."

"Well, I hope not."

"No, the thing is, about a month after this man approached you, a set of Mayan jaguars was stolen from one of my clients here in Massachusetts."

"Well, sir, I do not have those pieces."

"That's not—"

"I've heard nothing from that man except for that one conversation," he said quickly. "I want nothing to do with stolen property. It tends to be a bad investment. Quite aside from the legalities. Not even to mention the ethics."

"I believe you," I said.

"This theft you are talking about," he said. "It happened after that man called me?"

"Yes. Mid July."

"As if he was trying to arrange the sale of the jaguars before he stole them, is what you're thinking."

"Right."

"Assuming they're the same pieces."

"Yes," I said. "It does seem possible. How many Mayan jaguars can there be, available for sale?"

"None, as far as I know," he said. "And I would be likely to know."

"So—"

"Well, I didn't want anything to do with them. I told him that. That was it. I haven't heard from him again."

"Did he describe the pieces to you?"

"Sure. They were gold jaguars. Mayan, fourteenth century. With emerald eyes."

"Bingo," I said. "It has to be Jeff Newton's jaguars."

Masters paused. "He wanted five hundred thousand for the lot," he said, finally.

"Is that a good price?"

I heard Victor Masters chuckle. "Based on his description, assuming, of course, that the pieces are genuine, that is an unbelievable price. That is about one-third the value of the lot. That, Mr. Coyne, is why I turned him down cold."

"Because the price was too good?"

"If he had been legitimate, he would have been asking a legitimate price. I simply told the man I was not interested. He was polite. He thanked me. As I said, I haven't heard from him since, and I had more or less forgotten the whole thing. The other day Marla mentioned a theft, and that reminded me of that call."

"This man," I said. "Did you meet with him?"

"No. He called me on the phone."

"Can you recall the conversation?"

"Just generally. It was brief, businesslike, as if he had a list of names he was calling and I was on his list. He said he had these jaguars, described them, assured me they were genuine, mentioned his price, said it was not negotiable, and asked if I was interested. I thanked him and said no. That was it."

"Do you know where he was calling from?"

"No."

"His voice. Was there anything distinctive about his voice?"

"I didn't notice any particular accent, if that's what you mean."

I thought for a minute. "Talking to me, Mr. Masters, do you find anything distinctive about my voice?"

He laughed quickly. "Of course I do. You're a Bostonian, aren't you?"

"I think I told you that."

"I would have known. You do a peculiar thing with your R's."

"So this man you spoke with on the phone, the man trying to sell the jaguars—"

"He's probably a westerner, Mr. Coyne. Like I said. Nothing distinctive about his voice."

I tried to remember the voices of the two men who amused themselves by threatening me with a knife. They were wearing ski masks. Their voices were muffled. They could have been westerners. Or Bostonians.

"One more thing, Mr. Masters," I said. "Did this man on the phone mention how many pieces there were in the collection he wanted to sell you?"

"Sure. He said there were seven of them. Is that—?"

"Yes," I said. "My client owned seven jaguars. Can you think of anything else?"

"Actually . . ." He was silent for a moment. "No, I'm afraid not," he said. "I'm sorry."

"Well, if something should occur to you, will you call me?"

"Of course. As a collector, I have a stake in seeing that art thieves are brought to justice. Of course I'll call you."

I gave him both my home and office numbers, thanked him, and hung up.

I pondered what I had learned for the rest of the evening. It was interesting, but it didn't seem to lead anywhere. So the thieves planned their burglary at Jeff's ahead of time. So they knew what they were after. So they knew the names of some people who collected Central American Indian art. I had already surmised as much.

And maybe they were westerners, which very conceivably related to the phone calls from Montana, though I couldn't figure out how.

Martin Lodi's motorcycle was registered in Montana. But Lodi was in prison.

I kept coming back to Lily. Except in my gut I didn't believe she'd had anything to do with it, which no doubt qualified me as naive to the extreme. She told me it wasn't she, and no woman who slept with me could ever lie to me. That's how my reasoning, such as it was, went. *In sex veritas.*

Dumb, masculine ego.

I went to sleep wondering about it.

The telephone beside my bed jerked me awake. I fumbled for the light switch and glanced at the clock. It was ten of one. I picked up the phone.

"Coyne," I mumbled.

I heard a chuckle. "I'm sorry, Mr. Coyne. I forgot about the time difference. You were sleeping."

"Oh. Mr. Masters." I yawned and hitched myself into a semi-sitting position in my bed. "What's up?"

"I can call you tomorrow."

"I'm awake."

"I wasn't going to tell you this."

"Tell me what?"

"I mean, normally I don't give any credence to rumors. And this is a rumor. But I got to thinking. And I decided I would tell you, and you could decide for yourself."

I extracted a Winston from the pack on my bedside table and managed to light it one-handed with a match. "Go ahead. Please."

"A lot of rumors circulate among collectors. Who's buying, who's selling, who got a good deal, who got a bad deal. Each of us, we like to think we're the shrewdest. Most of these rumors you learn to discount. And, to tell you the truth, this one I'm calling you about I discounted when I heard it, and pretty much forgot about it. I just didn't make the connection."

"Does this have something to do with the jaguars, Mr. Masters?"

"Well, I don't know. If I knew, I certainly would've made the connection before now. Talking with you earlier this evening got me to thinking, and it reminded me of this rumor."

The cigarette tasted awful. I stubbed it out, mildly annoyed at the habit that had caused me to light it in the first place. "What is this rumor?" I said.

He cleared his throat. "The rumor is that a collector got himself an awfully good deal on some Mayan artifacts recently. The rumor is that the deal might not have been entirely aboveboard."

"Jaguars? Were they gold jaguars with emerald eyes?"

"I don't know what they were, Mr. Coyne. Just that they were Mayan artifacts, and very valuable. Pre-Columbian."

"You don't know the name of this man, do you?"

"Yes, I do. It's one of the reasons I hesitated to call you. Because I knew you'd want his name. And, as I said, I don't like to spread rumors."

"But you did call me."

"Yes. I decided I'd tell you his name. It's a man I have met. A real estate developer. Very wealthy. Builds condominiums. Rather tasteless condominiums, in my opinion. Sells time-sharing on them. He's only started collecting recently. He collects for the same reason he builds condominiums. Investment. Profit. He doesn't love art. He buys it and sells it. From what I hear, he has considerably better taste in what he collects than in what he builds. And his scruples in both pursuits are dubious. His name is Timothy McBride."

"Hang on a minute, Mr. Masters," I said. I fumbled on my bedside table and found a scrap of paper and a pencil. When I'm awakened by a phone call in the middle of the night, I don't trust myself to remember anything I'm told. I wrote down Timothy McBride's name. "What else can you tell me about him?"

"That's all I know," said Masters. "Just this rumor. I connected that phone call I got with the rumor about McBride acquiring some Mayan pieces. Anyone who'd know enough to call me would also probably call McBride. The timing of it all seemed to fit, so I decided I'd pass it on to you."

"He's into real estate, you said."

"That's right."

"Real estate in the West, I understand, is not very lucrative these days."

"That is very true."

"Do you have any idea where this McBride lives?"

"He lives in West Yellowstone, Montana, Mr. Coyne."

I wrote that down too. Not that I needed to. There was no way I'd forget that Timothy McBride lived in West Yellowstone, Montana.

ELEVEN

• • • • • •

I HAD THE COFFEE brewed by the time Julie came into the office the next morning. I filled her mug, added sugar, and handed it to her. She accepted it with arched eyebrows but didn't say anything. She sat behind her desk and lifted it with both hands to her mouth.

I stood in front of her desk, watching her.

After a minute she looked up at me. "So what do you want?" she said.

"What do you mean, what do I want?"

"You want something. I can tell. The way you gave me the coffee. The way you're standing there with that little-boy look on your face."

I shrugged. "When you've finished your coffee."

"I'm fine," she said. "Had a cup before I left this morning. Let's have it."

"Well, okay," I said. "The thing is, I have to go to Montana for a few days."

She nodded. "I thought as much. I knew it'd be something like that. The way you've been moping around. You and who—Mr. McDevitt? Dr. Adams? Trout, right?"

"This is business. For Jeff Newton. My client. Who's now lying comatose in a hospital bed, being kept alive by machines."

"Who you really ought to visit," she said, peering up at me.

"You're probably right," I said. "Though I don't see why. He wouldn't know the difference, and it'd just depress me."

"They say sometimes people in comas know."

I shrugged. "Maybe. Somehow I doubt it. Anyway, now I'm in a position to do some real work for him. A business trip, Julie."

She rolled her eyes. "A business trip to Montana. Sure."

"Those jaguars that were stolen from him? I think they've showed up in West Yellowstone."

"West Yellowstone. Absolutely."

"I know how it sounds." I stopped. "Why do I feel that I need your approval?"

"Because you feel guilty."

"I'd go if it happened to be Detroit, where's there's no clean water, or San Diego, where there's no fresh water at all, never mind trout. It just happens to be West Yellowstone—"

"Where there's all kinds of clean fresh water full of trout," she said. "You've told me all about Montana. I know how you love it out there. So what do you want from me, Brady? It's your law practice, if you want to abandon it. Your clients won't mind. They're probably used to it by now." She sighed in a heavy, exaggerated way, then cocked her head at me and grinned. "I do love to give you a hard time."

I smiled and nodded. "Me, too. I love it when you give me a hard time. It's one of your important responsibilities. I depend on it. When you do it, I don't have to. It saves all kinds of wear and tear on my conscience. So see if you can clear the calendar for next week and get me reservations into Bozeman. Oh, and arrange for a car rental at the airport. I'll need a Cadillac, or at least a Lincoln—"

"Pardon me?"

"I said—"

"I heard what you said, Brady. I just don't believe it. A Cadillac?"

I nodded. "Yes. Or a Lincoln."

"You always want compacts when you rent cars. From places like Cheepo Flybynight Rentals."

"Well, for this trip I want the biggest, glitziest car they have. I'll need a room, too."

"A big and glitzy room, too?"

I grinned at her. "Exactly."

"You are the boss, I suppose." She shrugged. "What about your friends?"

"Doc and Charlie? They're not going. This is business. Really."

Julie got up and walked out of my office. As the door shut behind her, I heard her mutter, "Cadillac. Holy shit."

Later in the morning I called Lily at the bungalow in Orleans.

"Lily," I said when she answered. "It's Brady."

"Oh." There was a long pause. "Well, hi."

"How have you been?"

"Just fine, thank you. You?"

"Okay." I paused. I hadn't spoken with her since she drove away from me in Scituate. "Look—"

"Brady, it's all right. I'm sorry how I reacted that night. I guess you had a right to ask those questions."

"Well, I'm sorry, too. But that's not why I called."

I heard her exhale into the receiver. "I guess I knew that. You're not one to apologize."

"What do you mean?"

"Forget it. So why did you call, then?"

"I got a line on someone in Montana who might've bought Jeff's jaguars from those guys who stole them."

"Does this mean I'm no longer a prime suspect?"

"Look," I said. "I don't know what to think, and I really didn't mean to hurt your feelings. It's just that—"

"Don't worry about it," she said quickly.

"Well, anyway, I just wanted you to know. So if Jeff . . ."

"He's not going to regain consciousness, if that's what you mean."

"Well, they say sometimes people in comas can hear things. Tell him I'm working on his cats."

"Can you tell me more than that?"

"Not really. My friend Dan LaBreque—he's a curator at the MFA—he has a friend in Phoenix. I called her, and it turns out she has a friend who heard a rumor, so . . ."

"That's it?"

"That's it."

"A rumor?"

"That's all."

She didn't speak for a moment. "What'd you have in mind, Brady?"

"I thought I'd go," I said. "Check it out."

"Why?"

"Why?" I paused. "Jeff can't very well go himself."

"How quixotic of you."

"That's what Julie thinks, too," I said. "She thinks I'm going out there because it's trout mecca."

"You're not?"

"Remember how Jeff looked when we found him that morning?"

"I'm not likely ever to forget."

"Remember me, when you found me in bed?"

"Yes." She hesitated. "It was pretty scary."

"It sure was."

"I'm sorry, Brady. It was a nightmare. Still is."

"I haven't lost my thirst for revenge, Lily. I want those bastards. For Jeff. And for me."

"So you're going to go riding out there with your spear and your banner."

"If you want to look at it that way. Julie looks at it that way, I think."

She was silent for several moments. Finally she said, "So exactly why are you telling me?"

"I don't know. Maybe it is sort of an apology. Anyway, I thought if you visit Jeff, talk to him, you could tell him. If anything is registering, it might make him feel better."

"You could tell him yourself, you know."

"He'd probably rather hear it from you."

I heard her snort a quick laugh. "Well, have fun. I'll tell Jeff."

"I'll call when I get back."

"Sure you will."

Around noon Julie scratched on the door and came into my sanctum. She had a manila folder in each hand. She sat in the chair beside my desk. She put one folder on the desk and opened the other one. She sighed heavily. That sigh reminded me of Gloria, back when we were married, sitting beside me in the den of our Wellesley home after I returned from a day's work. She would hand me a gin and tonic, take a tentative sip of her own, give me that weary sigh, and share "her day" with me. She told me little tales with no climax about faulty mechanical devices, supermarket ripoffs, neighborhood squabbles. I would listen politely. It was, after all, her day, and all her days taken together constituted her life. And whether she intended it or not, there was a purpose to her telling me about it. It took me a while, but I finally got Gloria's point. Her life was as pointless as her stories. Mine, by extension of her implied logic, was exhilarating and infinitely fascinating.

All of this she managed to convey in a single, exquisitely expressive sigh.

She was not happy. This, cumulatively, made me unhappy.

Ultimately, we got divorced.

She remained vaguely unhappy. Nor did I find instant ecstasy. But although from time to time we halfheartedly tried, we knew that we could no longer blame each other for it.

"Your flight," sighed Julie, "leaves Friday at 6:40 A.M. Delta, if it matters. You've got a two-hour-and-ten-minute layover in Salt Lake City. You arrive in Bozeman at 1:35 P.M. That's Rocky Mountain Time, of course. Hertz will have a car waiting for you. I reserved a room for you at the Madison River Inn, which they claim is the swankiest place in West Yellowstone, those things being relative in the Wild West, I assume. It's the most expensive, at least. It's on the outskirts of town. A view, I was assured, of mountains and forests. Elk and pronghorn antelope, I think they were called, presumably graze out back. Sauna, hot tub, masseuses on call. Okay?"

"Perfect," I said.

She cocked her head at me, a question I declined to answer.

"You're scheduled to return on Wednesday," she continued when she realized I wasn't going to explain myself. "If that's not enough time to wet a line in enough trout rivers, you can change it." She closed the folder and slid it under the other one. "You can pick up your tickets at the agency downstairs. Any questions?"

"This isn't a fishing trip, Julie."

She smiled and nodded. "Right."

"What about the car?"

"You got a Lincoln Town Car. I gather it was the least tasteful car available."

"Good. A Lincoln Town Car is sufficiently tasteless."

"Next question?"

"Why Friday? I said next week."

"The rates are better if you're gone over a Saturday."

"I knew that."

"Sure you did."

"I'm speechless at your efficiency."

"You better be, buster," she said. She picked up the other manila folder. "Now, if you're going to be out of the office for four days, and I've got to play lawyer for you, there's a bunch of things we have to discuss." She tapped the folder with the long nail of her right forefinger. "Ready?"

"Ready," I said. But already I was trying to decide which fly rods to pack, and whether I'd need my insulated waders, and if I should call Charlie and Doc to gloat a little. Maybe I just would try to squeeze in a little fishing. If nothing else, it would be a good cover for my real business.

I had to stay up until midnight—ten o'clock Rocky Mountain Time—to reach Flask Dillman.

"Yuh?" he said into the phone.

"Brady Coyne."

"Brady. Be damned. How'n hell are you?"

"I am presently terrific, since I'm flying into Bozeman this Friday, laden with fly rods. Any fishing these days?"

"Madison up back of the Slide Inn's been fishin' real good. Caddis comin' off toward dusk. Little hopper action on the Yellowstone. Spring creeks've been hot. The usual stuff."

"You still know where all the big ones are?"

He chuckled. "Every goddam one of 'em. Got a couple with your name on 'em, if you're interested."

"I could be persuaded," I said.

When I first knew him, Flask Dillman was a highly respected Montana fishing guide, a small, lithe man with a scraggly sun-bleached beard, sun-fried skin, and a boundless capacity for rum-and-Cokes.

He lost his guide's license when one of his clients nearly drowned in the Box Canyon section of the Henry's Fork of the Snake River, a place where several less fortunate fishermen have actually succeeded in drowning by carelessly wading in the heavy boulder-strewn currents. It wasn't exactly Flask's fault. But the client happened to be an influential Wall Street banker who believed that Flask's failure to leap to his rescue was attributable to his having consumed the entire contents of the engraved silver flask he carried in his hip pocket before he curled up under a lodgepole pine and fell asleep, while the client tumbled downstream past him.

After that, Flask kept the rum out of his Cokes. He placed his silver flask on the windowsill over the sink in his kitchen and left it there as a sort of trophy of his comeuppance. And every year he applied to the state's licensing board for reinstatement. Every year he was turned down. That Wall Street banker had powerful friends. Flask always said he wished to hell the fat shit had drowned. Since then Flask and I have fished together as partners.

"Saturday, then?" he said.

"It's a date. I'll call you when I get in Friday. You can do me a favor in the meantime."

"Name it."

"Ever hear of a guy named Timothy McBride?"

He was silent for a moment. Then he said, "Might've. Rings a bell."

"Real estate developer. Supposed to be building somewhere in your neck of the woods."

"Yeah, okay. Him. Got himself a spread up by Hebgen Lake. They say he's gonna build a big fancy condominium resort. Sure. I heard of him."

"See what you can find out about him."

"Okay."

"Quietly, Flask."

"Goes without saying, Brady."

The thing I liked about Flask was that he didn't ask questions.

"I'll buy you dinner Friday night," I told him. "I'm staying at the Madison River Inn."

"Hoo, boy. The Inn. Some client must be payin' your way this time."

"As a matter of fact."

"Business trip, then."

"Mainly, yes."

"This McBride," he said. "Folks don't like him much."

"I hope to draw my own conclusions," I said.

The next morning, unable to restrain myself, I called both Charlie and Doc. To gloat. I left out the whole part about the jaguars and Jeff Newton. They responded as I'd hoped they would. They were jealous as hell, and, good friends that they were, both of them expressed enormous resentment and promised they'd hang up on me when I got back and tried to tell them about all the big fish I'd taken. They knew this was the reaction I wanted.

I also phoned Dan LaBreque to thank him for his indirect contribution to my trip.

"So you're going out there?"

"I owe it to Jeff."

He chuckled. "Sure."

"I don't understand why I get the same reaction from everyone."

He was silent for a moment. "Well, listen," he said. "The blues'll be blitzing for the next month. When you get back?"

"Definitely. It's a date."

"Hey, Brady. Be careful, huh?"

"Don't worry about me."

"I'm jealous."

"It's strictly business, Dan."

"Right."

West Yellowstone is a simple grid of twenty-eight blocks on the western border of Yellowstone National Park in the narrow south-central tongue where Montana meets Idaho and Wyoming. West Yellowstone exists for two reasons: It's the western gateway to the Park, and it's smack in the middle of the greatest concentration of fine trout fishing in the lower forty-eight. Within one hundred miles of the town flow more than two thousand miles of blue-ribbon trout waters—the Madison, Yellowstone, Lamar, Gallatin, and Henry's Fork are just the better-known. And the lakes—Henry's, Hebgen, Quake, Island Park Reservoir—teem with huge trout.

Mecca.

Around seven hundred people actually live in West Yellowstone. Their businesses cater almost exclusively to fly-fishing and Park-visiting tourists. Over a million every year. Souvenir emporiums vie with motels and restaurants and gas stations and fishing shops for the vacationers' bucks. Generally there are more than enough bucks to go around.

Many of the roads in town are still unpaved. The sidewalks are elevated from the street and made of wood. Storefronts are low, featuring log structure and rough-hewn vertical planking. The Old West.

The natives are friendly. They all fish for trout, or pretend they do when they talk with patrons of their businesses. Western beef is the specialty of all restaurants except the odd pizza joint. Steaks are cheap and thick. If you order one rare, it gallops into the dining room under its own power.

They had my Lincoln Town Car waiting for me at the Hertz booth. I loaded my duffel into it, drove south for a little under two hours on Highway 191 from Bozeman into West Yellowstone, where I checked into the Madison River Inn. A big, open-faced kid held my car door for me and insisted on lugging in my gear. I folded a ten-dollar bill twice and slipped it into his hand, and he shoved it into his pocket without looking at it. A classy joint.

A teenage girl with sleek black hair and an olive complexion checked me in and then tapped a bell. An old guy with stooped shoulders materialized and hefted my bags and rod case. I took the bags away from him and let him carry the rods. I didn't want to be responsible for his coronary. I followed him to my room while he told me about all the good stuff at the Inn. I gave him a ten-spot, too.

I tested the bed and the television. Then I flopped down and dialed Flask Dillman. No answer. I asked the operator for Timothy McBride's number. A computerized voice told me Timothy McBride's number was unlisted.

I took a shower, slipped into my Montana outfit—jeans and moccasins and an old flannel shirt—and went outside. I climbed into the Lincoln, feeling as out-of-place among all the four-wheel drives, vans, and trucks that populated the West Yellowstone streets as a water skier on Walden Pond. I drove a few diagonal blocks to the Blue Ribbon Fly Shop, where I bought a Montana fishing license. Then I wandered around the store, ogling the rods and reels and fly-tying stuff, and to justify my time I bought half a dozen No. 16 Pale Morning Duns. The young guy behind the counter told me that the Madison was fishing well, as was the eastern end of the Madison arm of Hebgen Lake. So, naturally, I bought half a dozen Adamses in size eighteen. It was hard to leave.

I got back to my room at four thirty and tried Flask's number again. Still not home. I kicked off my shoes and lay down on the bed. I'd try Flask again in a few minutes and we could go fishing, hit the evening hatch somewhere. He could tell me about McBride while we cast dry flies toward rising trout. Talk about combining business with pleasure! I closed my eyes and thought about it.

I awakened to the jangling of the phone beside my bed. I opened my eyes reluctantly. My room was dark. Dusk had arrived. So much for fishing.

TWELVE

• • • • • • •

MR. COYNE?"

"Yes?" I mumbled from amid the cobwebs.

"This is Janice, at the front desk." She had a professionally cheerful voice, which, right then, irritated the hell out of me. "Mr. Dillman is here to see you?" She made it a question. She sounded as if she assumed there was a mistake.

"Sure. Okay." I creaked my neck and yawned extravagantly. "Send him up."

"Certainly, sir," she said, after just an instant's hesitation, and by her tone I surmised that Flask, clad and groomed, no doubt, in his usual fashion—faded blue jeans blotched with outboard motor oil and dried fish slime, flannel shirt with the elbows out, scuffed leather boots, untrimmed beard, tobacco-stained teeth—did not fit the Madison River Inn image.

I swiveled into a sitting position on the bed, took a deep breath, stood, and staggered into the bathroom. I filled the sink with cold water and immersed my face in it. I was toweling myself dry when I heard the knock on the door.

I went and opened it. Flask Dillman, all scrawny five-foot-seven of him, stood there. He held his shapeless canvas fishing hat in his left hand. Flask's hat is studded with dozens of bedraggled flies and smeared with ancient dirt and trout gore. It's a great hat. Every time I saw it I wished I had a hat like Flask's. His right hand was extended. I grasped it and was instantly reminded of the sinewy strength of the little man.

"Flask," I said. "Come on in. Damn good to see you."

"Me too," he said, grinning.

At the window end of my room a pair of maroon satin wing-backed chairs sat on either side of a round Queen Anne table. They were angled to encourage the guest to gaze westward over the meadow toward the sunset behind the distant mountains. In the evening I supposed the elk and pronghorns really did venture out there to graze. Flask and I sat down and dutifully gazed. No animals appeared.

Although I had fished with Flask several times since he lost his guide's license and climbed onto the wagon, I still remembered him the way he was when I first knew him—often red of eye, slurry of speech, and hesitant of gait, but always vastly knowledgeable and reliable. He was a good companion, drunk or sober. Now his gray eyes were clear and his bearing almost aristocratic.

"You're looking terrific," I said.

"One day at a time. Fightin' them demons." He crossed one leg over the other and hung his hat on the toe of his boot.

"Looks like you're winning."

"Oh, the fight never ends. I just keep my guard up, look sharp, try to keep on standin'."

"I tried to call you when I got in," I said.

"I was cuttin' brush down to my sister's place in Ashton." He shrugged. "It's work. I take what I can get."

"You should be guiding."

He nodded once and looked out at the mountains.

"Cigarette?" I said, fumbling in my shirt pocket for my pack of Winstons.

"Factory-rolled?"

"Yep."

"I got my makins." He extracted a cloth bag of tobacco and a package of cigarette papers. He poured, rolled, and lapped a nifty cigarette.

We lit up. He turned to face me. "You want to talk fishin' or McBride first?"

"Let's get McBride out of the way, then we can move on to the important stuff."

"Rich fella," said Flask without further preliminary, returning his gaze to the darkening plains outside the window. "Come out here maybe two years ago. Bought himself a spread up north. Near five hundred acres. Few horses and cattle. Fella I know did some wranglin' for him. Says this McBride don't know shit about ranchin', and don't seem particularly interested in learnin'. Plannin' to build some kind of big resort up there. Already's sunk lots of money into it and ain't even broke ground yet. My friend figgers McBride's got himself a serious case of the shorts. Folks around here don't think much of him. California-type boy. Loud talker. Likes to shoot partridge and pronghorn out of season, bomb around the back roads in his Jeep chasin' rabbits."

"I heard he was an art collector," I said.

Flask nodded. "I hear that, too. Don't seem to fit, though. Big crude fella, McBride. Hear he likes to throw his weight around. Big fanny pincher when he's had half a dozen Coors. He's on his third wife. Keeps her at the ranch. He's got somethin' goin' with one of the gals in town. Pretty little thing from Helena name of Jenny. College gal, waitin' tables for the summer. 'Bout half his age, I reckon."

"You didn't ask," I said, "but I want to tell you why I'm interested in McBride."

"Fact that I didn't ask don't mean I ain't interested." He picked a speck of tobacco off the tip of his tongue.

"I'll give you the short version," I said. "One of my clients back in Massachusetts had some priceless art objects stolen back in July. Got his head smashed in by the crooks. Irreversible coma. I picked up a rumor that the bad guys were shopping them around. This McBride might've bought them."

Flask reached over and tapped my knee. "You playin' detective again, Brady?"

I shrugged. "More or less, I guess. It's sure nice to be out here, for whatever reason."

"I ain't heard nothing about him buyin' stolen art."

"I'd like to find out."

"I got an idea," said Flask.

"Good. I need one."

"It's Friday night. McBride'll be sittin' at the bar, swiggin' Coors, pesterin' the girls, waitin' for Jenny to get off. Whyn't we go ask him?"

"What bar is that?"

"The Totem."

I sat up straight. "The Totem Café?"

Flask cocked his head at me. "Why, sure."

"That's where McBride hangs out?"

"Yup. Him and lots of others. Why?"

I smiled. "It fits, that's all. This McBride. He's my man."

Flask suggested we walk, since it was only a few blocks to the Totem Café from the Madison River Inn. I told him I wanted to take my car. He shrugged. Flask wasn't one to ask questions.

Even when the boy delivered the Lincoln to the front door and I slipped him another ten-spot before sliding behind the wheel, Flask didn't say anything. For some reason I felt I had to explain myself.

"You're probably wondering about the Lincoln," I said as I pulled out of the circular drive.

"I might be wonderin'. Don't mean you gotta tell me."

"I'm trying to make a certain statement."

"You sure'n hell are makin' one, all right."

"To McBride, I mean."

He was silent for a few moments. "I get it," he finally said.

I parked directly in front of the Totem, and Flask and I went inside. I had eaten there several times on previous trips, and I knew the beef and the ribs were good. The decor isn't much, but the service is fine and the prices are right.

We walked through the big front dining room, through the smaller inside dining room, and found two empty stools at the horseshoe-shaped bar in the back.

The bartender was a beefy guy with close-cropped red hair and a big Irish grin. He swiped at the bar in front of us with a rag that looked like a diaper. "Usual, Flask?" he said.

Flask nodded.

"Mister?"

"Daniel's on the rocks," I said.

The bartender was back in the space of time it took me to get a cigarette lit. He placed a glass of Coca-Cola in front of Flask and a generous slug of sippin' whiskey in front of me. He leaned his elbows on the bar. "Been up to the Madison?" he said to Flask.

"T'other day," said Flask. "Took a few on Prince nymphs. Right out back of the Grizzly Bar."

"Been meanin' to get up there," said the redheaded guy. He cocked his head inquiringly at me.

"This here's Brady Coyne," said Flask. "Buddy Gleason. Picks a mean banjo."

I shook hands with the bartender. I didn't bother trying to remind him of our phone conversation a month earlier.

"Gonna try some fishin'?" he said.

"Little fishing, little business," I said.

"What sort of business you in?"

"Investments," I said with a deprecatory wave of my hand. "Whatever."

"Mr. Coyne's got lots of money," said Flask. "Mr. Coyne's from back East." I thought he was speaking more loudly than necessary.

"Well, nobody gets rich around here," said Gleason, " 'less you like sunsets and trout rivers."

"I like both very much," I said.

Buddy Gleason grinned and wandered down toward the other end of the bar.

Flask tapped my leg. I looked at him and he darted his eyes across the bar. I lifted my drink to my mouth and from behind the glass I mumbled, "McBride?"

Flask nodded.

He was sitting directly across the U-shaped bar from me. He had a thick neck and small eyes and a wide mouth. There was a gap between his two front teeth you could wedge a matchbook into. He wore a green-and-black-checked flannel shirt with the sleeves rolled halfway up his ropy forearms.

I realized after an instant that those small eyes were looking directly at me and that wide mouth was smiling at me. I arched my eyebrows and lifted my glass in his direction. He nodded, chugged from his beer glass, and resumed his conversation with the two swarthy men sitting on either side of him.

"You got his attention," muttered Flask.

"You got his attention, you mean."

"Wasn't that what you wanted?"

"Yes, I guess it was. I just don't know what to do next."

"You'll figure it out."

I thought about it, but nothing came to me.

Flask and I sipped our drinks and he told me trout stories, for which I have an insatiable appetite. Occasionally I glanced across the bar toward Timothy McBride, who seemed to have forgotten me. He had his head cocked to the side so that he could listen to what appeared to be an impassioned sales pitch from the man on his left while still keeping an eye on the waitresses who came up to the bar with drink orders. The two men sitting with McBride looked as if they were Indian or Spanish—or a mixture of both—neither typical tourists nor typical West Yellowstone natives.

After I finished my drink, I said to Flask, "Ready to eat?"

"Don't you want another?"

"One's enough for me. Let's eat."

"You payin'?"

"You taking me fishing?"

"Yep."

"Well, then, I'm payin'."

Buddy Gleason brought the bill and I spread some money on the bar. Flask and I climbed off our stools and Flask got the attention of a hefty woman whose gray hair had been braided and wound into a beehive on top of her head. She waddled toward us.

"Evenin', Flask," she said. Her smile revealed a random scattering of stubby teeth.

"Evenin', Cora."

"You boys ready to eat, are you?"

"We're starved," I said.

She led us to a table in the smaller dining room adjoining the bar, dealt us menus, and wandered away. A moment later a girl wearing a white blouse and tight blue jeans appeared at our table. A small plastic pin-on plaque over her left breast had "Jenny" imprinted on it.

"Want drinks, men?" she said. She had blond hair, cut short and straight, and a tan the color of honey.

"Had 'em," said Flask. He glanced at me. "Unless—?"

I waved my hand. "I'm fine. I'm ready to order, though."

"Me, too," said Flask. He glanced at me. "One of them great big sirloins, rare."

"I've been dreaming of a rack of ribs with that sauce since I was here three years ago," I said.

Jenny bit her lip as she wrote this down, a gesture that made her look about nine years old. "Salad bar's in the next room. You want fries or baked?"

I took the fries, and Flask asked for baked with sour cream.

When the waitress left, I said to Flask, "Is that the same Jenny, the one McBride's chasing?"

He nodded.

"Pretty one."

Flask frowned and nodded again.

From where I was sitting I could see into the bar. As I watched, McBride swiveled off his stool and walked around to the left. "Excuse me," I said to Flask.

I found the men's room beside a big-screen television set off a small room behind the bar. I pushed open the door and walked up to the urinal beside McBride. I saw then that he was about my height and considerably broader across the back and shoulders.

I unzipped. "You're McBride, aren't you?" I said.

He turned to look at me. "That's right."

"My name's Coyne."

McBride grinned. "I'd shake hands, but . . ."

"I know. Your hands are full."

"They sure'n hell are, friend." He zipped up and stepped away. "How'd you know my name?"

"I imagine everyone in this little town knows your name, Mr. McBride."

"I suppose they do at that. But that doesn't answer my question."

I finished and went to the sink to wash my hands. "No," I said, "it doesn't. I heard of you before I came here. I heard you were like me."

"That right?"

I turned to face him. "Heard you liked to make money."

"Who doesn't?"

I smiled at him and reached for a paper towel.

McBride ran his damp fingers through his hair and inspected himself in the mirror. "So what do you want with me?" he said.

"What makes you think I want anything with you?"

"You followed me in here, didn't you?"

"I had to take a leak."

He shrugged. "My mistake." He turned toward the door.

"Mr. McBride?"

He stopped but didn't turn. "What?"

"I'm looking for investments."

"So?"

"I heard you might be looking for investors."

"Where'd you hear that?"

"Does it matter?"

He turned to face me. "Yes, it does."

I shrugged. "Forget it, then. When I'm asked to keep something quiet, that's what I do."

"What the hell is that supposed to mean?"

I shrugged. "I heard you were hurting. I might be interested in helping."

"Why?"

"Like I said. I need someplace to park a little money."

He narrowed his little eyes at me for a moment. Then he

nodded. "Maybe we'll talk sometime," he said. He pivoted and pushed out of the room.

I dried my hands slowly, then followed him. He had returned to his place between the two Indians. I went back and sat across from Flask. He lifted his eyebrows at me. I shook my head quickly.

When we left the Totem Café an hour later, Timothy McBride was still at the bar, still drinking draft beer and still talking with his two Indian friends.

Flask's old Ford pickup was parked in the lot beside the Inn. I steered the Lincoln into the empty slot beside it and we got out. A full moon bathed the broad plains in pale orange light. I looked up. The Big Sky. You can see way more stars in the Montana sky than in Massachusetts. Our breath showed in little puffs.

Flask climbed into his truck. I stood beside it. "Fishin' tomorrow?" he said.

"Yes. Where will you take me?"

"Lemme think on it. Suppose I pick you up about nine?"

"I'll be ready," I said.

He started up the truck and rumbled away in a cloud of exhaust. I went up to my room. Although it was only nine thirty, my internal clock was still set on Eastern Time, and I suddenly realized that it had been a long day. I showered and crawled into bed, and I had nearly drifted off when the phone rang. I picked it up.

"Yes?"

"Mr. Coyne?"

"Hello, Mr. McBride."

He chuckled. "You knew I'd get ahold of you, didn't you?"

"No," I said. "I knew you couldn't be predicted that easily."

"Not many people drive into town in a rented Lincoln."

"They have them at the airport. Somebody must rent them."

"People who do that are trying to say something."

"What do you figure they're trying to say, Mr. McBride?"

"They're trying to say they've got money. They're trying to say that real loud."

"I think I already told you that, straight out."

"Not many people tip the kid who parks their car ten bucks, either."

"The boy did a good job."

"So do you want to talk business?"

"Depends."

"On what?"

"What kind of business."

"You said it yourself, Mr. Coyne. Investments."

"Sure. We can always talk."

"Tomorrow?"

"I had planned to go fishing."

"Cancel it."

"Okay."

THIRTEEN
• • • • • • •

MCBRIDE GAVE ME directions to his ranch. I agreed to be there at ten the next morning.

I disconnected from him and phoned Flask.

"Change of plans," I said.

"McBride?"

"Yes. He wants to talk with me."

"About art?"

"No. Investments."

"Well, you take care."

"I intend to. I'll call when I get back. I'd still like to get fishing."

"I should be hangin' around."

I slept soundly and awakened with that familiar keyed-up sharpness I used to get on the day of a ball game, and which I continue to get when I'm due to make a court appearance. I worry when I don't feel that way. It means I won't perform well.

And today, I realized, I'd have to perform. I'd do it the same way I managed most of my courtroom performances, a combination of careful planning, meticulous research, and inspired improvisation.

I'd make it up as I went along. I'd wing it.

I ate a leisurely breakfast of steak-'n'-eggs on the patio

outside the elegant dining room of the Inn and glanced through the *Billings Gazette*. The box scores were two days old. At nine forty-five I had my Lincoln delivered to the front door. Ten-dollar tips were getting out of hand, but I seemed to have established a precedent.

I headed north out of town on Route 287, crossed the Madison River, and two miles later found the gravel road Mc-Bride had described angling off to the left. It cut straight through a second-growth forest of lodgepole pine. Here and there rutted dirt roads branched off it, with signs indicating campsites and areas where firewood could be gathered.

One sign warned of bears. It advised would-be campers to use hard-sided tents.

A couple miles down the rippled roadway the forest ended. Spread out in front of me stretched a broad expanse of plains that rolled down for several miles toward Hebgen Lake, which had been created by damming the Madison River. Beyond the lake rose the peaks of the Madison Range in the Beaverhead National Forest. I stopped the car and got out to drink it in.

I love the corrugated topography of my New England. Nowhere in the New England countryside, it seems, is there a flat place to stand. Oak and maple, beech and poplar, pine and birch—the trees everywhere grow thick and tall. Streams and brooks trickle through every rocky crease in the earth. The New England landscape hugs you to its bosom. It's cozy, intimate, comforting. Except from the tops of our tallest mountains, and discounting Boston skyscrapers, which should be discounted, you find very few long views in my part of the country.

Perhaps that's why I find Montana so spectacular. Everything's on a different, grander scale. No matter where you stand in Montana, you can see forever. The sky seems to extend more than 180 degrees overhead. The plains appear to roll away into infinite space, as far as the human eye can see, and then beyond them hills poke up, and beyond the hills rise peaked mountains, and so on, and there's no end to the land or the sky.

So I stood there beside my rented Lincoln for the amount of time it took me to puff a Winston down to the filter, and I reflected on the courage of the pioneers who challenged these awesome spaces in ox-drawn wagons, while I, in my computer-driven Town Car, worried about snapping an axle on the bumpy road.

I stubbed out the cigarette in the car's ashtray and pulled forward. I found the hand-painted sign a little farther on. "McBride's Ranch," it said. The arrow pointed toward a narrower gravel roadway on the left.

I followed this road as it snaked down a long gentle slope, and soon a cluster of buildings appeared in view. "Ranch" seemed to me to overstate the case. There was a square two-story farmhouse constructed of weathered planks, an outbuilding shaped like an airplane hangar, which I guessed served as a barn, and three smaller structures that could have been bunkhouses. Rail fencing meandered and intersected here and there beyond the buildings. Inside one of the crude fenced-off squares a half dozen horses stood with their heads hanging. A few clusters of steers grazed in the unfenced pastures farther out back.

The roadway bent around the buildings and ended there. Two ancient pickup trucks, with rifle racks mounted inside the back of the cabs and weapons hung on the racks, were parked beside a new Jeep Wagoneer and an equally new Buick. I pulled alongside and got out.

I clunked the car door shut, which signaled a dog to start barking from inside the barn. A moment later a golden retriever came bounding out to sniff my pants. Behind him came Timothy McBride. He carried a Stetson in his left hand.

"Mr. Coyne," he said, his broad smile of welcome revealing the wide gap between his front teeth. "Welcome. Never mind old Jed, here. Jed," he said to the dog, "you get your ass out of here."

Jed looked up at McBride, lowered his tail, and scuttled back toward the barn.

McBride extended his hand to me. "Glad you could make it."

I took his hand and we briefly administered to each other the Western test of manliness. We both passed. "Happy to be here," I said. "Gorgeous spread."

"Isn't it pretty," he said. He held up both hands like an Old Testament prophet, indicating the horizon. "Five hundred acres, all the way down to the lake. I've got some big plans for this place, Mr. Coyne."

"Call me Brady, why don't you."

"Great, great. I'm Tim. Look, how about some coffee? Or would you maybe like something more bracing?"

"Coffee would be fine."

I followed him up the wide front steps and across the porch into the house. We paused in the foyer while he yelled, "Jessie! We got company!"

As I stood there I glanced through an archway into a large room that was dominated by a great fieldstone fireplace. On the mantel stood an angular wooden sculpture stained in dull earth tones. It appeared to be a primitive version of a horse. I walked past McBride into the room to examine it more closely.

"Mayan, isn't it?" I said, guessing wildly.

He came up behind me and nodded, frowning slightly. "By Jesus, not many people know that. This old thing isn't worth much, but I kind of like it." He took in the rest of the room with a sweep of his hand. "All this stuff's Mexican." Hung on the walls instead of paintings were woven rectangles that could have been serapes or blankets or small area rugs, dyed in drab oranges and blues. In one grouping hung a series of flat carved wooden masks that appeared to mimic primitive gods. Another sculpture stood on the glass-topped table in front of the sofa, this one of a naked woman fashioned from a dark metal that looked like crudely smelted iron.

There were no golden jaguars in the room.

"You're a collector, then?" I said.

"Tim?"

Her voice was hesitant and soft. She stood uncertainly in the archway, looking at McBride. She was short and busty in her sky-blue T-shirt and tight faded jeans. She had fat round cheeks and a small rodent-like mouth. Her dark hair had been pulled severely back from her face into a ponytail. She squinted slightly as she shifted her gaze from McBride to me.

I guessed she was twenty-five years old. Timothy Mc-Bride's third wife was at least twenty years younger than he.

"Jess, honey, this is Mr. Brady Coyne. He's from back East, and he's here to take a look at our place."

She examined her feet, which I noticed were bare, and nodded. Without looking up, she said, "Is he—?"

"We'd like some coffee, now, Jess. Let's treat our guest courteously."

She stepped forward and held out her hand to me. She couldn't quite bring her eyes up to meet mine. They seemed to stop somewhere around my fly.

"Mr. Coyne, nice to meet you," she said in a small voice.

"Call me Brady," I said.

"I'm Jessica," she said. "Jessica McBride." She glanced at

McBride, then said, "Well, come on out to the kitchen, then. Coffee's all hot."

We followed her down a short passageway into a large kitchen. Its walls were decorated with copper-bottomed cookware and little framed squares of needlepoint that said things like "If you don't like it, give it to the dog" and "Quitcherbellyachin'." Half a dozen little ceramic pigs were lined up on the windowsill.

The counters were crowded with gleaming appliances. There was a wall oven, a big restaurant-sized stove, an oversized refrigerator, a freezer chest, and, beneath the broad picture window where the pigs stood, a big double sink.

In the center of the room stood an oval maple table. McBride and I sat at it, while Jessica poured coffee from one of the machines on the counter.

"Cream and sugar, Mr. Coyne?" she said.

"Brady," I reminded her. "No, I take it black."

McBride took his black, too. After she delivered our coffee, Jessica stood there uncertainly for a minute until McBride nodded at her. Then she left the room.

"Nice kid, that Jessie," said McBride when she was gone, and I liked him better for saying it.

I nodded. "She's very attractive." This was a lie, but it seemed appropriate.

He grinned. "She can be hell on wheels, if you know what I mean."

I knew what he meant. I liked him less for saying that.

"Mind if I smoke?" I said after a minute.

"Hell, no."

I lit a cigarette and sipped my coffee. "I like your collection," I said, gesturing with a jerk of my head in the direction of the living room.

"Junk," he said, dismissing it with a quick flap of his

hand. He leaned toward me. "Let me tell you about my plans."

I shrugged. "Sure."

He reached across the table and touched my wrist. "I'm going to build a sort of combination condominium resort and dude ranch," he said. "A fancy one. The biggest, most expensive, fanciest goddam dude ranch in the West. Horses, heated pools, tennis, golf. Private airstrip with our own jet. Boats for the lake. Water skiing, sailing, fishing. The works. Condos'll have a hot tub and sauna in every unit. I've got it all designed and surveyed, and I'm starting to bring together some investors." He cocked his head at me.

"Investors? You mean private investors?"

"Yes. Sure."

"What about banks?"

He narrowed his eyes for a moment. Then he said, "Look, Brady, I'm not about to bullshit you. I've looked into banks and other financial institutions. You won't believe how goddam conservative they are. Since the summer of the fires, eighty-eight? And the droughts? Hell, business in the Park's been off, touring in this part of the country's off, fishing's off, real estate market's down, and the damn banks can't see beyond their own stuck-up noses. They don't get it. See, that's exactly why this place is going to be pure gold. It's an alternative. This kind of place'll be the wave of the future. Not just out here, but all over the country. I've got big plans. West Yellowstone first. This'll be the showplace. Then Scottsdale. Then maybe up north of Boise. Listen. Folks're already lining up to buy themselves one of these condos, and we're marketing some of them for time shares, which is lucrative as hell. We'll get our investment money back as soon as we get it built. All the rest'll be gravy. I hired a firm to do a little market research. This is the kind of place that's going to be big in the next ten years. Real big. They gave me projections from their computers. The smart man who gets in on the ground floor of this'll make himself a quick bundle. I've got brochures—"

I laughed and held up my hand. "Whoa. Slow down, Tim. I just got into town."

He grinned. "Sorry, there. I get all excited about this thing." He shrugged. "Feel like riding?"

"Riding?"

"Ever been on a horse?"

I smiled and patted my rump. "I still remember how it felt."

He stood up and twisted his Stetson onto his head. "Come on."

I followed him out of the house and into the barn, where a rawboned young guy, a cowpoke straight out of a Remington painting, stood hunched over a bench, working on a small engine. He had a slim black cigar wedged between his teeth. "Hey, Hank," said McBride.

"Yep," said the cowpoke without looking up.

"Saddle up Jill for my friend here, and old Zeke for me."

Hank put down his tools, turned and nodded once to McBride, and walked out of the barn without saying anything.

"You're a friend of Flask Dillman, then," said McBride as we strolled out to the front of the barn.

"A very old friend."

"Back from his guiding days."

"That's right."

"That boy's had some problems, I hear."

"I guess he has."

McBride shrugged.

A few minutes later Hank appeared leading two horses by the reins. McBride hoisted himself onto the chestnut, and Hank handed me the reins of the other, the mare named Jill.

She was gray and placid. Her great eyes rolled back at me as I stood by her side.

"Know how to mount her?" said Hank.

I nodded. "I know how. I'm not sure I can do it."

The stirrup was about waist-high, but I managed, by hanging on to the saddle horn, to get my left foot into it and swing up onto the horse.

"Don't shove your foot all the way in," said Hank. He kept his teeth clenched on his cigar when he talked. He touched my foot. "Just put the ball of your foot here."

"I remember," I said.

"She'll obey the reins," he said. "Just lay 'em over her neck the way you want to go. You find yourself goin' too slow, give her a kick with your heels and talk nice to her."

"Thanks."

"Ready?" said McBride.

"I think so."

His horse began to move. "Giddyup," I said to Jill, and, to my amazement, she moved alongside. Soon I got the rhythm of it. I enjoyed being so high up, and once I remembered to trust the horse to find her own footing, I began to enjoy the landscape.

We angled away from the buildings and followed a length of rail fence. Half a mile or so from the ranch we stopped our horses. "We'll break ground here first," said McBride, gesturing to the edge of a planting of evergreens. "Twenty units. Get 'em built fast, so our buyers can see what they'll be getting. It'll be the showplace. A one-bedroom'll go for one-thirty-five, a two-bedroom for one-sixty. What could you get for those prices back East?"

"Not a helluva lot."

"Right," he said. "I figure folks from Connecticut and New Jersey'll think they got themselves a real bargain at these prices. Condo fees'll be high, but look at what you're getting. Down there," he added, gesturing to a broad flat area, "that's where we'll put in the airstrip. We can build a runway long enough to handle a Learjet. Also a helicopter pad alongside."

Our horses ambled along. McBride chattered about his plans. I had to admit that it sounded good. He was an enthusiastic salesman, and his enthusiasm was contagious. It even occurred to me, however briefly, to invest some money with him.

Under that great blue sky, surrounded by limitless miles of open spaces up on a gentle horse, I had to remind myself why I was there. Was it McBride who had made four collect calls from the Totem Café to Jeff in Orleans? Did McBride set up the theft? Did McBride and Jeff know each other? Where did Martin Lodi fit into the picture? What about Lily?

McBride did collect Mexican artifacts, although I doubted that anything I had seen in his living room qualified as a valuable piece of art. But of course he wouldn't display stolen pre-Columbian pieces in his living room.

In spite of his enthusiasm for his ambitious project, McBride struck me as a desperate man. Why else would he invite me, whom he knew, or thought he knew, only as a wealthy and ostentatious Easterner, out for a prolonged sales pitch?

He was undercapitalized and overextended, I felt certain. Spending half a million dollars on stolen Mayan jaguars—a real bargain, according to Victor Masters, but still a lot of money—could undercapitalize a man pretty fast.

It occurred to me that such a man would be eager to turn a quick profit by reselling the pieces. That, in all probability, was why he had purchased them in the first place.

Having reasoned that far, I was left with the question: Did Tim McBride in fact have Jeff's jaguars? I had to find out, and I figured that Flask's approach was as good as any.

I would, at the right moment, ask him.

We rode down to the edge of the lake. "Let's sit a spell," he said.

We dismounted and hooked the reins around the saddle horns. My legs were cramped and sore. I strolled along the water's edge to stretch them out. McBride walked beside me.

"What do you think?" he said.

"Impressive."

I sat on a boulder and lit a cigarette. McBride scootched down next to me. He took off his Stetson and ran his fingers through his hair. He cocked his head and looked up at me.

"Hell," he said, "I know it's impressive. I'm looking for investors, Brady."

"I don't know. I'd have to look into it."

"Sure. Naturally. I can give you the names of some folks who've already bought some shares. Bank references if you want. This is an up-and-up deal here. Question is, are you interested?"

"It's not the sort of thing I usually get involved in, truthfully."

"All the more reason. Diversification, right?"

I shrugged. The surface of the lake was mirror-smooth. Here and there I saw the boil of a big trout eating insects off its surface. It reminded me of what I was missing and made me impatient for it.

I turned to face McBride. "Mainly," I said, "I buy and sell art."

His face revealed nothing. "Is that right?"

I nodded. "You like Mayan stuff?"

"Sure. You saw what I have."

"You said it yourself," I said, watching him. "Junk. Tourist art. No market for that sort of thing."

He was staring out over the lake. "I like it. That's all."

"I would've figured you'd go in for more substantial things. Things with real value."

He swiveled his head around to look at me. "Funny goddam thing," he said. "Couple boys at the Totem last night were saying the same thing to me. How do you figure that?"

I remembered the two men at the bar, the Indians. "I don't know how to figure it," I said.

"You don't know those two, huh?"

"I never saw them before."

"They were talking about Mayan art. One of them, called himself Carlos, he said he collected old Mayan things. Now why in hell would he be telling me that, and then next thing I know this dude comes into the john to take a leak, and by Jesus if he's not saying the same thing to me. Makes a man wonder."

"I can see why it would."

"So why, Mr. Brady Coyne, are you here, driving that godawful automobile, calling attention to yourself, throwing around big tips in West Yellowstone, Montana, asking me about Mayan art?"

I looked him in the eye. "Because I heard you might have something to sell. If you do, I'm interested in buying."

"Where'd you hear this?"

"Rumor. I need to know if it's true, or if I'm wasting my time."

"You heard a rumor like this back East?"

"I have sources all over, Tim."

"A couple names might help."

I gazed out over the water. "Martin Lodi, for one."

"Can't say I know him."

I glanced at McBride. He showed no reaction.

"What about Jeff Newton and Victor Masters?"

He shook his head. "Nope. So you just hop a plane to

track down these rumors like a man might go to the drugstore for a pack of cigarettes."

"About like that." I shrugged. "There's always the fishing."

He stood up, put on his hat, and brushed off the seat of his pants. He clapped his hands and the two horses, which had been drinking from the lake, lifted their heads and began to amble toward us. "We best be getting back," he said to me. "You don't want to miss a whole day of fishing."

On the ride back to the ranch McBride showed me the sites for the rest of the condos and the tennis courts and the heated pool and the health club. It was as if the previous conversation had not happened.

We galloped the last few hundred yards, and I enjoyed the feel of the air rinsing my face and the bouncing rhythm of the horse beneath me. When we handed over the reins to Hank at the barn, McBride walked me to my Lincoln. "You're welcome to stay for some lunch," he said. "But I expect you're pretty anxious to go fishing."

I understood that this was a dismissal, not an invitation. I held out my hand to him. "I'll think about your proposition," I said.

He nodded. "You do that."

"Thanks for the tour. And thank Jessica for the coffee."

"You bet."

"Perhaps we'll be in touch."

"Surely."

I climbed into the car and backed out. Then I started up the roadway. From my rearview mirror I could see McBride standing there, tapping the side of his leg with his Stetson, watching me.

I still didn't know if he had Jeff's jaguars.

FOURTEEN

• • • • • •

"I FIGURE," I said to Flask that night as we were eating at the Totem, "that if he has those jaguars, he'll get in touch with me. I think I made it pretty clear what I was after." I carved another slice out of my prime rib and stuffed it into my mouth. Prime Western steer. Probably exactly the same thing I got at Durgin Park back in Boston. But it always seemed to taste much better out there in beef country.

"Or," said Flask, spearing a French fry on his fork and pointing it at me, "maybe you scared him off. Sounds like you mighta come on kinda strong."

"I don't think so. He's hurting for money. He thinks I've got lots." I shrugged. "Anyway, I did what I could. I don't know what else I can do. All I want is to find out if he has the pieces. Then I'll figure out what to do next. Down the line, I just want to look into the eyes of those guys who bashed in Jeff's head."

Flask shoved the French fry into his mouth and chewed on it thoughtfully. "Folks around here are feelin' mixed about him," he said. "They figure, on the one hand, if he builds his place out there, it'll bring in a goodly amount of business. On t'other hand, they don't like him much. Outsider. And they don't like to see their open spaces dug up and built on. Mc-Bride's pissed a lot of people off. They see what's goin' on with little Jenny there, and him with a young wife back at the ranch. Folks're quick to judge a man around here, and slow to change their minds once they make 'em up. McBride's taken a swipe at a married gal or two, and that don't set well, neither. It's a little town, Brady. Word gets around. Folks take sides quick. Friend of McBride . . ."

I looked up. Flask was frowning at me. "Are you saying that because I went out there . . . ?"

He shrugged. "You're either for him or agin him. That's how they think."

I nodded and smiled. "And if you happen to be a friend of mine . . ."

"I can pick my own friends," he said quickly. "And you're one of 'em. Regardless of what folks might want to think. Still, I gotta live here."

I cut another slice of beef. "If he calls me about the jaguars, that'll tell me what I want to know. I'll just say I'm not interested, I changed my mind, and put the authorities on to him. If he doesn't call, I suppose I'll never know. I'll have done what I could. No need for me to spend any more time with Tim McBride."

"Hey," said Flask. "Not on my account."

"No. On my own account. I'm ready for some fishing. So let's talk about tomorrow . . ."

I was waiting under the broad portico in front of the Madison River Inn at nine the next morning, letting the warmth of the early sun wash my face, when Flask's old pickup chugged and belched into the driveway. I picked up my fishing gear and went to the driver's side of the truck. He rolled down the window. The stub of a hand-rolled cigarette drooped from his bottom lip. "Mornin'," he said.

"A beauty," I said. "Why don't we take the Lincoln."

He grinned at me. "You don't think this old thing'll make it over the divide?"

"I know better than to insult a man's truck. I'm just offering to drive. It'll take us half, three-quarters of an hour to get over to Idaho. The Lincoln rides nice."

Flask didn't argue, so we stowed our fishing gear on the backseat of the rented Lincoln and headed west on Route 20. Flask fiddled with the radio until he found a country-western station he liked. The Lincoln had a good stereo system. Front and back speakers. Graphic equalizer. Flask grooved on some banjo music. He jiggled his leg and tapped his fingers on his knee. It sounded pretty good to me, too.

A few miles outside of town I patted my shirt pocket and muttered, "Damn!" An Exxon sign loomed ahead. I pulled in beside the square, shingled one-bay garage, away from the pumps, next to a row of cars that had seen hard use. I threw the Lincoln into park, left the motor running, and opened the door. "Be right back. I'm out of cigarettes. Want anything?"

"I'm fine," said Flask. "I'll sit tight and listen to your radio."

I slammed the door shut and walked around to the front of the gas station. Hand-lettered signs in the window indicated that shiners and night crawlers were for sale, along with soft drinks and cigarettes, motor oil and antifreeze. The attendant, a bulky young guy wearing stained overalls over a T-shirt that probably was originally white, was leaning against a mud-streaked Blazer at the pumps, filling the tank and chatting with the driver.

"Be right with you," he called to me.

I waved and went inside.

I stood there admiring the girl in the leopard-skin bikini who was posing with a set of heavy-duty shocks on the calendar, and I happened to glance out the window as the Blazer pulled away from the pumps and the attendant started my way. I was watching as he suddenly lifted off the ground and then seemed to throw himself sideways, simultaneous with the long hollow thump of the explosion. It rattled the wood-frame building and shook oilcans off the shelves and knocked me to my knees.

It was over as suddenly as it had happened, but the roar seemed to echo and roll away toward the mountains outside. The silence that followed seemed absolute. I wondered if I had been deafened. I shook my head and staggered to my feet.

I opened the door and went outside. The heat from the fireball beside the garage was a physical force that pushed me backward. I moved against the wall and edged along the sheltering side of the building until I could look around the corner.

My rented Lincoln was a blackened skeleton filled with roiling orange flames and spewing black smoke. I started to sprint toward it, but the heat forced me to the ground. I began to crawl toward the car. My eyes ran wet, and my skin felt afire. I was on my hands and knees. I kept my head turned away from that terrible heat.

"Leave her be," came a soft voice from behind me, and then I felt hands on my sides.

"Let go," I mumbled, twisting away from him.

His arms went around me. He half lifted me and dragged me away from the inferno that had once been my rented car, and that now, I knew, had become Flask Dillman's pyre. I tried to hit backward at the attendant with my elbows, but I seemed suddenly to have no strength.

"It's only a car, mister. Lucky you weren't in it."

"You don't get it," I said. My voice came out a hoarse whisper. "Flask's in there."

The attendant wrestled me to the front of the building and propped me into a sitting position against the wall. "Now you sit tight," he said. He left me for a moment, and came back with a can of Coke. He squatted in front of me and held the can to me. "Drink this," he said.

I did as I was told. The carbonation was harsh in my scalded throat.

"Must've had a leaky fuel pump," he said. "I seen cars go up like that before. You're a lucky man. Hell, we're both lucky you didn't park near the pumps, or we'd all a been blowed sky-high."

I looked at him. I felt tears coursing down my cheeks. The heat of the flames. Frustration. Agony. "My friend was in the car," I said.

He stared down at me. "Oh, shit," he muttered. "Holy fucking shit. Look, mister. Don't move, okay? I'll be right back." He got up and went inside the building.

I pushed myself to my feet and went to look at what was left of the Lincoln. The fireball had died, but flames still licked up around the sides and darted out from under the hood. I edged nearer, but the heat prevented me from getting close enough to see Flask.

"Come on, buddy." The attendant's hand grasped my bicep and tugged me away. "Nobody coulda got out of there. He's done."

I let him lead me into the front room of the garage. I sat in a plastic chair and sipped from the Coke can.

"I called the firehouse. They'll be along in a minute." He frowned at me. "You okay?"

I nodded. "You got it worse than me, it looked like."

He shrugged. "Knocked me down was all."

"What could've happened?" I said.

"Hard to say. She blowed up, 'bout all I know. That was a brand-new car, looked like."

"I rented it," I said irrelevantly. "Hertz."

"I'd sue the hell out of 'em."

"Jesus," I whispered after a minute. "Flask. Oh, Jesus."

I heard the sirens growing louder, and then an engine pulled in. The attendant went outside. I slumped in my chair and closed my eyes.

A minute or two later I felt a hand on my knee. I opened my eyes. A thirtyish blond woman wearing a white jacket and blue jeans was squatting in front of me, peering at me. "You all right, sir?"

I nodded. "My friend was in the car."

"We saw him."

"Is he . . . ?"

She nodded her head once. "I'm sorry."

"Good Jesus." I felt the tears come again. "Oh, shit."

"Let me get your pulse," she said. She put a cool hand on my wrist, frowned, and studied her wristwatch. Then she unbuttoned the cuff of my shirt. She pushed it up to my shoulder and strapped on a blood pressure gauge. She pumped it up and studied the dial. Then she nodded once and unstrapped it. She took a penlight from the pocket of her jacket and shone it into my eyes, bending close as she studied my pupils, her fingers gentle on my cheek. Her scent reminded me of the delicate Cape Cod mix of aromas from the forested garden that Lily cultivated for Jeff Newton. Salt air, raw earth, sweat, and flowers. That all seemed long ago and far away.

"BP's a little elevated, your pulse is kinda high, but I reckon you're all right," she said, smiling. She gave my face a quick grandmotherly pat before she rocked back on her heels.

"You're looking for shock."

She nodded.

"I'm shocked, all right," I said. "But I'm not in shock. The other man, the attendant. He was knocked down."

"My partner's checking on him." She stood up. "You just

relax for a minute. I think Sheriff Hawkins wants to talk to you."

My Coke can was empty. I patted my shirt pocket before I remembered why I had stopped at the gas station in the first place. Then it hit me all over again. I had parked beside the garage, left the motor running, and after I got out, the car caught fire and exploded. Had I not stopped, it probably would've happened with me in it, somewhere on the highway.

My addiction to cigarettes had saved my life.

Flask hadn't been so lucky.

A tall man—six and a half feet, at least, I guessed, in his Western-style boots and ten-gallon hat—strode into the room. He had a long, thin face, deeply creased, with pale eyes that drooped on the outside corners, and wisps of white hair hanging around his king-sized ears. He reminded me of Lyndon Johnson. He stood in front of me, looking down.

"I'm Sher'f Hawkins," he said.

I nodded to him, not trusting my voice.

"You all right, son?"

"My friend was in the car."

"You got a name for us?"

"Brady Coyne. I'm from Boston. Out to do some fishing."

"Uh-huh. And the pore fella in the car?"

"Flask Dillman."

Hawkins removed his hat and scratched what I now saw was a bald head fringed with white. Without his Stetson he looked nothing like L.B.J. "Ol' Flask," he said softly. "Be damned. Sure'n hell couldn't recognize him in the car out there. What were you boys doin' here?"

"We were on our way to the Henry's Fork for some fishing. I was out of cigarettes . . ."

He nodded absentmindedly. "So you come in and pore

Flask stayed in the car. You leave the motor runnin', did you?"

I nodded. "I figured I'd just be a minute. He was listening to the radio."

The sheriff turned and looked out the window. An ambulance was pulling away. Its lights flashed but no siren sounded. They were in no particular hurry.

"What happens now?" I said.

Hawkins smiled without humor. "They'll take Flask over to Judd's funeral parlor, try to locate a relative. State police'll want to have a look at your automobile. Somebody oughta have themselves a nice lawsuit outa this one, car blowin' up like that."

"Flask has a sister in Ashton."

He nodded. "That's a help."

"What about me?"

He shrugged. "I'd get myself another car if I was you."

"I mean, do you need to question me?"

"Why?"

"A man was just killed."

"Hell, boy. You didn't kill him." He cocked his head to the side and rolled his eyes toward the ceiling for a moment. Then he looked at me again. "Did you?"

"No."

"Didn't figure you did. Still, I'd just as soon you hung around a few days."

I nodded. "My plane doesn't leave until Wednesday."

"That oughta be just fine."

I walked out of the building behind the sheriff. Most of his imposing height, I realized, came from his erect carriage plus his boots and hat. In stocking feet he'd be about my height.

I accepted a ride back to the Madison River Inn with

him. I learned he hunted elk and pronghorn with scope-sighted high-powered rifles and fished for trout with spinning gear. Although he didn't say it, I inferred that he believed fly fishermen were sissies, and somehow not the sort of folks who got blown up in automobiles. I also learned that he liked Flask, as did everyone else who knew him.

He let me off in front. "Any problem, Mr. Coyne, you just give my office a call," he said before he drove away.

I lay on my bed for the rest of the morning studying the ceiling. I tried to organize my thoughts, which darted and buzzed in my brain like a swarm of hatching caddis flies. The crump of the explosion, the rolling power of the ball of flame that engulfed the car, the searing heat of it—they recalled Vietnam newsreels and, later, feature films, of the war I had not witnessed firsthand. I flirted with an understanding of the men I knew who had been there and made it back. They always seemed inarticulate to me when they tried to explain how their experiences had scarred their souls.

And I allowed myself to remember Flask, an ordinary, gentle, tragic little man, who loved the outdoors as much as any person I knew. I couldn't pray for his immortal soul or meditate upon thoughts of eternity. But I could remember my friend well. It was the best I could do.

Had we taken his truck, he and I would be stalking big trout at this moment.

Had I turned off the engine before going in for a pack of cigarettes, maybe he'd still be alive. Or maybe the car would have waited to blow up later, with both of us in it.

Had I minded my own business and stayed in Boston . . .

I sat up. Enough what-iffing. I swiveled around, dangled my legs over the side of the bed, and reached for the telephone.

I had to answer an overpowering urge to talk to Gloria and my sons.

I got the answering machine. I listened to her recorded message. Somehow I found comfort in it. I waited for the beep. I sighed once, then hung up.

The Hertz people not only gave me another car to use, but they delivered it themselves all the way from the airport in Bozeman. They brought another Lincoln. Two of them came, one in the Lincoln and a second man in a little Chevy to drive the two of them back to Bozeman. I told them I really didn't like Lincolns that much, that the Chevy would be fine. They insisted I keep the Lincoln. I had no spirit to argue with them.

I wondered if I'd soon have a visit from a slick young man with a liability waiver he hoped to persuade me to sign.

Flask's sister came up from Ashton Monday morning and took Flask home with her in an urn. I got to Judd's an hour after she had left and didn't like myself for feeling relieved that I'd missed her.

I wandered around West Yellowstone all afternoon. I visited every fly shop in town. I made a pain in the ass of myself, buttonholing all the clerks, asking about current insect hatches at the rivers, the flies they recommended to match them, tying techniques to make those flies, anything that occurred to me. All my fly-fishing gear had burned up in my car. I supposed someday I'd mourn that loss, too.

What bothered me was that I had no desire to go fishing.

I stopped at most of the bars between fly shops. There are lots of bars in West Yellowstone.

I avoided the Totem.

After a while I found myself able to avoid thinking too much about what had happened.

And so I passed the entire day.

I was having breakfast on the patio the next morning, Tuesday, wondering what to do with myself on this my last day in West Yellowstone, when I saw Sheriff Hawkins approaching me. A younger man was with him.

"Mornin', Mr. Coyne," said Hawkins.

"Good morning, Sheriff."

"How you doin' today, son?" The sheriff squinted at me. I nodded. "Okay. Better."

"Well, that's fine," he said. "This here's Mr. Langley. He's from the state police up to Bozeman."

I shook hands with Langley. He wore a summer-weight suit and carried a briefcase. "Coffee, gentlemen?" I said.

Hawkins shook his head. "Not me."

But he sat down at my table, and so did Langley. "I don't mind," said the Montana state cop.

A waitress came over and refilled my cup. I asked her to bring one for Langley, and she returned with it in a minute. After she left, Langley said to me, "How are you feeling, Mr. Coyne?"

I shrugged. "I'm okay."

"Bad experience."

"It was."

"You got any enemies out here, Mr. Coyne?"

"Why?"

"Just asking."

I shook my head. "Not that I know of."

"What about Mr. Dillman?"

"I don't think so. I can't imagine Flask having an enemy. There was nothing to dislike about him." Hawkins was watching me placidly, nodding.

"I hate to contradict you," said Langley.

"What do you mean?"

"One of you's got an enemy, all right."

"I don't see—"

"Your car," interjected Hawkins, "was blowed up."

"Well, sure," I said. "It caught fire and exploded. I know that."

"No," said Langley. "It was blown up, Mr. Coyne. Dynamite. It was wired."

I frowned and shook my head. I had already thought of that and rejected it. It happened in movies, not in real life. It happened to mobsters and DEA agents, not gentle fishing guides and Boston lawyers. "That can't be right," I said. "It would've blown up when I turned on the ignition if it was wired. We'd been driving for ten or fifteen minutes before it caught fire. There was a gas leak or something. Otherwise—"

Langley reached across the table and put his hand on my arm. "Slow down, Mr. Coyne. Listen. The way it was rigged, one of the wires was wrapped around the tailpipe. When it heated up, it melted the plastic coating on the wire, and then the wire made contact with the pipe, which completed the circuit, and . . . ." He shrugged.

"You're trying to tell me that somebody was trying to kill me."

Langley nodded. "You or Mr. Dillman. Yes."

"They wanted it to happen somewhere on the highway, where it would look like an accident."

"That's how we figure it," he said. "The way it was rigged, it wouldn't go off for ten or fifteen minutes, enough time for you to drive out of town and get into the country. Your car would explode, go off the road, probably smack into a tree or roll over a few times. Most likely, no one would actually see it happen. When it was found, it would be in flames, of course, but it'd just look like reckless driving, like it caught fire after it crashed. Out here people drive fast. Too damn fast. Wide open spaces, all that. No way to patrol our highways. We have these kinds of accidents. Probably no one would ever think to examine the wreckage too close, looking for a bomb, if it had happened that way."

"Where I come from they'd sure as hell examine it."

He shrugged. "This is Montana."

I shook my head slowly. "Jesus," I whispered.

"So let me ask you again," said Langley softly. "Who'd want to do that?"

I sipped my coffee. McBride. He was the only candidate. I decided not to tell this to Langley. Not yet. I wanted to work on that idea for myself first. "I suppose there are people who don't like me," I said. "Maybe some of them are even enemies. But someone who'd want to kill me? Anyway, they're all back in Boston." I spread my hands. "I don't know."

Langley nodded. "That's a hard one, I realize. Listen. You think on it. We'll talk again."

He stood up and Hawkins followed suit.

"Mr. Coyne," said Hawkins, "I want you to be careful. Best if you stick close to the Inn for a few days."

"Are you trying to frighten me?"

"Mean to say you ain't frightened yet?"

I tried to smile. "Okay. I hear you."

"We'll be in touch," said Langley. He and Hawkins turned. I watched them walk away.

I had one more cup of coffee. Then I left the table.

I went up to my room, sat on my bed, and called Delta Air Lines. Then I called my office.

"Julie, it's Brady," I said when she answered.

"I know, I know," she said. "You don't have to tell me. The fishing is so terrific you're staying another week."

"You're half right. I'm coming in Saturday, not Wednesday."

"Oh, brother," she said.

"It's not at all what you think."

"Of course it isn't."

"Julie, I'll tell you about it when I get back."

"You're supposed to be in court Thursday."

"Who's the judge?"

"Crowell. Your favorite."

"The Berger thing?"

"Yes."

"You know what to do."

"I ought to by now."

"Thanks, Julie."

I heard her sigh. "Well, you must really be having fun."

"You bet."

FIFTEEN

• • • • • •

I FELT FOOLISH getting down on my hands and knees and twisting my head around to check the undercarriage of my replacement Lincoln Town Car, but feeling foolish didn't stop me. I also lifted the hood and looked around among the engine parts. The fact that I wouldn't know a bomb from a catalytic converter didn't stop me from doing that, either.

And the fact that I found nothing that looked as if it was designed to kill me didn't stop my heart from pounding for the fifteen minutes it took me to drive out of town to the turnoff to McBride's ranch. After bumping over the gravel roadway for a few minutes, I figured that any dynamite wired to my car would have gone off if it was going to, and I began to relax.

I swung onto McBride's driveway for the long, curving descent to his ranch. The road wound tightly through low scrub. It was barely wide enough for one car to pass, so I went slowly. I didn't want to meet McBride head-on at a corner. I wanted a different kind of meeting.

As it was, I nearly crashed into the brown Pontiac station wagon that had stopped in the middle of the driveway. I sat there for a minute, resisting my city-bred impulse to lean on my horn, before I noticed that the wagon's hood was up. This time I turned off the ignition before I climbed out of my car.

I went around to the front of the Pontiac. A man was

bent at the waist, leaning into the depths of the engine. Both of his hands were reaching down into its guts. He was working with some sort of tool.

"Problem?" I said.

The man grunted without looking at me.

"I'd offer to help," I said, "but I know absolutely nothing about engines."

The man said nothing.

I cleared my throat. "Think you'll be long here? Something I can do?"

He grunted again. It sounded like a curse. I could sympathize. It was a lousy place to have engine problems.

"Look," I tried again, "if we can push your car to the side a little so I can get by, I'll go down to the ranch and phone for help for you."

The man muttered something and turned his head to look at me.

"You look familar," I said. "The Totem, right? You're a friend of Tim McBride."

It was one of the two Indian types I had seen the night I met McBride. Up close the man looked more Mexican than Indian. He was squat, big-bellied, round-faced, with dark liquid eyes that I couldn't read.

"And you," he said in the careful English of someone who had studied it but used it rarely, "are Meester Brady Coyne." His Spanish accent was heavy.

I nodded. "McBride must've mentioned me to you." I stepped closer to him and held out my hand.

The man straightened up and withdrew his hands from the bowels of the engine. He showed me the tool he had been using on it. It was an automatic pistol.

I smiled. Then I frowned. "I don't get it," I said.

"That ees not important."

"Am I supposed to reach for the big sky or something? Is that how we do it out here in the Wild West?"

"You will seet on the ground, please," he said without smiling. He gestured with his weapon. I did as he requested.

"Your hands," he said. "Seet on them, please."

"Then I won't be able to smoke."

"I am sorry. It will not be for a long time."

I sat on my hands. "Can I ask a question?" I said.

"No, please."

He leaned against the side of his car with his arms folded, the gun in one hand, and looked at me as if I was inert. He struck me as a man with infinite patience, a quality I lack. But I figured under the circumstances I'd have to do my best.

After what was probably five minutes, but seemed like an hour, my hands and arms began to tingle and ache. It reminded me of having them taped to bedposts.

"Can I move my hands?" I said to the man. "They're falling asleep."

"Poot them on top of your head."

I obeyed. After a few minutes of that, I removed them and folded them in my lap without asking permission. The man did not object.

"You must be the guys who wired my car," I said. "Where's your friend?"

He did not change his expression or answer me.

"What I don't get is why," I continued. "I mean, does this have something to do with those jaguars? Because if it does, I assure you that I don't want them that badly. You don't need to blow me up. Hell, you can have the damn jaguars, I don't care. I just want to know if McBride has them, that's all."

This outburst caused his eyes to blink. I figured I was really getting to him.

"Tell you what," I said. "Just let me climb back into my car, and I'll be gone. I was hoping to go fishing today. That's what I'll do. I'll drive away and go fishing. You can have the damn jaguars."

He shifted his weight from his left leg to his right. He continued to stare at me. I gave up.

Ten or fifteen minutes later I heard the sound of a car coming up the hill from the direction of the ranch. It was a compact Ford, dark blue under its coating of road dust. It nosed up to the Pontiac and stopped. The second Indian I had seen at the Totem—this one, too, looked Mexican close up—got out and came around to where I was sitting.

He said something in rapid Spanish to the man holding the gun on me. I caught the name "Carlos," which I remembered McBride mentioning. Carlos, I deduced, was the name of the man who was pointing the automatic at me.

I thought I caught several other words, but the Mexican was talking too fast and his accent was too unfamiliar for me to sort many of them out. He repeated the word *chinga* several times until, from the various inflections he gave it, I caught its meaning. *Gato,* he said a couple times. He pronounced "Mc-Bride" with a Spanish accent. He used several other words and phrases that I thought I recognized but lacked time to consider for translation, so rapidly did he speak.

Once Carlos interrupted him to repeat one of the words. *"Muerte?"* he said, and the other nodded, glanced at me, and repeated the word. *"Muerte."*

This word I knew. It meant death. In Spanish it's used as part of several unpleasant idioms. I did not like the sound of that word.

When this little speech was over, Carlos nodded, waved his gun in my direction, and delivered his report in equally unintelligible Spanish to his partner, who, I deduced, was called Tomas. When Carlos finished talking, Tomas shrugged and said, "*Sí.* Okay."

With his empty hand held flat, palm up, Carlos gestured for me to stand. I did. Tomas moved in front of me. He was short, no more than Flask's height, but broad and muscular. He wore a thin mustache, and a triangle of black hair grew from beneath his lower lip. He could have been Carlos's older brother. He smiled broadly at me, showing large yellow teeth.

"You are Meester Coyne," he said. "Why are you here, please?"

"I'm a friend of Tim McBride," I said. "I came to—"

His hand flicked out and caught my cheek. I staggered backward. My face burned, more from the humiliation of being slapped than from the pain.

"Now, goddam it—"

"Meester Coyne," he said. "The truth ees, you are not a friend of McBride. The truth, please, for you, will save more problems than eet will save for us."

I shrugged. "Sure. What the hell." I rubbed my cheek. "I came to see if he owned some art pieces."

"Good. That ees better. What art pieces, please?"

"I think you know."

His black eyes stared at me. "Continue, please."

"The jaguars."

"Ah, yes. You intend to steal them, no?"

"No."

"To purchase them, then."

I shook my head. "No. I pretended to be interested in buying them. But I just wanted to know if he had them."

"Continue, please," he said when I hesitated.

"I'm a lawyer. One of my clients back in Massachusetts owned a set of Mayan jaguars." I spoke more slowly, and enunciated more carefully, than usual. Tomas studied my face as I talked. He had intelligent eyes. I was certain that he understood everything. "The cats were stolen from him. He was hit on the head by the thieves, and he is in a coma. They do not expect him to recover. They hit me on the head, too. I'm not really interested in the jaguars. But I am interested in the men who stole them." I paused and cocked my head at Tomas. "I know you weren't those men. I would recognize your accents. I figure McBride bought the cats from the thieves. I was hoping I could persuade him to tell me who they are."

He smiled again. *"Gracias,* Meester Coyne." He turned to Carlos and said something. Carlos handed him the gun. Then Carlos opened the door of the wagon and brought out a length of rawhide, while Tomas pointed the automatic at me. Carlos came to me and pushed me down into a sitting position. He began to tie me up. I hadn't liked it when I had duct tape wrapped around me, and I didn't expect to enjoy this much, either. He wound and stretched the rawhide around my ankles, up my legs, then extended it through my crotch. He pulled my arms behind me and tied my wrists and wound the thin rope up my forearms, pressing them together painfully. When he was done I was immobilized.

He stood up and Tomas returned the gun to him. Carlos took up the task of pointing the automatic at me, while Tomas climbed into my rented Lincoln. He started it up and drove it completely off the road so that it was half hidden in the roadside brush. He shut off the engine and got out. He jangled the ignition keys in the palm of his hand for me to see, then shoved them into his pocket. He reached into the car, unlatched the hood, then went around to the front. He bent inside. A moment later he emerged. He held something in his hand. He showed this to me, too, before putting it into his pocket. I guessed it was a distributor cap, or something equally essential to the running of the engine.

Then he nodded to Carlos and went back to his dusty little Ford.

Carlos came over and squatted in front of me.

"You gonna kill me?" I said, with considerably more bravado than I felt.

Carlos grinned.

"I sure hope not," I added more humbly.

"Meester Coyne," said Carlos, "we did not put a bomb in your automobile. We do not want to keel you. You are not our enemy. You are in our way, but you are not our enemy."

"Well, then—"

I didn't see it coming. The crack on the side of my head tumbled me onto my side. It hurt terribly. The second blow separated me from my consciousness, and from the pain, and from the confused memory of a previous time when I had been lying in bed in Jeff Newton's house . . .

I was probably out for no more than a minute. When I regained consciousness, I heard the high-pitched whine of the Pontiac moving up the hill in reverse and I saw the rear of the blue Ford disappear around the corner behind it. I listened to the engine sounds fade. Then there was silence.

The side of my head hurt terribly. My vision was clear, however, and I felt no nausea, so I figured I had not suffered a concussion. I maneuvered myself into a sitting position. I tried to move my arms, but the harder I tried the tighter the rawhide bit into my flesh. I shoved myself backward by digging my heels into the ground until I backed myself up against a boulder. I felt for a sharp edge, then began to rub the rawhide around my wrists against it. It was awkward and painful, since every movement tugged the rawhide into my groin, but I kept at it until I felt the rawhide behind me snap. This served only to loosen the wraps around my wrists, but it was enough for me to wiggle my fingers and hands. With great difficulty, I twisted and picked at the loosened strands of rawhide behind me until my hands and arms were free.

I quickly unwrapped my legs. I rubbed circulation into them, then stood up. The two Mexicans were gone. They hadn't killed me. I found that confusing, not that I wasn't appreciative.

I didn't even bother to check my Lincoln. Without the keys, it was useless to me. The Mexican had taken them. I could have told him he didn't need to disable it. I didn't know how to start it without the key.

I began to walk down to McBride's ranch.

It took me fifteen or twenty minutes to descend the sloping driveway. Each step sent a little dart of pain to the place on my head where I had been pistol-whipped. Otherwise I felt fine. Happy to be alive.

Jed the dog greeted me as I approached the farmhouse. I bent down and stroked his neck. He dropped onto the dusty ground and rolled onto his back. I accommodated him by scratching his belly for a minute.

Then I went to the house. Jed followed behind me, poking at my legs with his nose. I knocked on the door. When no one answered immediately, I called, "Tim? Jessica? It's Brady Coyne. I've had car trouble."

I waited a minute or two, and when no one came to the door, I went over to the barn. The Wagoneer, the Buick, and the two pickups were still parked there.

I stepped into the dimness of the barn and called, "Anyone here?"

There was no answer. Hank, the cowpoke, was not at his bench.

I went back outside and wandered among the buildings. The horses were in their stalls. The cattle grazed in the pasture. But I found no people.

I returned to the farmhouse and again knocked on the front door. There was still no response from within. I tried the knob. The door opened. I stepped into the foyer and again called, "Tim? Jessica? Are you here?"

I waited for a moment, then tried again. No answer. I didn't like it.

I went quickly into the kitchen. Jessica was there, sitting in a chair at the table, her head bowed, her chin on her chest. She looked as if she was sleeping. Except she was tied to the chair with rawhide.

I moved beside her. "Jessica," I said.

She didn't answer.

I slapped her face gently. Her head lolled to the side. I pried up an eyelid. She stared blankly back at me.

I felt for a pulse under her jaw. There was none.

I found the wound at the base of her neck, just under the skull at her hairline. It was a small, neat black hole, and it hadn't bled much.

"Oh, Jesus," I muttered. Then I yelled, "McBride!"

He didn't answer. I didn't expect him to. The house echoed its silence.

There was a door. It stood a few inches ajar and opened into a small room off the kitchen. I hadn't noticed the door or the room on my previous visit to McBride's kitchen. I pushed the door all the way open and stepped into the room. Tim McBride was there. He lay on a hand-woven Mexican carpet, facedown. The dark splotch that spread out under his chest was not part of the carpet's design.

I knelt beside him and found what I expected. No pulse. No life. I resisted the urge to roll him over to examine his wound. That was for the police.

I stood up and looked around. The room was no more than ten feet square. Vents near the ceiling hummed almost subaudibly. The walls were dark stained wood panels, fitted so perfectly that the joints between them were barely noticeable. The door opening into the room from the kitchen was a single slab of solid oak, a good three inches thick. No windows admitted sunlight into that room. Only a dim floor lamp in the corner gave shadowy visibility. But it was enough for me to see the room's function.

A low counter along one wall held a row of eighteen or twenty rectangular glass cases, similar to those in which Jeff Newton had kept his jaguars. All the cases were empty. Another wall had built-in shelves. A few small statues and sculptures were scattered at irregular intervals among them. There appeared to be many empty spaces where other pieces had once stood.

A small rolltop desk and a straight-backed wooden chair were the only furnishings in the little room.

This, I deduced, was the vault where Tim McBride had stored and preserved his collection of illegally obtained pre-Columbian artifacts. It was designed for the job—temperature- and humidity-controlled, dust- and chemical- and sunlight-free.

I returned to the kitchen and examined the outside of the door that opened into the little treasure room. There was no knob. It was wallpapered to match the rest of the kitchen. Built onto it was a single wooden shelf that held a row of cookbooks. I pulled lightly on the shelf and the door eased shut. It was perfectly balanced, and it swung as if on ball bearings. When the latch clicked, the seams of the wallpaper matched up perfectly. The door became invisible, just part of the kitchen wall. A secret room. I moved my fingers along the underside of the shelf and found a little button. When I pressed it, the door silently swung open.

I sat at the table across from Jessica McBride's body and lit a cigarette. I had a little trouble with the match.

It wasn't hard to reconstruct what had happened. The Mexican, Tomas, had tied up Timothy and Jessica McBride and held them at gunpoint at the kitchen table, demanding the jaguars. The McBrides refused to cooperate. Tomas threatened them with his weapon. Tim McBride was shrewd, stubborn, willful. He would not easily be bluffed. So, to demonstrate his sincerity, Tomas shot Jessica. Tim was undoubtedly impressed with Tomas's sincerity. Tomas then untied him, and McBride pressed the hidden button and led the Mexican into the secret treasure room.

After verifying that the jaguars were there, Tomas shot Tim, too.

The room, I guessed, judging from the fact that there were more than seven empty glass cases, had held more treasures than just Jeff Newton's jaguars. Tomas cleaned out all the valuable ones, leaving only a few less worthwhile pieces, or perhaps pieces that he recognized were not authentic, on the shelves. He loaded his booty into his blue Ford and drove away.

Meanwhile Carlos was standing guard halfway up the driveway to intercept people like me who might come along to interrupt the job.

I looked at Jessica's body slouched across from me. I wondered if I had reconstructed the events accurately. Had Tim purchased Jeff Newton's golden Mayan jaguars from the men who stole them? Had these Mexican thieves, Carlos and Tomas, followed up a rumor the way I had, and come here for the jaguars?

Had I, in fact, accomplished my mission? Had I succeeded in tracking down those jaguars, only to lose them again?

I looked at Jessica McBride's body. In death, she looked about fourteen. Too young to die that way.

She had no answers for me.

I got up from the table and doused my cigarette under the faucet. Then I picked up the telephone on the counter.

The line was dead. I was not surprised. My car was dead, the telephones were dead, and Jessica and Tim McBride were dead.

I was not dead.

I wandered back into the room where McBride's body lay bleeding on the rug. I wanted some answers.

I found one answer on the floor of a small closet in the corner of the little room. It was a suitcase. The suitcase was empty. But attached to its handle was a white tag. It was the kind of tag the airlines string on to luggage. The tag said BOS.

That suitcase had flown to Boston. I assumed McBride had flown with it. It all fit.

McBride hadn't bought the jaguars from the thieves. He had stolen Jeff's jaguars himself. He had smashed in Jeff's skull. McBride and an accomplice had tied me up, cut me, and knocked me out.

I felt like a fool. He had undoubtedly recognized me the moment I walked into the Totem with Flask. All my juvenile playacting—Lincoln Town Car, big tips at the Inn, poses as a potential investor and buyer of stolen art objects. He must have been laughing the whole time. He knew exactly who I was. He had held a flashlight in my face and seen my fear.

I looked down at his body. I felt like kicking it. I silently cursed Tomas and Carlos. They had deprived me of the pleasure.

I found a second answer in a manila envelope in the bottom drawer of the rolltop desk. It was a list of names, neatly typed, with telephone numbers beside the names. There were nine names. The second name on the list was Victor Masters. I didn't recognize any of the others, but that one was enough.

Each name had a pencil line drawn through it. McBride had struck out.

There was a third answer in the same envelope. It was a Western Union telegram, dated July 16. It read: MAKE IT FRIDAY STOP DO NOT HURT THE DOGS.

The telegram was unsigned.

I calculated quickly and figured out that July 16 was the Wednesday before the theft. The same day I had agreed to spend the weekend with Jeff Newton.

I walked out of the house. Jed greeted me at the steps. I squatted down and scratched his ears. He whined and darted toward the barn. He stopped halfway there and turned to see if I was coming. I stood up. He ran back toward me, wagged his tail, and again made for the barn. I followed him.

Jed led me inside and through the big main part. There was an open door beside the workbench. He went through it.

It was dim in there, and it took my eyes a minute to adjust. When they did, I saw Jed standing beside Hank, the hired hand. Hank was lying on his back. His chest was sploched with blood. A carbine lay beside his outthrust arm.

I didn't need to check his pulse.

A single small dust-caked window let in just enough light for me to see the cases of dynamite stacked in the corner.

McBride and Hank. The two of them. For some reason, I had no particular desire to kick Hank's body.

I did check his pockets for car keys, but found none. I went outside and looked in all the ignitions. No keys. I went back to the house and tried Tim's and Jessica's pants, too, and looked in what I thought were all the logical places. I concluded that Tomas had taken the keys and disabled all of Mc-

Bride's vehicles, as he had mine. So I went back outside. Jed the dog was sitting by the steps waiting for me.

I reached down to scratch his neck. He looked up at me. "Come on, fella," I said. "Looks like you're an orphan, now. You might as well come along with me. I've got quite a way to go, and I wouldn't mind some company."

He wagged his tail and followed me out of the barn. We started up the driveway. Jed bounded ahead of me. We began the long trudge back to the main road.

SIXTEEN

• • • • • • •

A WHITE PATCH was held in place on the front of his throat with cloth strips extending around his neck. From the middle of the patch emerged a clear plastic tube attached to hoses that led to a rectangular box on a cart beside his bed. On the front of the box was an imposing array of dials and switches and buttons. On top of the box perched a small bellows, which hissed and sucked like a sleeping asthmatic. It sounded like the machine was breathing—which, of course, it was.

A white opaque solution that looked like baby formula dribbled from a bottle suspended from a rack beside the bed through another tube that disappeared under the sheet to his abdomen.

A third tube snaked out from under the covers to a plastic bag hooked onto the side of the bed. The bag was half filled with urine.

Four wires crawled out of his gown and plugged into a small monitor beside the breathing box. Green lines dipped and danced across the screen, ticking softly in the silence of the room.

He lay flat on his back. The sides of the hospital bed were raised. It didn't look as if he was going anywhere, though.

The small square room was painted pastel green. It was

separated from a warren of other rooms just like it by a glass wall. Aside from the bed, a straight-backed wooden chair was the only furnishing there. Except for the machinery.

I stared at the screen of the monitor, watching it form regular jagged lines.

A nurse was in there with me and Jeff. She was young and thin, with premature vertical lines etched like parentheses alongside her mouth from frowning too much. She adjusted dials, checked IV lines, and smoothed the sheet that covered Jeff up to his waist. Her movements were quick, precise, nervous. She ignored me.

I hitched the chair up beside the bed and sat in it. "They tell me it's possible your brain might be registering what's going on out here," I said to him. "That you could be hearing my voice. Even recognizing it, although they claim you couldn't actually understand what I'm saying. They assure me that you'll never ever be able to answer my questions, even if you were willing. This is damn inconsiderate of you."

Jeff Newton lay there, motionless as death except for a spooky random tic at the corner of his mouth and the barely perceptible rise and fall of his chest to the rhythm of the mechanical suck and whoosh of his ventilator. His face was pale, thin. Someone had shaved him recently. His hair seemed sparser and whiter than the last time I had seen him.

The triple scar on his cheek shone neon pink against the paper-white of his skin.

I glanced around the room. The nurse had left.

"I had some things to tell you," I said to him. "Before I figured it out, I was going to regale you with tales of my adventures out West. I wanted to tell you about my friend Flask Dillman, and how he got roasted in my rented Lincoln Town Car, and about Timothy and Jessica McBride and their hired hand, a guy named Hank, a handy fellow with batteries and wires and dynamite, and how they all got assassinated. I was going to boast just a little about tracking down your jaguars, and then I was going to apologize for letting them get away again. I was going to tell you about these two Mexicans, Tomas and Carlos, who spared my life but killed the McBrides and Hank. It puzzled me, their not killing me, too. They pissed me off, though. They stole from me whatever chance I might have had of getting revenge for what McBride did to you and me. Oh, well. They got there first. McBride would probably have murdered me anyway. Tomas and Carlos took the jaguars back to Mexico with them, where I guess they belong."

Underneath his closed eyelids, Jeff's eyeballs rolled and twitched. I wondered if this was some kind of response to my recitation.

"I had lunch with Dan LaBreque the other day," I went on. "He explained to me about Tomas and Carlos. He said that those two are bounty hunters. A cross between Robin Hood and Long John Silver. They don't really work for the Mexican government, certainly not in any official capacity, but the government apparently tolerates their methods. They get results that the government likes. They find missing things and bring them back. They enforce the law. The law you broke when you smuggled in your jaguars. The specialty of guys like Tomas and Carlos is tracking down and recovering pre-Columbian art. They turn it over to the appropriate government agency. They are well paid for doing it. They use whatever means seem suitable. Sometimes killing people seems suitable to them. The Mexican government apparently doesn't query them too closely about their methods. They just pay them for results. Our government's going after them. It's a tricky extradition problem. No one's expecting much."

I sat back and looked at him. Jeff didn't say anything. I

stood up and went to the window. I could see the Holiday Inn sign at the corner of Cambridge Street and beyond it the lights from Beacon Hill blinking fuzzily through the rain-sheeted glass. I turned my back on the window. "Damn you," I said to the motionless figure on the bed. "I envied you for a long time, you know. You had your dream. You didn't let it get away. You actually chucked your boring career and went to Africa. You did what you really wanted to do. That put you one up on most of the rest of us. Even when you came back from Africa half dead, I was still a little jealous. At least you did it your way. Nobody escapes death anyway. It's not bad, if it comes to you on your own terms. Of course, then you became different, and I began to realize that dreams are complicated things, and nothing comes without a cost."

I went back and sat down. "They said it didn't matter how long I stayed in here with you. I guess you're beyond being worn out by company. I doubt if you've ever been this patient with guests before in your life. Lily's been here several times since they moved you here, you know. They don't know how long you'll stay. After a while they'll probably move you to some kind of chronic care facility. They would've done it sooner, I understand, if you hadn't had that heart attack. That's when they moved you up here to Boston from Hyannis. It's been nearly two months since the theft, since you've been gone from us, and still counting, and it looks like you'll be lying somewhere with machines doing your living for you for as long as your organs continue to function, since no one's likely to pull the plug on you, even though I suspect that's what you'd prefer. Your daughter, Ellen, was here once, Lily said. She was sad but resigned. James couldn't make it. He said he saw no purpose to it. Lily promised to keep in touch with both of them, let them know if there's any change. That, I believe, is a euphemism for your expiring. Passing away. Leaving us. Shit. Dying. I'm afraid Sheila decided not to come, but I guess you can understand that. It's not like there's anything she can do, and it has no connection to whatever residual bitterness she may feel. Anyway, Lily's the one, and the fact that you treated her like shit doesn't matter to her. She's still keeping house for you, and she drives up twice a week to sit here, holding your hand and talking to you. She's out in the waiting room now. So you and I can be alone. Knowing you, you'll be stubborn about this."

His eyelids twitched and a tiny sound came from deep in his throat. The box beside the bed buzzed softly for an instant. "They told me not to be startled if you made a noise," I said to Jeff. "You might gurgle and grumble, and I shouldn't read anything into it. Involuntary muscle contractions, a bit of congestion in your throat, that's all. Meaningless. If there's a problem, they'll come running. All this gadgetry is wired into another room where there's a nurse to watch over it."

I took a deep breath and let it out slowly. I pondered the fact that breathing could be a conscious, autonomous act, and that, had I wanted to, I could have held my breath. "I don't mind telling you," I said to him, "I feel a little strange, talking to you. Not that you have been particularly forthcoming in recent years. But usually, at least I could get you to curse or say something cynical. I could use a cigarette. Give you a chance to make fun of my weakness, huh? You know, I suspected Lily for a long time. I figured she set it up. God knows she had motive to rip you off, the way you treated her, how she'd given you a big chunk of her life and got nothing back for it. Hell, all she wanted from you was a little tenderness, a little appreciation. The cops thought it was her, too. You know how it is when you suspect someone? Everything they say and do is colored and distorted by your suspicion. I mean, there was Lily, heartbroken at what happened to you, a simple, warm, loving woman, and she came to me for—for comfort, that's all, to be held—and I interpreted it as a ploy."

I got up, went to the window, then went back to the chair and sat down. "And Sauerman. He was a prime candidate. The cops even had their eye on me, for God sake."

I looked down at him and resisted the impulse to shake him by the shoulder. "Well, I knew it wasn't me. That left Lily and Sauerman. But there was one thing about it that bothered me, and even after I realized that McBride and his wrangler did it, that thing still was there. It was this. Why did they come into my room that night? There was no reason for it. It got me to thinking. And the thought I had was this. I figured that my being there that night was no coincidence. It was a key part of the plan. Once I got that far, the rest was easy. And when I saw that telegram you sent McBride, that clinched it."

I touched his leg under the sheet. It felt soft and lifeless. "Look, dammit. I wish you could tell me why, that's all. Why would you arrange to have your own jaguars stolen? Yes, okay, the insurance money. That's obvious. And your good buddy Martin Lodi set it up for you with his Montana friend Tim McBride. Maybe it was even his idea. You needed money, you complained about it to him, and he had a surefire plan for you. But why? You had enough for your own meager needs. And why, for God's sake, did you let them slug you like that? Was that part of the plan, too? A gentle tap on your skull to fool us, except they hit you too hard? Or did they double-cross you? I don't know, and I guess you're not going to tell me. But here's what I think. I figure you went after them when they killed your dogs, right? That was your last instruction to McBride. Don't hurt the dogs, that telegram said. So it was one last quixotic act of courage, going after McBride and Hank the cowpoke in defense of those two nasty Dobermans."

I sat back and smiled. "Whatever it was that got your head smashed in, I'm sorry. Because this is a lousy way to finish up your life." I stared out the window for a minute or two. "As for setting me up, I can't really forgive you for that. I know. You needed a reliable witness in order to get the insurance money. I'm your lawyer. I was the perfect candidate for the job. So when you talked me into going down there for the weekend, you telegrammed McBride. You knew what they were going to do to me. I didn't like it much. It made me fear death. It showed me a part of myself I'd just as soon not have seen. Same thing you learned after the leopard got you."

I had nothing left to say, but I continued to sit with him, trying to remember how he was before the leopard got him. I couldn't do it. All I could remember was the mean, hollowed-out Jeff Newton that came home from Africa.

After a few minutes I reached over and put my hand on his arm. "Be seeing you," I said. Then I got up and left. Lily was in the waiting room. She held a styrofoam cup in one hand. A magazine lay open on her lap. Her head was back and her eyes were shut. I sat beside her.

"Hey," I said softly, touching her arm.

She opened her eyes and turned her head to look at me. "I was just resting my eyes."

"Let's go get some food."

"I'm not that hungry."

I held out my hand to her. She took it. "Come on. Let's eat," I said.

She frowned. "Are you all right?"

"Me? I'm fine. It's a little weird, talking to him."

"I know."

"Come on. Let's get out of here."

She nodded. "Okay."

We walked along the brick sidewalks without talking.

Lily's heels clicked and echoed, and the evening air created misty orange halos around the streetlamps. When we crossed Cambridge Street, she held on to my arm. When we got to the other side she let it go. We entered La Trattoria, a little store-front restaurant at the foot of the Hill renowned for its Italian wines and homemade manicotti. We were led to a table near the back. We asked the waiter to select a wine for us, which he did with obvious pleasure, and after he opened it, presented the cork, sloshed a bit into my glass for inspection, and, upon my nod, poured our glasses full, he left.

"Tell me what happened," I said to Lily.

She shrugged. "He hadn't changed much. They had de-cided they'd keep him there in Hyannis. Then I got a phone call. It was a week ago Friday. He'd had a heart attack during the night. A bad one. So they shipped him up here." She shrugged.

"Only difference now," I said, "is that he's one big step closer to death."

She stared at the candle that flickered on the table be-tween us for a moment, then raised her eyes. "That's about the size of it."

"But you still visit him."

She lowered her eyes. "It's not much of a problem. I don't have a helluva lot to do with my life."

I touched her hand. Her fingers twisted around my wrist and held tight. "You are a loyal person."

"You thought I was a crook."

"I'm sorry. I'm trained to be objective. I objectify. It's a flaw, I know. The evidence, how I put it together—those phone calls from West Yellowstone, for example, I figured it was you who'd taken them—Martin Lodi, you know, the mo-torcycle, I thought you and he . . ."

She smiled—a little sadly, I thought. "You don't trust anybody," she said.

I nodded. "Yes, I know. Including even myself."

"Especially yourself," she said.

I shrugged. "I've been fooled too often to accept my own emotional reactions to people, to trust them and go with them."

"To take risks."

"Right. Okay. To take risks."

"To love," she said. There was an edge to her voice.

"That, too. Yes. Look. People I care very much for have done things that surprised me. Like Jeff, for example."

She had been staring into her wineglass, stroking its side with the edge of her forefinger. Now she looked up at me. "Jeff? What do you mean?"

"He arranged the theft of the jaguars."

"Oh, come on."

"Actually, I think it was your former husband Martin Lodi who set it up for him. Lodi, I figure, knew McBride from his travels in the West, knew McBride liked Mayan stuff and wasn't above a little burglary, especially when the victim was a willing accomplice to the crime. Jeff liked it. He organized his own theft. He needed money, and the cats were all he had. He had them stolen for the insurance money. He knew he couldn't sell them legitimately. He'd smuggled them in when he was hunting in Mexico. The papers were forged. They'd never pass muster. Any legitimate buyer would know that, and instead of buying them would report Jeff to the authorities. Then he'd lose the cats and get nothing for them."

"That's fantastic, Brady," she said. "Why would he do that? He loved those jaguars."

I shrugged. "Money, obviously. I don't know why he wanted money, but it's the only answer I can come up with.

See, that's why he wanted me down there that particular weekend. It was very important that I be there on the night of the
theft. And that's why McBride and Hank came into my room
and did what they did to me."

"I don't get it."

"So there'd be a reliable witness. He wanted to be sure of
my testimony. The insurance adjuster told me how easy this
particular investigation was for him. Rarely are there wit-
nesses to burglaries. But he had me, a lawyer, no less. As
reliable as you could get. Remember the cop, Maroney?"

Lily nodded.

"He accused both of us. He believed it was an inside job.
So did I, actually. I suspected you. We were both right."

"Except it was Jeff."

I nodded.

"What makes you think it wasn't me?" she said.

"McBride had no reason to come into my room if all he
was after was the jaguars. What he did to me was completely
gratuitous, unless it was to set me up as a witness for the
insurance. If you were stealing the cats, you wouldn't care
about the insurance. The only one who would care was Jeff." I
shrugged. "Q.E.D."

"It hurt me very much," she said after a moment. "You
suspecting me."

"I'm sorry."

"I mean, that night, after we went fishing . . ."

"I figured that was part of it. Your way of—"

"Distracting you?"

"Of making me"—I waved my hand in the air—"of making me love you. So I wouldn't suspect you."

She let out a long breath. "Shit," she said softly.

"Yeah. I'm sorry."

"You really—"

"I know. I don't know much about women."

"I mean, I really needed you, and you . . ."

I nodded.

"I thought that we had gone beyond that."

I shrugged. "I'm not sure I'm capable of going beyond that, Lily. It's me, not you."

She smiled. "Yeah. I got that figured that out. It's your loss."

"I guess it is."

She had the manicotti and I had the cannelloni. I asked her what she planned to do after Jeff died. She said she hadn't thought about it, didn't want to think about it. She'd worry about it when the time came. It wasn't exactly that she loved him, she said. It was just that her life would be different. She supposed one day she'd recognize it as a chance to begin over again. Just then, though, she felt lost. It was the second time a man had left her. "The third time," she said, gazing into the candle, "if I count you."

"You shouldn't count me."

"You're right," she said. "You don't count."

She said that for a long time after Jeff was slugged on the head she was angry at him. After a while her anger made her feel guilty. She found it all confusing.

I couldn't think of anything comforting to say.

We were sipping espresso when Lily suddenly reached across the table and gripped my wrist. Her fingernails dug into my skin. "Brady, Jesus!" she said.

"Lily, ow! What is it?"

"Morphine. It was the morphine."

"Huh?"

She shook her head slowly back and forth. "The doctor. Not Sauerman or the one in Hyannis. The new one, here. They did blood tests and so forth. He told me, he said that Jeff was a morphine addict. That he'd been taking huge amounts of morphine, or morphine derivatives, and he'd been doing it for a long time. It's what brought on the heart attack, he thought. Not an overdose. The opposite. An acute opiate withdrawal, he called it. He asked me—hell, Brady, he practically accused me—he wanted to know where Jeff was getting all the drugs."

"I'll be damned," I said. "Sauerman."

"Had to be," she said. "I'll bet—"

"Sauerman was putting the squeeze on him," I said. "Come up with some big money, pal, or I'll cut you off."

"See," she said, "the morphine. That's why he—he turned into the man he became. He was so different when he came back from Africa. Grouchy, nasty. Twisted. Those awful dreams that used to wake him up, when he'd want me to hold him while he slept. The morphine. It's why he slept all the time. Why Dr. Sauerman's visits were so important to him. Why he lived for those shots on Friday nights. The pills I kept giving him. There's a new kind, the doctor said. Morphine pills. It's why he wouldn't eat. Why he wouldn't—couldn't make love, and didn't want to."

"All he wanted was his fix," I said. "Everything else— you, the jaguars, even his dogs—nothing mattered in comparison. So he was completely dependent on Sauerman. Sauerman says raise some big bucks or it's the end of the happy trips. Jeff'd do anything. So he had the cats stolen. For the insurance money."

Lily reached across the table and covered my hand with both of hers. "Oh, Brady," she said.

"It's kind of sad when you think about it, isn't it?"

She nodded. "The real sad thing," she said quietly, "is that it makes you right."

I cocked my head. "What do you mean?"

"I mean, you objectify, you don't trust, you won't risk

your emotions, you don't allow yourself to love. And something like this happens, and all that gets reinforced."

I nodded. "It keeps me from getting hurt, though."

"That," she said, "is a helluva way to live your life."

EPILOGUE

• • • • • •

O N A CRISP October Sunday Dan LaBreque and Charlie McDevitt and I steered *Cap'n Hook* down toward Provincetown, where it had been rumored that the blues were schooling up for their migration.

The whales had already left.

As far as we could tell, so had the bluefish.

We drank quite a bit of beer and didn't talk about pre-Columbian art at all.

A squall came up on the way back to Gloucester. The three of us huddled in the cabin while *Cap'n Hook* slogged through the rolling seas. Charlie told a few jokes, but otherwise we watched the gray ocean through the rain-streaked windshield in comfortable silence, and when we finally pulled into Dan's slip at the marina, darkness had already fallen. We agreed it had been a very good day of fishing. After all, there was no blood and slime to wash out of the boat and there were no fish to clean.

I talked with Gloria on the phone a few times, mostly polite conversations updating each other on our respective businesses. She seemed to be enjoying the life of the professional photographer more than I liked lawyering. She offered no complaints about Joey, nor did I inquire.

Joey brought Debbie to my apartment to try my famous chili one autumnal Friday evening. He introduced me to her as his old man. He found a sock under the sofa and he tried to tease me because he knew I'd tried to clean up the place for company. Debbie, I noticed, called him Joe. She exclaimed over my view of the harbor and claimed to like my chili. Joey pretended to sulk when I refused to serve them beer. I enjoyed having them there. Neither Joey nor I mentioned his moving in with me.

Even with all the wires and tubes and machines, Jeff didn't make it through his next heart attack. He died on the day before Thanksgiving. Maybe the doctors didn't run to him as fast as they could have when the alarms rang and the red lights started blinking. Nobody had the inclination to inquire.

Ellen and James donated what was left of his body to Harvard Medical School. Aspiring doctors could dissect it, study Jeff's anatomy.

They could study it all they wanted, and they'd never figure out what made him tick. Or what killed him. Or the fact that he had been dead for many years before his heart quit.

The kids decided not to hold a memorial service. Perhaps they assumed nobody would attend, I don't know. They didn't consult me.

Lily would've gone to it.

I would have, too.